Miranda's Destiny
by Candace Smith

The Atlantis Series
book one

Published by Strict Publishing International
Copyright © 2012 Candace Smith
All rights reserved.
ISBN-10: 0857792911
ISBN-13: 978-0857792914

CONTENTS

Prelude

The ship traveled silently through space, and the look of hope was evident on all the pale faces. It had been well over a year since the planet had been discovered, but the evasive maneuvers necessary to protect them from their enemies had made the journey painfully slow. After several months, with no other ship appearing on the star charts, they felt confident they had not been followed. No one traveled to the primitive, dangerous outer worlds.

The three couples held hands and, communicating in their telepathic way, they encouraged each other that their plan would work. It had to; it was all that was left to them. They slowly parted and retreated to their quarters.

Mahana and Laryan lay back on their mattress, excited and more than a little nervous at the enormity of their tryst. The survival of their species depended on a successful coupling, and the mates felt the burden of this weight lingering in the background as the sexual heat of the moment was building.

Mahana's liquid blue eyes stared up at her lover, and her pale face showed a slight hint of the flush of desire as her lips trembled with passion. The smoothness of Laryan's hand traveled down her flat chest, the surface of which was barely rippled with the tiny light pink nipples of their kind. The mere brushing of his porcelain skin across the slight protuberances caused her to writhe in ecstasy, and her azure eyes sparkled with anticipation as his hand continued to the bared vee at the junction of her thighs.

Mahana's small hand quivered as she

reached between Laryan's legs to find his finger-sized organ stiff and pulsing. He lifted his head, gasping and gritting his teeth in lust. The diminished size of their sex organs belied the unparalleled passionate nature of their species. The exotic advanced creatures had heightened nerves, exciting them and keeping them in a constant state of arousal for their mates.

As they gazed into each other's watery wide eyes, Laryan swept Mahana's juices along her cleft, and slowly inserted a long, slender digit deep within her. When his thumb gently stroked her, her fist tightened on his shaft and she moaned, "Laryan, how I love you."

He shifted his slender body on top of hers. "And I love you, Mahana, with all my soul." He thrust deep within her, as she gripped and pulled at him, refusing to release him. He drove his need into her, feeling almost unbearably squeezed and stretched with every plunge.

Mahana answered his desire with her own clenching demand until they could not hold back, and their eyes became blank stares as the automatic trance induced by their climax showed them a vision of the future. He fell onto her, spent. Their ivory arms held each other while they studied each other's eyes in silence, understanding their vision and the decision the remaining clan had agreed to. Mahana was now pregnant for the first time in five hundred years. This would be their race's last chance to survive, and she gently caressed the pale skin over her womb with a mixture of love and sorrow. She would have so little time to be with her only child.

They were Atlantians, the last brave vestige of their dying kind. Only one insignificant planet in the far reaches of the outer world could support their species, but the child must be born and raised on its surface. The parents could last only a few years, a decade or less, in the rich suffocating atmosphere, so their children were to be left behind on this unknown planet to be raised by natives. As the centuries passed and the Atlantian bloodline thinned, there should be three children in every generation that held their Atlantian parents' gene. It was their species' only hope of survival.

The remaining six Atlantians, three mated pairs, had traveled the worlds for centuries, outrunning those who wished to see them extinct. The enemies had destroyed the temples and the halls of learning, and only a few scrolls were safely sequestered on the ship before their planet was swallowed back into the black fathomless universe. Finally driven to the outer worlds, they found the planet of hope they had been searching for.

The three babies, two girls and Mahana's son, were born the day after the clan reached the surface of the planet. Already, the adults could feel the weighted pressure of the atmosphere and the unfamiliar sensation as their bodies began to decay. They studied their struggling infants calmly, mentally scanning the tiny bodies trying to adapt and accept the challenging surroundings.

Mahana's son's fist clenched her finger as his lungs worked desperately to process the heavy air, and her eyes filled with tears as she looked at Laryan. "He decays, my love."

Laryan gazed at her sadly and gently gripped her arm. "We knew to expect that, Mahana. Our son will survive long enough to procreate, but he will wither young and none of our babies will see a single century." The couples held hands to comfort each other's misery.

Their leader, Yatsema, finally broke the silence. "It is time to separate. There is so much to be done before we leave this place. Does anyone wish to speak before we begin?"

"I think we have planned as well as we can, considering the primitive environment. The signs and our teachings should provide the native species of this planet with the knowledge they need to ensure our genes survive until we return. Shall we discuss our visions?" Laryan suggested.

The clan agreed it would be wise to have some idea of what the future would hold for their efforts on this uncomfortable world.

"Mahana and I see our gene survives, but how it is transported from this planet and what the future holds beyond that, we do not know. We only know that our gene will survive to leave this place."

There was a collective sigh of relief, and Yatsema's mate stared at Mahana, her watery eyes filled with hope. "Did you see the other genes survive, as well?"

Mahana felt a wave of despair for her friend. At least she knew her ancient heritage would live on. "No." She quickly added, "That does not mean your lines do not survive, only that our vision was limited to our own gene, because it was our combined focus."

Yatsema's voice was slightly contemptuous as he revealed his vision. "I see this planet being swallowed not long after the Great Calendar's cycle ends. The primitives here have a barbaric sense to the nature and balance of this place, and they are greedy and driven. If not for your vision of a gene surviving, I would suggest not wasting our time with the instructions. Thank the gods that apparently some of those among this species will protect what we leave with them."

Alderian was the last to speak, and the bewilderment of his recanted vision was etched in his pale features. "Our vision was of a battleship and a warrior standing in full armament before a sun and a moon, protecting them. We do not know what to make of it." The Atlantians closed their eyes to meditate on this unusual vision. If the warrior were no enemy to the heavenly bodies, what role would he play in their future? In the end, they had no answer.

"It is time to prepare our messages. We must meet back on the ship in nine years and nine months. If we remain on this planet any longer, we will be sacrificing ourselves for no reason. Agreed?" Yatsema searched the faces for any hint of indecision, and he was pleased to see the faces looking back at him were filled with hope and anticipation as they nodded. The mates gathered their infants with determination, and traveled to their assigned locations.

It had been decided years ago which signs each artisan of the clan would leave for their children. The locations to which the Atlantian couples had been assigned contained the most advanced of the species of this world. They began the work that would take almost a decade to complete, but many years from now the natives would believe these works took centuries, and conclude that they had been constructed many years apart.

The children had been sequestered with kind families, and Mahana spoke with her son every day while the work was being completed. When the great stone beacon was finished, and it was time to leave or perish, she placed her small hands on his shoulders and looked into his liquid blue eyes. "You carry the hope of our people, Larinth." She kissed his forehead and released him to the surrogate mother she had chosen.

The beautiful stone carvings of massive proportion were arranged in a circle, like an altar, in accordance with the angles and formation the artisans had calculated. Tears flowed down the peasants' faces, as they watched the keepers of the towers walk down to the beach and across the surface of the water, until Mahana and Laryan could no longer be seen.

The pyramids were complete and in the lower level, far beneath the harsh rays of the sun and damaging dry climate, the sacred scrolls lay protected in their tubes. The dark Egyptians thought the authors of these great works, startlingly beautiful people with pale skin and luminous blue eyes, were gods, and they built shrines and statues of them. As the artisans left the great pyramid, they gazed back at the lights of the city one last time. "Be well, my child," Alderian whispered, and then he took his mate's hand as they walked across the desert sands and disappeared.

Half way around this world, frenzied sacrifices were being offered as the last of the Great Calendar was carved. The masons, their beautiful ivory skin contrasting with that of the exotic ebony tribe, silently walked south. The Mayans followed for months until they reached the base of a mountain. There, the masons smiled compassionately at them, yet told them to follow no further. The tribe waited at the bottom, their dark eyes watching the carvers as they traveled to the summit until they were out of sight. One brave warrior dared to climb to the top, and returned to tell his people the masons had vanished.

Years passed, and the legend of the artisans became distorted and blurred. The sacred scrolls from the pyramids were feared by the new rulers and considered dangerous works, filled with political and religious anarchy, and they were burned in Alexandria along with most of the teachings of the great philosophers who had struggled to learn from the artisans. One of the many wars broke out, and Alderian's precious Atlantian gene was lost.

The masons' Great Calendar remained undisturbed, for the most part. Many years after its completion, a deadly plague disbursed the panicked tribe in all directions after claiming the gene carried within Yatsema's great, great grandson. Credited to the Mayans, the Great Calendar ended in the pre-destined year of the artisans' visions, but no one was left to explain what was to happen. Wild stories of the end of days circulated among the natives of the planet as they watched the ancient calendar nearing the last of its etched symbols. Yatsema would have shaken his head in disdainful sadness at their ridiculous conclusions. The calendar simply ended when the clan was to return for their children.

The great stones of the beacon remained, weathered and worn by time and the elements. Stories of altars and sacrifices spread among the species as with each successive generation fewer people remembered the truth. It was dangerous to practice what little of the Old Religion the artisans had shared, and the believers were ostracized and condemned for their rituals. A wizened woman with knowledge of the stones traveled across the great ocean to the Americas, hoping to evade the inquisitors' time in Europe. She was soon condemned as a witch, and killed. Her pale blonde daughter cried in her father's arms. Laryan and Mahana's gene had survived.

No one remembered the true story of the great artisans, and the legends became nothing but myths, fantasized and scorned. A popular rumor spread of an advanced people traveling to the planet, only to sink with the mythical land of Atlantis into unknown waters. It was easier, at the time, to believe the Atlantians sank into the ocean, along with their fictitious homeland, than to understand the incredible truth.

The great works of art, the signs so patiently designed by the artisans, remained. The pyramids in Egypt and South America, reminiscent structures of the crystal temples the Atlantians had loved on their home planet, the Great Calendar spanning thousands of years, marking their return, and the beacon of Stonehenge, where their children would be waiting, were all shrouded in mystery and half truths.

Like dominos on their fallen collision course, the teachings were lost and forgotten. The scrolls had not survived the politics of their discovery, the magical wizened folk with the knowledge of the beacon did not escape the killing times, and the Mayan tribe had been separated or killed by the conquerors' plague. If the Atlantians had not misjudged their length of stay on the planet by the two days it had taken to birth the babies, they would not have continued to slowly decay when they returned to their ship. If just one of these events had not happened, the child would have known.

CHAPTER I

Miranda gazed around the clearing and sighed. The basket of apples in her arms smelled sweet, and she looked over at her small orchard silently blessing the trees for their fruit. The sound of a fish slapping the water in the pond at the edge of the woods caught her attention. Leaves decorated the trees in the colors of Samhain, the sabbat quickly approaching, and Miranda and Tempest still had ritual preparations to complete.

The weather was cool, but not too cold for this time of year, and she studied the orange and red leaves on the maple, reading their curls. November would be harsh this year, and Miranda made a mental note to bring the herbs inside. She smiled and thanked the goddess for Tempest's insistence to grow them in pots instead of the garden. The rocker on the porch moved to the slight breeze as if to remind her, and she wandered over to it. *I might as well get it over with.* She sat down and closed her eyes.

Tempest always did her reflecting after Yule, making her resolutions on the traditional first day of the year, and cleansing herself for the new wheel. Miranda thought it was too depressing to think about her lonely past in the isolated coldness of December. Her grandmother had taught her the rituals, and since she was a child Miranda had done her reflecting before Samhain. She welcomed cleansing herself of the sad memories of her life so she could meet and bless her ancestors with a clear mind. Miranda missed her grandmother terribly. She was the only one who understood and could explain Miranda's differences to her.

The wide planks creaked as she rocked on the porch of her little cabin in the woods that she had purchased with the money from the sale of her parents' house and the insurance settlement after they were mugged and killed on a weekend trip celebrating their twentieth anniversary.

Miranda's trances and premonitions had labeled her 'weird' since she was a child. Thank the stars for Tempest. The spiky haired girl had been her only friend in high school, when the first whispers of 'witch' followed her through the halls from the cheerleaders and chess geeks.

She remembered the day Tempest sat down in the empty chair next to her in the back of English class. The new student stared down at her desk with a resigned look on her face, and Miranda shrugged and returned her attention to the essay she was writing. She knew that before the last class was over, the girl would learn that Miranda was a freak, and she would choose a different seat the next day.

Miranda was suspicious the following afternoon when the new girl once again plopped down in the chair next to her. Miranda glanced sideways at her, and the dark haired girl grinned, her green eyes peaking out from under her shaggy bangs mischievously. "A witch, huh?"

Miranda prepared to defend herself, and answered calmly, "That's what they tell me."

"Any chance you can get this dipshit teacher to drop the Shakespeare and throw us some Poe?"

Miranda relaxed a little and stifled a laugh. "Shakespeare had his dark moments, too."

Emerald eyes flashed with amusement. "I'm Tempest." She held out her hand.

"I'm Miranda, welcome to Midpoint High."

Tempest smirked. "Spoken like an admiring

alumni... which you're not."

"True, I'm not," Miranda agreed.

Tempest was a new age outcast from Arizona, and became her best and only friend. No one messed with Miranda when Tempest was around, and she usually was. Over the next two years, Miranda told Tempest some of her secrets, and she was pleased when Tempest never asked her for proof. She believed her completely, and said she just wished she could gain Miranda's focus to experience some of her own potential.

Tempest's mother ignored them, and spent her time involved in a vague quest for her own truth. "I need to find myself, Tempest. I will never be whole until I do." She would take off on strange weekend retreats, saying she was 'searching for herself'.

Tempest used to laugh and say she might as well stop looking. "Cripes, Miranda, she can't even find my father. I don't think she even knows who he is."

After two harsh West Virginia winters, the confused woman finally decided she would 'find herself' back in Arizona, and she told her daughter she was returning the day after Tempest graduated. She made no mention that Tempest would be accompanying her.

Miranda leaned on Tempest's strength through the struggle of her parents' funeral, and she accompanied her to the attorney's office where Miranda signed documents making her their official and only heir at the age of eighteen years and three days.

When they had left his office, Tempest said, "I have an idea."

"What kind of an idea?" Miranda asked with suspicion. She had suffered the backlash of a few of Tempest's 'ideas' in the past.

"Mom can't wait to head back to the desert, and our rent is due in two days. What if we tell her I can stay at your house, and she can take off?"

"Would she do that, just leave you like that?" Miranda was astonished by this suggestion.

"Hell yes. She's been a great mom, but she's already decided it ends at eighteen, and then she figures she gets her life back. I'm cool with it. I love her, but face it, Miranda, she was never cut out for the Mrs. Cleaver life." Tempest looked expectantly at her friend.

"I guess that would be okay. I mean, it's not like we will be throwing wild parties or having any guys over." The two had accepted their isolated friendship years ago.

Tempest's mother pounced on the offer, and never looked back. She did not write, there were no calls, and she did not give the girls her new address. Miranda and Tempest held a ritual wishing her well, but never tried to find her.

The girls graduated high school with no parents, family or friends to congratulate them, and a few days later Miranda had the attorney sell the big house with too many memories and she found her cabin in the woods.

Miranda pictured her broom sweeping the sadness from her thoughts, and she slowly opened her eyes knowing she would never think of those events again, or, at least, not with the despair those times had caused her in the past. She rose from the rocker and smiled out onto her orchard.

Tempest worked ten miles away in the small town at a nursery and studied botany at the junior college. Miranda made soap and candles to sell at a gift shop on Main Street. They were perfectly content with their quiet life.

Miranda only traveled to town once or twice a month to stock her display shelves and collect the money from sales. It was as she returned from one of these trips she saw a flyer on the window of the coffee shop announcing a pagan meeting the first Monday morning of the month, and Miranda discussed it with Tempest. She was lonely and she wanted to find others like her.

Tempest absently swirled the whipped cream into her cappuccino while Miranda studied the group. There was no sense of power from any of them, not even the little glimmer Tempest cast, but there was also no sense of animosity and that in itself was a relief. The group was an eclectic gathering of witches and new age believers, and the tall woman orchestrating the meeting invited the girls to a gathering in the woods to celebrate the full moon.

Miranda loved esbat rituals. The feeling of peace and renewing power charged her for the month, and she was excited at the prospect of a larger gathering honoring the goddess. The girls wandered out onto the glade and approached the bonfire and rough altar arranged on a large rock, waiting for the ritual to begin. Miranda noticed the woman who had invited them standing by the altar wearing a cape and ornamental jewelry, and someone whispered to Miranda that she was their coven's priestess. The prospect of a teacher to finally guide her and help her understand her abilities was exciting. She scanned the priestess and was confused that she detected no power from the woman. She decided it must manifest during the ceremony.

As the Priestess began, Miranda tried to understand the calling of the elements and the repetitious words. The whole ritual made no sense to her, because she instinctively knew the gods and goddess were always present. It made her more than a little nervous when the woman in the cloak 'summoned' them, and Miranda could not bring herself to repeat the words to 'summon' the gods. She believed they would 'summon' her, if they needed to.

Words passed between the priestess and a young handsome man standing beside her, and the group repeated the words reverently, hands clutching athames pointed towards the moon. They seemed to be impassioned by the act, and Miranda looked at Tempest and shrugged her shoulders. Tempest whispered, "Maybe it depends on where you're from. Let's just do it the way we do at home."

Miranda silently nodded in agreement and held Tempest's hand. She lifted her other open palm towards the moon and silently blessed the goddess for Tempest's friendship, their cabin in the woods, and their health. She praised her for her wisdom, and felt the familiar filling of light that traveled through her body and into Tempest by their joined hands. Her trance was so complete she never noticed the rest of the coven was quietly staring at her with their gaping mouths hanging open. It was as if all the light cast from the moon had formed a single beam and was shining on the strange new girl's hand.

When Miranda came out of her trance, the group gathered excitedly around her asking questions. Miranda was overwhelmed, and Tempest, as usual, took control. "Back off a little, will you? She needs a little time to ground herself."

The angry priestess realized her leadership with the coven was in jeopardy, and she narrowed her eyes. "We must give thanks to the goddess for allowing the power of our ritual to manifest within the new believer."

Several from the group had been joining the rituals in the glade for years, and they had never witnessed anything like what had happened to Miranda. Their questioning eyes glanced in confusion at the priestess.

When Miranda had grounded, she felt the unmistakable hostility thrown from the priestess towards her. The woman's robe shifted in the slight breeze. "Thank you for joining our full moon ritual honoring the goddess." In a regal 'do-not-mess-with-me' voice she continued, "Your ways are that of a solitary, and I am afraid you draw from the power of our group to support them."

Miranda looked the fanatical priestess in the eye. "I understand," she replied calmly. "Thank you for the opportunity to share this ceremony with you." She took Tempest's hand and left the glade, obviously dismissed from further contact with the group.

Tempest muttered quietly, "What a bitch!"

"It has been a struggle for her to keep the group together, and I think she sees me as a threat," Miranda sighed in disappointment. "They do worship in their own way, and believe in the wisdom and balance of nature. I guess that's the important thing." The sadness in Miranda's voice was clear as she discovered she was even an outcast with these people.

The next time Miranda was in town stocking her displays, the handsome man from the pagan group caught up with her as she walked back towards her car. "Miranda? That's right, isn't it?"

Miranda turned and looked up at him. His blonde curls flopped in disarray around her face, giving him an even more youthful appearance.

"Yes, I remember you from the glade."

Johnny invited her to have coffee. Miranda had never had a real date before, and she nervously swirled cream into the dark beverage until she read the signs in the design on the surface, and then she calmed.

Over the next week, Johnny began to show up at their cabin frequently. His one annoying habit was to badger Miranda with questions about her abilities. Something told her to be evasive, and Tempest agreed it would be better not to divulge too many secrets.

The weekend approached, and Tempest told Miranda she would be staying in town with a man from work that she had been dating. "Why don't you invite Johnny to stay over? I know you're lonely, and he seems like a nice enough guy. At least he doesn't freak out around you."

Tempest had managed a few short trysts since high school, but shrugged off anyone who either tried to get too close or avoided Miranda. Her relationships lasted a matter of weeks, not months or years, and she always explained they just were not what she was looking for. She was adamant that she would know 'Mr. Right' when he came along.

Naturally, Miranda had thought about sex. She was almost nineteen and had never even been kissed. Of course, she really never had the opportunity, because by high school most of the kids walked on the other side of the hall to avoid the strange girl.

It certainly was not her looks. As wild as Tempest was with her dark pixie spikes and emerald eyes, Miranda was the complete opposite, with an almost ethereal beauty. Her golden hair shimmered down her back like a cape, and her eyes seemed like reflective pools of crystal blue water. Her pale skin never burned or tanned, and Miranda thought it was just another oddity she possessed.

She meditated by the pond and decided it was time, and as if to confirm her decision she felt an unfamiliar stirring of anticipation. Miranda made a stew with vegetables from the garden and a large loaf of herb crusted bread while she waited for Johnny to arrive with a bottle of red wine. After dinner, they sat in front of the fire and she could sense that he was nervous, too. It was becoming apparent he was a little afraid of her, and Miranda panicked as depression began to take hold that she would be cast out once again.

Miranda finally broke the awkward silence and said softly, "I've never done this before, Johnny. I wish I did not make you feel so uncomfortable." She looked down in her lap and twirled a golden strand of her hair around her finger. "It's been this way for me with every guy I've ever met. No one has ever come as close to me as you have."

Johnny put his arm around her, and pulled her head onto his chest while he trailed his fingers down her side. "I'm not uncomfortable, Miranda. I'm in awe of you," he admitted. "You know that. I've believed in the path for many years, but you are the first one I've met who actually had powers."

Miranda sighed. "To me, it's never been about power. It's about balance and trying to help nature offset the damage we're doing. I know I'm different, and all of my life people have avoided me." She studied the flames in the fireplace. "Sometimes I wish I had the confidence of your priestess."

"She's not my priestess," Johnny scoffed. "I was left a hefty sum of money, and I've spent my time traveling trying to find someone like you. I am so glad to have met you. I know this is real."

He lifted her chin, and for the first time, Miranda felt the warmth of a man's lips against hers. At least, at first it was warm. By the time his tongue had slipped past her lips, she felt fire in her womb and her nipples were erect and throbbing. An unexpected rush of energy passed through her, and her nails dug into his shoulders as she pulled him closer, plunging her tongue into his mouth.

"Whoa, slow down a little," he gasped. He was trying to be gentle with her, and found a wildcat in his arms. She quickly pulled his shirt over his head and ran her fingers along his slender chest. When he brushed her nipple through her sweater, she crushed herself closer to him.

She hastily threw off her clothes and dragged him down onto the rug in front of the fire. Johnny's own responses were becoming heightened, and he quickly kicked off his jeans as she fisted her hand in his hair, pulling his mouth against hers again.

His hand traveled slowly towards her breast. A part of him was still trying to be gentle, to make the act meaningful for her, but it was becoming difficult with all her grabbing and clasping. "Easy, Miranda, let's slow down."

Miranda groaned and pulled him closer. She had no idea what was happening to her. Her body was in control and not listening to the embarrassing warnings of her mind, because her Atlantian heritage demanded the throbbing pulse between her legs had to be satisfied.

In one last futile effort to prepare her, Johnny's finger slipped between her legs to find her highly aroused and more than ready. She bucked wildly at his touch and she pulled him on top of her. Her hand fumbled quickly for his shaft, and she had no time to recognize its velvet smoothness before she centered it in front of her, wrapped her legs around him, and drew him inside.

Johnny found himself holding on for dear life. Her hands were everywhere, pawing through his hair and clawing down his back drawing rivulets of blood, while she clenched so tightly around him that he had difficulty providing any movement for the friction he needed. When he tried to draw back, his erection stayed wedged inside her, causing him to stretch almost painfully instead of slide. *Virgin, my ass,* he thought.

That nasty thought broke through Miranda's senses as she climaxed. She experienced a brief flash of a vision of a large man with long wild dark hair as she squeezed Johnny in a vise tight grip and he swore as he orgasmed. She fell back in exhaustion and he rolled silently off her. His penis was shriveled and was bruising with pain, as blood from her clawing trickled down his back. Johnny quickly gathered his clothes and dressed. He ran from the cabin, and Miranda never heard from him again.

Tempest tried to talk to her about it. She had no idea why Johnny had mysteriously disappeared, and mistakenly thought they had had a fight. Miranda finally broke down and told Tempest about the incident, and asked, "Is that what it's like?"

Tempest certainly did not remember it being like that her first time, or any other time for that matter. "Maybe this power you have has something to do with it?"

Miranda meditated, and decided that even

making love would be denied to her. She wondered why she had been saddled with the abilities that sometimes seemed to be more of a curse. She also wondered why, since the vision with Johnny, her dreams were filled with the big, dark haired man.

Over the years, Tempest's outgoing nature had her dating often. The short relationships never seemed to be satisfying, and the liaisons always ended. Miranda made it clear that she was more comfortable alone, and Tempest stopped trying to set her up on dates.

Tempest received her degree and opened a flower shop where she also sold their garden herbs and where Miranda kept a second display of her handmade soaps and candles. Miranda's crafting business had built a good reputation, as once again whispers of 'witch' began to follow her. It seemed to make her crafts more valuable, and her sales were modest but consistent. The two young women, not yet twenty-four, were financially comfortable.

For all the years she had spent watching and learning from Miranda, Tempest had never experienced her own gift of magic, if she had one. Yet, something drew her to the young woman, and since the first time they had met in high school, Tempest had the undeniable knowledge that she was supposed to protect her somehow.

Miranda was delivering Yule candles and soap to the gift shop next to the post office, and at the chiming of the bell over the door she turned to see a man with long white hair and a flowing black cloak lined in sapphire blue enter. *Another wizard,* Miranda thought, and dismissed him.

The man stood by the door scanning the store until his eyes focused on Miranda. Her back was to him as he approached her. "Do you make that yourself?"

She turned to face him and prepared to describe her crafts, but as soon as she gazed into his steely eyes, she felt herself fall into a trance. His eyes were like mirrors of swirling, fathomless emotion, and looking into them made her believe the man was older than time. There was an immense sense of kindness emanating from his aura, and Miranda found herself anticipating something from him.

He brushed his hand gently across her forehead and smiled. "He will be so pleased."

Miranda tried to shake herself out of the trance and ask him what he meant, but as she came back to awareness the strange man was gone. As the moments passed by, she found she could not recall what he looked like, and his words drifted away, leaving Miranda with no recollection of anything other than placing her soap on display. She shrugged her shoulders and completed the task.

She was walking back to her car to drive home when her mind seemed to go blank again, and she made her way into Elton Beiman's office. He was the only attorney in town, but even so she had no problem being ushered in to see him. Within an hour, she had transferred the deed to the cabin and land to Tempest and put her on all her financial accounts as joint owner. Miranda thanked Elton and drove home.

When Tempest asked her how her day had gone, she mentioned stocking her display and collecting two hundred dollars in sales, and the girls celebrated. Miranda did not remember doing anything else.

Three days later, Tempest awoke to find Miranda gone. At first, she was confused and she searched everywhere for her. When she discovered Miranda had transferred all her assets to her, Tempest dropped into a deep depression, reluctantly deciding her friend had gone in search of the grandmother who disappeared two decades ago. She prayed to the goddess she would be safe and return one day.

CHAPTER II

"This is unheard of, Ethram. Do we know her heritage?"

Ethram hung his cloak and ran his fingers through his shoulder length white hair. "I am sure she is an Ancient, but I think she is unaware of it. It is good she will belong to Zulien. She is going to need a warrior to protect her. She is completely innocent of her ancestry. We will try to discover her lineage when we bring her in."

"When will that be?" Ballion was pacing with excitement. He had been with Ethram as a student since he began his studies for his own procurement vessel some day. He had never secured or even seen an Ancient.

Ethram sat on a chair on the bridge. "I have some preparations to make." He tented his slender fingers under his chin. "This is a delicate matter, Ballion. She has been raised for centuries by barbarians and primitives." Ethram's nose wrinkled with distaste as he thought of his visit to the outer world. "They have destroyed their planet, and it will be swallowed very soon."

Ballion gasped in alarm. "Then we must act now to procure her. Zulien has waited beyond his time for her, and if she is absorbed with the planet he will be devastated."

"We have to be careful, Ballion. The outer worlds do not even know of our existence. I have no idea how she ended up on this planet, but her lineage has me curious. I sense great power within her, and this is why I choose to act with caution. We are not telling Zulien until she has been secured."

"How did you know to come here? No mates

have ever been discovered on the outer worlds." Ballion had been almost frantic since Ethram informed him they were leaving the relative safety of the inner worlds.

Ethram leaned back in his chair and sighed. "When I was training with my grandfather, he told me a story of finding a derelict ship at the very edge of the inner worlds. He thought it was abandoned. All on board were decayed with the exception of one Ancient male." He waved his hand dismissively. "I do not remember the specifics, or even who the race was for that matter." Ethram's voice dropped to almost a whisper, as though he was divulging a secret. "The Ancient told him they had placed their last genes in the outer worlds."

Ethram looked at Ballion as if searching for understanding. "You and I were so close when we procured from Prameton, I thought it was worth the chance. We have been honored with the mission to find the mates, and every one is precious. If there was even a remote possibility..." Ethram left the statement unfinished. He was still overcome with emotion at his discovery.

Ballion listened attentively. His teacher, the Commander of Isotant, was unparalleled in success. Ballion remembered standing before the Imperial Magistrates and learning he was to be Ethram's apprentice. Ethram's request came at a price. It was a two edged sword, because Ethram's mate was discovered decayed on a small planet already scanned and rarely visited. He would have no son of his own to carry on his work, and thus he issued the request to the Magistrates for an apprentice. Perhaps, his own experience was why the old man filled with emotion and drove himself to extremes to secure every destined mate.

A procurement chamber was prepared for the young woman containing the sparse furnishings for her temporary sleep, along with comforting scents and sounds of her planet. He made sure he plugged Zulien's genetic sexual profile into the enhancers. The Commander continued to search the knowledge banks for information about her and, after exhausting all known data sources concerning the Ancients, he finally admitted he needed her on board to study her further. "Ballion, it is time."

"Her compartment is ready. Shall I collect her?" the green Minoc asked hopefully.

Ethram stood. "She is to be the mate of a primary warrior." He adjusted his cloak. "I must collect her myself." Ethram noted the slightly dejected lowering of Ballion's shoulders. "I leave you with the important duty of guarding the ship and the other three mates on board."

I am to be trusted with three of the precious procurements? Ballion's chest puffed out, dark ribs etching his scaled skin with pride, and the green antennae protruding from his forehead stroked across his chin, displaying his obvious pleasure at the trust Ethram had bestowed upon him.

Ethram noted Ballion's reaction and decided to prolong the moment. "Are you prepared for this responsibility? Do you have any questions?" Ethram had no doubts. He knew Ballion was as impassioned with their commitment as any student he had ever met.

Ballion's antennae made an embarrassing frenzied motion across his chin as he fairly burst with emotion. "I have no questions, Commander. I will care for the ship and our precious cargo, and await your return."

Collecting mates was a lonely trade. It was,

perhaps, one of the highest honors, but ships could travel many, many years and come back with the news of no found mates, or worse. There were mates who had not been discovered in time, such as Ethram's, leaving their other half to settle for centuries of lonely emptiness, or never feeling complete by settling for a mating of convenience with another who had no true mate to procure. Every mate secured was the highest of rewards, and resulted in a hefty boon financially and earned promotions.

Ethram stroked a comforting thumb along Ballion's quivering antennae, and then dissolved with a sweep of his cloaked arm. Having scented the woman, he found himself in a small wooden structure in the woods. He smiled at her sleeping friend. "You have brought much comfort to this Ancient. May your remaining days be filled with the same." He gently lifted Miranda's small form and issued a feeling of peace, and she shuddered slightly as she curled into his chest.

For all Ballion's pride and emotion, Ethram was gone less than ten minutes in Earth world time, and he returned with one of the most unique creatures Ballion had ever seen in his arms. Her hair, spilling half way to the floor in shimmering waves, was the color of the suns, and her pale skin was the color of the moons. "She is of Celestial lineage," he said in awe.

"I also see the signs of this." Ethram gazed down at the little Ancient. "So many of those worlds have been swallowed. It will be a challenge of great magnitude to find which of them she was from."

"Zulien has been honored." Ballion bowed his head in respect.

Ethram glanced again at his procurement. "Have you read his sexual profile? Zulien will rip her apart if we do not prepare her. See how fragile she is? I trust our gods with their decision, but to mate such a small woman with a warrior?" He shook his head, bewildered.

Not to be distracted from practicality, Ballion reminded Ethram, "The boon on her will be high. We may get recognition from the warrior as well."

Ethram smiled. *Yes, the rewards for this Ancient would be large. She was worth more than the other three procurements tallied together.* "Locate Commander Zulien while I secure her, but tell him nothing."

"Yes, Commander." Ballion began searching star charts for the location of Zulien's battleship, the Quillant.

Ethram laid Miranda on the pallet in the sleeping chamber. Here, she would sleep and dream undisturbed in her suspended state, while her genetic sexual profile was enhanced to meet her mate's needs.

The Procurer removed her clothes and brushed his thumb across her forehead when she quivered, relaxing her into deep sleep. He placed the enhancers on either side of her head and attached probes to her nipples and between her legs, and he inserted the vaginal wand. He noticed with interest that even in deep sleep she became pleasurably aroused, and she pulsed against the wand as the enhancers fused the warrior's sexual genetic profile to her. *At least she will sleep in comfort until Zulien arrives to claim her.* Ethram turned once before leaving the chamber, and he studied the beautiful creature. "Lucky dremont," he muttered, and closed the door.

When he returned to the bridge, Ballion proclaimed, "The stars are with us. The Quillant is in Stanquest Three. We are just within communication distance and our ships can rendezvous in two days."

Ethram confirmed Ballion's information, though he was still nervous about turning over the fragile Ancient to the warrior. Reluctantly, he decided this was the gods' business and the decided mating was not his responsibility. "Get him on screen." Ethram's fingers strummed the arm of his chair. Warriors always made him anxious, because they were ruthless strategists and somewhat explosive in nature. Ethram had once met Commander Zulien on planet, and he knew he had a good reputation. Still, he was a warrior, and Ethram hoped he would be good to the little Ancient.

While the ship was contacted, Miranda lay on the pallet feeling as though she was floating in darkness until she eventually settled on something soft. She was so weary, but the sounds of a rippling brook and a breeze through the trees could not calm her. She was frightened as she lay alone in this dark void, and she wondered if she had died and how to find her way out of the pit to the goddesses' realm of the Summerlands.

She felt pinched feelings on her nipples and sensitive bead, and a soft cool bar was inserted into her. In her mind, she whimpered in fear until her thoughts began to fill with the man of her visions. His strong, golden hands caressed her, and he murmured assurances as impulses traveled through the probes and wand, arousing her.

Miranda felt the desire and passion building to frightening aspects, and she was frustrated to be limited to merely squeezing to satisfy her need to thrust. She felt as though she was being held on the edge of the precipice of release, and struggled against the trance that was denying her.

After an eternity, a strong hand brushed across her forehead. "I will come to you, my little Ancient," a deep voice echoed. She reached out into the blackness, blindly searching for comfort. Sobs wracked through her as she continued to throb in frustration, and she realized she was once again alone. Perhaps it was most frightening because she knew it was all in her mind.

The Quillant had finished securing the planet Fleighten after small skirmish had erupted concerning land boundaries, and they returned to space, scanning the planets for their next mission.

Zulien lay back against the headboard of his heavy wooden bed, waiting for the Parina to arrive. With three unmated warriors on board, they were allocated one of the unique androids to relieve their sexual urges every third night.

These androids had been designed with a long split tongue, and tiny suckers gripped and released as their sensors ordered. Full breasts were tipped with nipples that stood alarmingly stiff when suckled, and their clean-shaven mound excreted a sweet musk when stroked or licked. The Parina would gasp, moan or coo appreciatively, and her arms would hold and comfort while her lips continued to whisper and kiss.

Zulien despised them. No, it was more than that. He despised the need for them. Warriors were a lusty bunch, becoming sexually aroused with little provocation... and they needed to be satisfied, or rational judgment of the burly men was jeopardized. No one needed the Commander of a battleship fighting in the midst of sexual frustration.

As with any man, Zulien yearned for his mate, the one woman in creation with a gene matched to his. Over the centuries, he watched his crews' mates board the craft, and he waited for the day a procurement ship would contact the Quillant to announce his own mate had been secured.

It had been a century since a procurement vessel had hailed them, and the three remaining warriors were reluctantly admitting their mates had most probably decayed. The thought ripped at Zulien's heart, and he could not quite let go of a tiny bit of hope she was still out there, longing to be wrapped in his protective arms.

The door to his quarters opened, and the Parina entered his chamber. "Commander," she said in her low, overly seductive voice. Zulien would not let her call him by his name because it seemed too personal. He waved her in.

She pulled her shift over her head and swayed her hips with exaggerated movements as she approached him. He rarely spoke to her. It was not her animated words of comfort or desire he wanted to hear. She merely knew how to please him, and she used her red mannequin-like arms to spread his thighs.

"Oooh, Commander." She trailed a slender finger down his length and lightly squeezed. Her eyes blinked rapidly as the data was digested for the next appropriate response. "I see you have great need for me. My tongue salivates over the thought of your..."

"Voice off, dammit." Zulien wanted to grab her by her white hair and rip the speaker from her throat. She was nothing more than a masturbation toy. He lay back again, and her tongue stroked his length, splitting to coat both sides with its suckers as he closed his eyes.

The slow pumping of her head finally relaxed him, and he let himself get swept up in her rhythm. He wondered if, when he finally ejaculated, he would again have the vision of the tiny goddess lost in the darkness and searching for him. It had happened the last three times.

He had meant to communicate with his mother about this, because she might be able to decipher the meaning of these visions. Things on the ship had been hectic though, and he kept putting off the call. Zulien began squeezing his muscled ass as he thrust his hips towards the Parina. Soon he would orgasm, and, vision or not, he could send the horrid machine back to its closet.

Her fingers gripped him, and as he ejaculated in violent spasms, he once again saw his goddess, and this time she was sobbing with fright.

Zulien ordered the Parina to leave, and he dressed to go back to the bridge. He decided to let Taliquant have her for the rest of the night, if he desired. When he arrived on deck, Lieutenant Letang was leaning towards the communicator screen. "Who calls Battleship Quillant and for what purpose?"

"This is Commander Ethram of the procurement ship, Isotant. I wish to speak with Commander Zulien."

Communicator wristbands spread the news quickly through the battleship that a procurement vessel had signaled, and crew and mates rushed to the bridge. It was possible, though unlikely, they were seeking transport for a mate. More likely, was the possibility that someone on the Quillant was about to learn of his mate's discovery. Of the nine warriors on board six were mated, and these were very good statistics for a regiment. So good, in fact, that the three unmated warriors had begun to give up hope many, many years ago.

Two of them were planning to mate with unattached females. These matings usually culminated in frustration, as even with enhancers the female would not totally accept a substitute partner's sexual profile. This was especially true for the domineering warriors who required a truly submissive partner.

Berslan was to join with a member of royalty whose true mate had been murdered for political reasons. It was quietly discussed among the crew that he was mating for ambition, because a royal would never subject herself to satisfy a warrior's needs.

Taliquant was deciding between two warriors' widows, and everyone was in agreement that his joining might stand a chance. He would never experience the fulfillment of claiming his true mate, but at least a female destined to be with a warrior would understand a warrior's demands.

Zulien sometimes quelled his sexual frustrations with a serving girl when he was on planet, but he remained promised to no one. Resigned that his mate was most probably decayed, he decided he would not distract himself with the frustration of a substitute.

The Parina serviced all three of the unmated warriors. Her data banks contained their genetic sexual profiles, and her sole function was to provide climatic release for the men.

When he was young, Zulien had asked his mother how he would know his mate, and she closed her eyes to raise her golden head towards the northern stars. A few minutes later, she looked at her son and relayed her vision. "She will be your suns and your moons," she smiled. Living in space, Zulien had never noticed the phenomenon, but trusted his mother's vision and had remained unattached.

Zulien switched on his screen. If the mate was for Berslan, it could be messy trying to disentangle himself from his fiancée, but if she was for Taliquant, things would be much less complicated, and he swore an oath under his breath that the mate would enrich Taliquant. The battleship had been through some rough conflicts lately.

"This is Commander Zulien. I understand you have news?"

Ethram eyed Zulien cautiously. His long dark hair fell well below his broad bronzed shoulders and his black leather vest was tight across his muscled chest. For the first time in his many centuries of procurement, Ethram felt unease at revealing his prize. "Yes, Commander. We have procured a warrior's mate from the outer worlds." Ethram wanted to make sure Zulien understood the extra effort on his part to procure the young woman. Warriors could be generous.

"I did not realize procurement ships searched the outer worlds," Zulien replied, with a hint of suspicion.

"As usual course, we do not, Commander, but I had previous information concerning this mate." Ethram was slightly irritated the warrior would question his motives.

Zulien sat back in his chair. "I see. Tell me, Commander, which of our warriors have benefited from your efforts?"

Ethram smiled. "You, Commander. It is your mate we have procured."

Zulien was speechless. It had not crossed his mind to hope it would be his mate. The gathering warriors stood in shocked silence. Seartock regained his senses first and recognized his Commander's stunned reaction, remembering his own emotion when his precious Ebonisha was located. He spoke up, ignoring formalities. "You have located Commander Zulien's mate?" They needed this news confirmed.

"Yes, Captain, and we would like to arrange a rendezvous. We are within two days of your present location."

The Lieutenant spoke up. "We have locked onto your position, Commander Ethram."

Zulien's shock finally abated somewhat. Most warriors were mated with the Amarzonians, a large, elegant woman for the formidable warriors. *What would an Amarzonian be doing on an outer world?* He finally composed himself enough to find his voice. "Might I ask what lineage she hails from?"

Ethram looked into the warrior's eyes and waited until he was sure he had his full attention. "She is a Celestial, a true Ancient, Commander, and with so many of their worlds swallowed long ago, I am still searching her heritage."

Zulien was bewildered, as he glanced at the other warriors' faces, and those of their Amarzonian mates who had joined them on the bridge when the news of the procurement vessel's hailing quickly circulated. Celestials were always petite, even the males, from what he had studied. Ethram saw the confusion in Zulien's face and smiled with relief at the warrior's concern. "There is no mistake, Zulien. She is your mate. Perhaps, it is because she will require your protection."

Zulien thought about that for a moment. "Commander, thank you for the extreme sacrifice of traveling to the outer worlds. I look forward to claiming..." He was still rattled by the news.

"Miranda, Commander," Ethram said softly. "She has been named Miranda."

"Miranda." The name rolled off Zulien's lips as if it was the first word, the only word, he had ever spoken.

The communication line was silenced. The warriors and their mates crowding the bridge quietly digested the news that a Celestial, an Ancient, would be joining their group. It was Taliquant who finally spoke up. "Commander," he cleared his tight throat, "Zule, I am so pleased for you, sir."

Zulien could hardly contain his feelings. "Thank you, Tali." He belatedly realized how badly his friend had hoped the mate was his own. "I guess this proves the gods do not want us to give up hope."

Berslan shuffled his feet in agitation. "Commander, I feel it in my soul that my mate has decayed."

"Berslan, this is every man's decision, and no one here faults your path or your judgment."

"Thank you, sir. I know my course is true."

The warriors and their mates retreated to the lounge for a celebratory toast. The mates were excited with the news another female would be joining their ranks, and everyone planned to research the archives on Celestials. None of them had ever met an Ancient before, and they wanted their Commander's mate to feel welcomed. Taliquant, second in command, realized Zulien would be distracted, and decided to ensure the ship maintained on alert with such a valuable mate soon to board.

Zulien had a queasy, light feeling from his stomach to his groin. His mother had some knowledge of the Ancient ways. She practiced what was remembered of the lost Old Religion, and was one of few who could manage visions. He decided he needed her advice. *How in the worlds am I supposed to mate with an Ancient?*

Zulien entered his quarters, studying his home for the last three centuries. A woman had never graced its interior and the colors and furnishings were dark and heavy, like his moods. The maroon carpet was wearing thin, and the bedclothes... when was the last time he had requested new ones? *By the stars, how can I bring my mate, much less a Celestial Ancient, into this dungeon?*

He poured himself some wine, and sat down in the heavy chair at his desk. A twinge of guilt tightened his gut as he realized he had not spoken to his mother in years. When her calm golden face filled his screen he said, "Mother, I trust all is well?"

"Zule," she always used his boyhood name, "you have found your mate."

Zulien was momentarily silenced by her statement. "Yes, she was procured in the outer worlds by the Isotant."

"It does not surprise me. Ethram's grandfather located me for your father. It is such a shame he will have no son; their instincts are rare. I am being rude and wasting your valuable time, Zule. Did you need to speak with your father?"

"No mother, it is you I need to speak with. Ethram has told me my mate is a Celestial."

His mother laughed in her musical way. "I told you that when you were a boy. Why are you so surprised?"

"Back then, I did not understand your vision. Mother, she is Celestial," he repeated. "This makes no sense to me. I am at a loss as to what I should do. If my mate were ever found, I always imagined an Amarzonian. Celestials are incompatible with warriors, but Ethram assures me there is no mistake."

"Zule, has Ethram discerned what Ancient race she heralds from?"

"No, mother. He says he has exhausted his means for searching."

"Then, I ask you son, do you seek my advice concerning your mate?" His mother's calm face stared back at him.

He knew she would never presume to offer suggestions to a named warrior, even if it was her son. His strong façade faded. "Please, mother, she is my mate, and I need to know how to ensure her well-being."

"Zule, you will need to protect her, and it will not be long before news of her discovery is known. I admire Ethram, but he is a practical procurer and will be returning to the Magistrates to collect his boon for her. Her mere existence, even if she is unaware of her importance, makes her a target for the hierarchy. You must claim her, and then make her as comfortable as possible until you can get back on planet for your mating ceremony. That is my advice to you, son."

Zulien digested his mother's warning. "Have you seen her lineage?"

Zalana's smile broadened further, and her eyes filled with emotion. "Zule, she is the last of the Atlantians."

His mouth dropped open. By the stars of all the inner worlds, why would the gods and goddesses trust him to care for the only known priestess of the Old Religion? It was presumed the race had been destroyed before the inner worlds reorganized, thousands of years ago in the confusing Battles of Chaos.

"Zule," his mother waited for his attention, "you have been chosen for a reason. You must bring her home to us for your ceremony."

The warrior felt a painful, anxious feeling. He needed to get to his mate and protect her. "Thank you, mother. I will contact you when we are nearing Shallistar. If you truly believe there is danger, would you be willing to arrange the ceremony so we can be prepared to leave the surface quickly?"

"Zule! If you dare deny me the privilege of honoring my new daughter-in-law with her ceremony, I will put you over my knee again. Trust me, your father will hold you down." Her laughter chimed through his bedchamber.

Zulien smiled. He had not realized how much he had missed his mother's laughter. "I do not wish my mate to see me in such a disadvantaged position, and I bow to your wishes. I will contact you when we are close to planet."

"I hope to see her before then, Zule. The ceremony must include her wishes as well for it to have true meaning for her. Be the considerate man I have raised. She will be highly intelligent but unable to protect herself, and goddess knows what abilities she may have. You must let her know you will protect her, and that she must obey you for her own safety. It may be wise to hold Taliquant's ceremony at the same time. Would you ask him if he would like me to contact his family and arrange it?"

Zule's brows knit together. "Mother, Tali's mate has not been procured."

The golden complexion blanched slightly. "I do not understand, Zule. In my vision, the two mates have been close for years and I did not see them separated."

"Is it possible she was left behind? Why

42

would Ethram not have sensed her?" Zule was already making plans to contact the Commander as soon as he finished speaking with his mother.

"I have no idea, but I have a bad feeling about this, Zule. Sign off and contact Ethram immediately."

Zulien could not remember ever seeing his mother look so scared, but that was her expression: scared. He walked quickly to the communication bridge, hoping he did not run into Taliquant. As boys, Tali often joked about the visions his mother had, until she had correctly predicted that he, the mere son of a merchant, would one day become a warrior.

Zulien stepped out onto the bridge, and was relieved to find Letang sitting alone at the helm. The rest of the crew was still in the lounge, gossiping about the Celestial.

"Commander, congratulations. I thought you would still be celebrating, sir. " The Lieutenant shook his hand.

"Thank you, Letang." Zulien studied the man a moment. Letang could be trusted to keep news contained, he was sure of this. "Raise the Isotant on screen. I need to speak with Ethram immediately."

Letang had been on board when two other mates had been procured, and he knew the warriors were anxious for any information about the women they had waited for so long to be discovered. They would call the procurement vessels for the slightest descriptions of their women, and he wondered what the Commander would be asking.

"Isotant, this is the Battleship Quillant."

"How may we be of service, Lieutenant?" Ballion had misjudged by a mere five minutes when the warrior would be calling for specifics about his mate.

"Commander Zulien would like to speak with your Commander."

Ballion was miffed at the slight. He knew almost as much as Ethram about the Celestial. "Is there something I can help you with?"

Letang repeated, "Commander Zulien would like to speak with your Commander."

Ballion sighed and stood up. "Yes, Lieutenant." Ballion found Ethram in the Celestial's chamber, watching her sleep. He relayed the Quillant's request and Ethram followed him to the bridge. "How can I help you, Commander?"

"We may have a problem," Zulien began.

Ethram noted the Commander's uncomfortable expression, and considered his words, trying to gauge the seriousness. "What kind of problem, Zulien?"

"There was another warrior's mate near the Celestial. You did not get a reading on her?" Zulien watched Ethram's face fall.

"The signal from your mate's gene was very strong, Zulien, probably because she is an Ancient. Why do you believe there was a second woman?"

"I just know there was, and we must leave it at that for now. Is there a way to check?"

Ballion considered the boon for a second Celestial and nearly fainted. Ethram glanced at the charts and replied, "It will take another day to get back within range of this outer world, and I am not sure I can read through your Celestial's beacon to discern a second one."

"Perhaps we should hasten our meeting with you and transfer my mate off your ship," Zulien suggested.

"You are that sure there is another?"

"There is," Zulien affirmed.

Ethram was completely distraught at the thought of leaving a precious mate behind. "We must hurry, Commander. I sensed the planet was to be swallowed soon after I procured your mate."

Zulien paled. How could he ever tell his best friend that his mate was decayed? Any argument from Tali that he had given up hope of finding his mate was dispelled when Zulien saw the tears he was holding back at Ethram's announcement that the mate procured was not his. "Letang, arrange the coordinates for the rendezvous."

Letang remained calm through the startling transmission. He had already anticipated the Commander's request and had quickly altered course to intersect with Isotant's path before it reached the outer worlds. "I have increased speed, Commander. We should meet up late tomorrow morning."

"I trust you understand the need for discretion?" Zulien asked.

"Yes, Commander." Letang reached out in total breach of protocol and gripped his arm. "Zulien, by the stars, we will get there in time."

Zulien cleared his throat. "We must, Letang."

After the Commander left to go to his quarters, Letang called down to the lounge. Nemiste was supposed to relieve him in an hour, but he told the warrior he could remain at the celebration with his mate. Vasilla arrived on the bridge shortly after the discussion.

"I was hoping you would be joining me soon, Letang," his mate pouted.

The young warrior smiled at his tall, gentle mate. He indicated for her to sit next to him, and he explained the situation. Mates kept no secrets from each other. His thumb began absently stroking her large brown nipple through her sheer caftan, and she purred. "I am the best pilot on board, and the only one other than the Commander and the crew of the Isotant who understands how imperative it is to expedite our travel."

Vasilla laid her head on his shoulder and stroked his swollen shaft through his breeches. "I am so proud to be the mate of a warrior who will do this for his friends, Letang. Commander Ethram should be commended on his willingness to transport back to that volatile outer world with his knowledge of its impending destruction."

Letang chuckled. "Trust me, Vasilla, the Commander will be taking his commendability in a large boon and a petition for promotion. His Minoc may end up with his own vessel after this." Letang made some adjustments to the course as Vasilla dropped to her knees and her hands worked to unclasp his breeches. The battleship sped through the darkness.

Her tongue began to lap gently at the smooth flesh, and her soft hand stroked him. She was careful not to distract him from his mission as she brought him to a gentle climax. Letang brushed through her curls and he gazed into her adoring eyes. He refocused on his navigation, determined to aid a brother warrior in the procurement.

Taliquant had secured the ship and gone back to his quarters where the Parina was already naked and waiting for him. She swayed her hips as she walked forward and wrapped her arms around him, quickly scanning the depressed emotions.

"What is your pleasure, Tali?" she purred.

"I just want to lie down for a while." The

dejection in his voice caused her scanning lights to blink rapidly.

The android took his hand and led him to the bed. Her fingers slowly worked at undressing him, and her lips followed her fingers down his chest as it was bared. "You are sad, Tali. What can I do to comfort you?" The android's banks were frantically scanning for the proper movements and responses to ease the warrior's discomfort.

"Just stay here for a while."

The Parina finally settled on the immense, oppressive despondency of the loss or decay of a mate. "Your mate is unwell?"

"I have no mate," Tali snarled. "Just shut up and suck me."

The Parina obediently followed his orders. She released unbuttoned his breaches and began to work on him with her split tongue. Taliquant gripped her hair and thurst forward, ending in an unfulfilling climax.

When the procurement vessel had hailed them, he had convinced himself the mate would be his, and when his best friend, Zule, was confirmed, his emotions collided between happiness for his friend and the bereft emptiness he had been living with for centuries.

Zulien slept fitfully. The impending mission to collect Tali's mate was second in his reeling thoughts only to those of his Celestial, Miranda. He sensed her in a black pit, alone and frightened, and she was trembling with a desire she could not appease. He tried to reach out to her, but he knew it was impossible until she received his sash and oath. The bedclothes tangled around him as he fought his way to her, finally waking him in a panic that his mate was lost to him. Her sobs echoed in his head, fisting around his heart.

Giving up on hope of further rest, he rose on shaky legs and sat at his desk. He began researching the little information he could find concerning the Atlantians, and was slightly dismayed when he discovered he was correct in his assumption they were a smallish race. Some data indicated they had pale, luminescent skin and large crystal blue eyes that always appeared moist, and it was thought they had the golden hair of the suns.

Zulien knew his mate carried the gene, but her physical nature would have been changed on this new, primitive planet as the bloodline thinned. He had no information on this outer world, and thus, no information as to what characteristics may have been altered through the generations. She could have the green scales of a Minoc for all he knew. Not that it would matter. Their mating gene was matched so they would be attracted to each other regardless of physical appearances, still… he hoped she did not have scales.

An hour later, Letang knocked on his door and waited to be recognized. Zulien opened the door. "We will be docking with the procurement ship in an hour. Commander, there is a vessel approaching us fast from the Raliquest Quadrant and I have had no success in hailing signals on any channels."

Zulien considered his mother's warnings. "Is there a chance our communication with Isotant was compromised?"

"Yes, sir. Absolutely. The Isotant was barely within the inner worlds and had to use an open communication port to hail us." The Lieutenant was shifting his weight in uncharacteristic agitation.

Zulien knew Letang remained calm in the fiercest of battles, and his tense demeanor, more than anything else, let Zulien know he considered this a crisis. There was a tightening in his groin as he recognized an instinctual fear for his mate. "Then we must consider they heard the entire transmission and know we are to procure an Ancient. Sound the readiness alert and get the Isotant on a secure communication channel."

"Major Taliquant has the crew on alert already, Commander." The two men were walking quickly to the bridge. "He has also sequestered the mates to quarters."

Zulien silently thanked the gods for Tali's foresight, and trying to sound detached, he asked, "What are the chances the vessel has locked onto Isotant?"

Letang understood the Commander's fears. "I do not feel that is the case, Commander, because they have not changed course to intercept her. They appear to be tracking us," Letang replied as they walked onto the bridge.

"Nemiste, change our heading five degrees and slow down. Keep a close watch whether the rogue vessel continues to track us. Perhaps we will get lucky and be far enough out of range that they miss the procurement ship. Letang, have you hailed the Isotant?"

"Yes, sir. Ballion has gone in search of Commander Ethram."

When Ethram appeared on the screen, they discussed the mystery ship. "We are making a slight change of course, but will remain within range should they veer in your direction. This means we must delay the rendezvous. Can you complete the procurement safely with my mate on board?"

Eyes shot towards the Commander at the

question.   Another procurement?   Of course the battleship would aid such an important quest, even if the Commander's own mate had not been on board the vessel.

"Yes, Commander. I keep a scanner on board and it can separate the beacons, but it will take a little longer."

"You have to have contact with the woman to use that.   How are you going to narrow your search?"   Zulien could not help glancing at Taliquant. Luckily, all eyes were on Ethram.

"The Celestial's scent is strong, and I should be able to track to the location I procured her from."   Ethram was already cloaking.   "You mentioned that the second woman should have been close to her?"

"She would have been a close companion for many years," Zulien affirmed.

Taliquant stared at Zulien. For him to be advising the procurer reeked of the telltale signs of his mother's visions. An involuntary thought shot through his system. *Please let it be mine.*

"It is possible I already know who she is. Your mate lived in an isolated structure with a friend, and when I planted the will to disburse her goods she transferred everything to the other young woman." Ethram checked the scanner and reached out a hand to snag the Minoc. "Ballion, sit down," he ordered.

The Minoc had been pacing the bridge. Ballion was overwhelmed with the thought of going back to the outer world so close to its impending destruction. He would be caring for the four mates, one an Ancient no less, while his Commander was on planet. Add to that the threatening, mysterious vessel approaching... it was too much. He did as Ethram ordered, but could not control the jerking, whiplash movements of his antennae.

Ethram noticed his apprentice's distress and he employed the surefire cure to settle him down. "Think of the boon, Ballion. We will have procured two warriors' mates, rescued under extreme measures, and I am sure we will be promoted."

The mention of the impending riches collected for the two mates worked, and Ballion's antennae slowly stroked his rough green chin, comforting the agitated man. "You can count on me, Commander."

"I want you to keep the secure communication line open with the Quillant. Commander Zulien will issue orders to you in my absence."

Zulien heard Ethram's order. Minocs were nervous little men, and Zulien tried to reassure him. "You will be fine, Ballion. Your ship carries my mate, so trust me, we will be close enough to intercept should the vessel change directions and head towards your location."

Ballion's nerves settled a bit as he listened to the calm, deep voice of the warrior. "Thank you, Commander Zulien. I await your orders, sir."

Ethram placed his hands on Ballion's shoulders and looked into his slitted yellow eyes. "You will be fine, son, and I will return quickly. I have no wish to be swallowed with that polluted planet."

"Good luck, Commander Ethram." Ballion turned back to the communication screen, anxiously waiting for the warrior's instructions and his Commander's return.

Ethram had no problem finding the cabin. Unfortunately, if was afternoon, and the woman was not in the structure. He appeared in town, and his sensors brought him back to the shop where he had first located Miranda. Something led him to her display, and the scanner blinked a light blue. *Yes, yes, but I already have her,* he thought.

He left the store and walked past other shops, checking his scanner and becoming frantic as no response lit up the panel. It was possible the woman had moved on when her friend had disappeared. He crossed the street, and at the second shop he thought he noticed the tiniest blip on the screen. He entered and saw the display of Miranda's soaps and candles on a shelf by the register. As he approached, the blue light began to pulse, and his hopes fell. *Another false signal.*

"They're homemade and the last of their kind, I am afraid. My friend made them."

Ethram turned to look at the owner of the wistful voice. It was her, thank the stars; short, dark, spiky hair, green eyes and all.

In the inner worlds, it was considered proper for a young woman to be procured for her mate, and celebrations were held to commemorate her leaving. The outer worlds, blissfully ignorant of the advanced civilizations, would find it a mystery, perhaps even an unsettling event if such a disappearance occurred. Ordinarily, Ethram would have researched the proper way to handle this. However, this was not an ordinary situation. He glanced at the scanner, and even without physical contact, it pulsed a steady red. His fingers flew over the gene panel, and it read: 'Taliquant'. Ethram made a mental note to question Zulien further on this.

"Are you all right?" the woman asked. She thought he looked a little pale. Of course, the black wizard cloak did not help.

"You are Miranda's friend?" Ethram

approached her, holding out his hand.

"You know Miranda? Have you seen her? She disappeared about a week ago without a word." For the first time in days, there was hope in Tempest's sad eyes.

"I am going to take you to her," Ethram smiled. The woman stepped back suspiciously, just before his hand grasped hers.

"Where is she?" Tempest was getting an odd feeling about this old guy, and her mind filled with thoughts of kidnapping.

"She is fine." He again held out his hand. "I am Ethram." He prided himself on procuring mates as gently as possible, but this one was being difficult and he was running out of time. If she did not take his hand willingly, Ethram decided he would grab her.

Tempest's automatic response was to shake hands, and that was the last thing she remembered.

The shop stood abandoned, as did the cabin in the woods. Police made a half-assed effort to look for the two unusual women, but no one reported them missing or seemed to care what had happened to them.

One year later, the property in the woods had been sold. The planet was swallowed before the new owners moved in.

CHAPTER III

Ethram returned with Tempest softly snoring against his chest, and a slight line of drool running down her chin from her open mouth. Her spiked hair flattened on the side resting against him, making the tufts still protruding from her skull look even wilder.

Ballion had expected another Celestial, not this feral creature his Commander had procured, and he stared in disbelief. "Are you sure she is the one? Her bloodline must have completely thinned. She does not resemble Commander Zulien's mate at all. Perhaps, there is a mistake." His little legs pumped madly to match Ethram's strides as he trudged down the hall towards Miranda's sleeping chamber.

"Yes," Ethram sighed wearily. "I assure you, she is much more presentable when she is awake." He had Ballion place another pallet in the room, because they did not have time to properly prepare and honor Taliquant's mate and this was the best they could manage. He laid the young woman on the cot and attached her probes and wand. It took only a minute for the enhancers to have her emit the proper response to the warrior's profile. Satisfied she was being comforted by her mate, he checked on Miranda and then slipped out of the room.

Ethram noted Ballion's concern. "She has aptly been named Tempest, and Major Taliquant will have his hands full taming her. She is far more primitive than the Celestial." Ethram rubbed his temples. "My head is spinning with these unexpected procurements. First an Ancient, now a primitive from the outer worlds? I hope this is not to become the way of it. The inner worlds are challenge enough to search for mates. If the outer worlds are going to produce them, the Magistrates will have to double our numbers."

Ballion's antennae stroked his chin as he thought about this. It could mean he would have his own vessel sooner than he had planned.

"I see your mind working, Ballion. Consider this: the Magistrates may decide it is the new Commanders they can risk to the outer worlds." Ethram sat at the communications portal.

Ballion's antennae jerked, as even the idea of commanding a ship into unknown space among the primitives petrified him. "Surely they would see the wisdom in sending the more seasoned Commanders into the new territory?"

Ethram was distracted while he studied the star chart. "I am not certain they would risk that. These are the only two mates I have ever heard of being discovered in the vastness." He glanced at his apprentice. "They would most likely keep us in the inner worlds where there is a predictable outcome to the search." He turned his attention back to the screen. "What has been happening since I have been gone?"

"The mystery vessel continues to track the Quillant, and the battleship is making a wide arc and should be headed back this way soon. I have heard the warriors' hailing signal, but the other ship still has not responded," Ballion reported.

"What a waste of time. I hope somebody makes a move soon. We have mates to deliver and boon to collect," Ethram declared.

A few minutes later, the rogue vessel shot sideways, predicting the battleship's course and attempting to cut across the arc. The Quillant continued its path, not changing position to engage.

Ethram and Ballion watched the star chart, fascinated and more than a little anxious at being so close to the impending fight. Zulien's deep voice boomed through the bridge. "Ethram, stay where you are. I think I have figured out their plan. They mean to take out the Quillant and leave you and the Ancient unprotected. I think they have known your position all along."

"We do have some weapons on board, Commander. We are trained in defense. Is there anything you would like us to do to assist you?" Ethram offered.

Ballion's antennae roamed nervously. *He was no warrior. By the stars, what was his Commander doing?* He calmed considerably with Zulien's reply.

"Thank you, but no, Ethram. Have you procured the other mate?"

"Yes, she rests safely beside the Celestial. You are certain you do not want our assistance?" Ethram confirmed.

"Your cargo is far too valuable and your weapons would not stand a chance against them. I still do not know if they mean to collect the Ancient or destroy her." Zulien squinted in concentration. "Did you get a further reading on the planet? Do you have any idea how long it has?"

"It will be soon, though probably not for another year." Ethram had upped his timeline of when the planet would be swallowed, based on readings from the scanner.

"It is hot though, right?" Zulien confirmed.

"Yes, I felt my lungs burning. I think that is why my initial estimation was off," Ethram admitted.

Zulien thought for a minute. "Ethram, if they mean to destroy the Ancient, they may break off from our challenge once they realize they are losing. If this was meant to be a suicide mission to destroy her, they would not have to be gentle on their approach to you. The Quillant will most likely annihilate the rogue long before it can get close, but I think I would like to secure the odds."

Ethram sat forward. "What do you have in mind, Commander?"

"We are not going to wait for them to attack. We are going after them. As soon as you sense the battle, swing your vessel behind the planet while we keep them distracted. Being in the outer worlds they will be disoriented, and even if they break free and try to run they will only have a vague idea of your location. The heat from the planet should camouflage your position." Zulien was pleased with the extra measure of protection he could provide his mate.

"I had no chance to categorize the primitive's advances. They have a few devices close to their atmosphere and two of them are armed with minor weapons. To be safe, we will hide behind the fourth planet. It is uninhabited." Ethram began to plot the new course, and looked up at the screen. "Commander, do you wish me to make the announcement now?"

"Yes," Zulien agreed. "I do not need the warriors' minds compromised, and they already know something besides this attack is going on."

Ethram did not have time for his usual formal announcement when presenting a warrior with news of his mate. These men often waited centuries in hope their mate would be procured, and to hurry through the proclamation seemed unfair. Due to the circumstances, he felt he had no choice. "Major Taliquant, your mate rests beside the Celestial aboard our vessel."

Taliquant felt as though he had been kicked

in the stomach by an arragon. Dazed, he asked, "Zule?"

"It is true. It was the vision my mother relayed to me while we discussed my mate. I am pleased for you, Tali. It is right that our mates have also formed a bond, and it will make it easier for them to adjust to their new lives." Zulien's relief that his friend's mate had been procured was visible on his face.

"Commander Ethram, she is safe?" Taliquant needed the reassurance.

"Quite safe, Taliquant, and I intend to see to it she remains that way. Are we ready, Zulien?" Ethram waved Ballion towards the navigation area.

"We will contact you on this channel when it is safe to return to the inner worlds. This should not take long," Zulien replied.

"We await the attack." Ethram looked at the other warrior. "Taliquant, her name is Tempest, and I think you will find her quite challenging," Ethram chuckled. He knew Taliquant was wondering if his mate was Celestial as well, and he did not want to tell him his young woman was an outer world primitive just yet. It might distract him during the attack.

"Stations. Taliquant, Redemis and Versheron force them towards the Quillant. Do not engage until they fire on you," Zulien ordered.

The warriors dashed to their crafts and began a wide circle to position themselves behind the rogue vessel. The ship continued its course designed to intercept the Quillant. The Battleship tried one last time to hail the vessel, and was surprised to receive a reply.

"Warriors of Quillant," began the nasal whining speech.

"Debayluths," Zulien muttered. "I should

have guessed. You are out of your usual territories."

The pirate ignored him. "You will not aid the procurement vessel. Even your Magistrates will support our decision to remove the threat of an Ancient."

Zulien laughed. "Yes, I am sure the Magistrates will take into consideration the decision of a bunch of thieves and marauders."

"You think only the Celestial have visions? It was our wizards who told us of this discovery," the creature whined.

"Were they also kind enough to tell you to plan your demise?" Zulien baited. He wanted to give the three warriors time to get into position behind the pirate craft. One thing you could count on with the self-important Debayluths was that their pride and misplaced arrogance overshadowed any sense of strategy. All you had to do was ask and they could not wait to divulge their 'foolproof' battle plans.

"Our mission is to weaken you. Two other ships are within a day's travel and will finish you off. The procurement vessel cannot outrun both of them." The insane creature sounded pleased to convey the news.

Letang scanned the star charts and made a discreet call to the Battleship Quistar. He scribbled a note on his wrist pad and smiled as he showed it to Zulien.

It was next to impossible to keep a straight face as Zulien said to the pirate Commander, "Your visionary wizards were not on the Blaytard by any chance... or perhaps the Dishton?"

The Debayluth's pink eyes widened. He was sure he had not divulged the names of the other vessels, and he decided to try to throw the warrior off balance. "Why would you suggest such a thing?"

Zulien knew he had the upper hand. "Of course not. They have visions. Certainly they would not have boarded the two vessels knowing they were to be destroyed by the Battleship Quistar in Starquist Four."

"You lie! The vessels are less than a day away, and your vessel was the only battleship on the star charts."

"Two days ago we were the only battleship in the quadrant," Zulien confirmed. "The Quistar was on planet gathering supplies and they re-entered space this morning only to find themselves engaged, for a brief time anyway, with your two rogue vessels." Zulien smiled at the shocked expression on his adversary's face, and he wondered what he would do now that he knew his support was not going to arrive. The Debayluths were natural cowards.

The rogue Commander fell back in his chair after another crewmate apparently confirmed Zulien's message, and he was shaking his head in confusion. They did not handle a change in plans well.

Even though the single ship provided little threat, Zulien decided the rogue vessel had to be destroyed so that they could not take news of the Ancient back to their hideout. "It is time to join your wizards, pirate." Zulien turned to Seartock. "Engage."

The lasers blasted towards the rogue vessel before it had time to maneuver, and Letang increased speed, heading straight for their ship while Seartock and Nemiste fired their weapons. The Debayluth's ship finally made an attempt to turn. It was unprepared to see Taliquant, Versheron and Redemis blocking them in and firing their smaller lasers in a joined line directly at the view port of the bridge.

The battle lasted less than fifteen minutes before Ethram noticed the brief flare and then the disappearance of the rogue vessel's position on the star chart. The Isotant had not even crossed into the outer worlds.

"Zulien, I take it the Quillant is the vessel I still see on the charts?"

Zulien chuckled. "We have this marker to ourselves, Commander. Apparently, the Battleship Quistar aided our cause by taking out two vessels that were supposed to join them for back up."

"I caught part of the communication. What are Debayluths doing this close to the edge?" Ethram was no warrior, but a Commander of any vessel would be remiss if he did not keep up with the charts.

Zulien answered, "I have no idea. They said they had some wizards who had visions of my Ancient."

Ethram caught the warrior's reference to 'his' Ancient. "Debayluths with visionary wizards? Never going to happen."

"I agree, but this is quite the mystery. Let me secure the Quillant and my returning warriors, and I will get back to you shortly to discuss this further."

Zulien's abrupt finish led Ethram to believe he had already formed an opinion on the matter. Their discussion later would be interesting, he thought, his tapered fingers stroking his chin thoughtfully. "Ballion, keep our weapons at the ready."

"Letang, meet me in my quarters to discuss the rendezvous. Berslan and Nemiste, take the helm and scan the charts in case there is a fourth ship we have missed. Seartock, you can release the mates from quarters." Zulien walked briskly back to his room with Letang at his heels. "Letang, freeze outgoing communications with your pass code. It should buy us a little time, and he will think you forgot to release the device when I ordered you to follow me."

Letang knew better than to ask questions and quickly did as he was told.

Zulien walked over to his desk and scanned the communications log. "Letang, call Taliquant and tell him to meet us here ASAP. I do not want to transmit over my band in case someone is scanning me."

Letang did as he was ordered. He was curious about the Commander's statement because Zulien was not a paranoid man. He must truly believe he was being observed by someone on the ship, and they waited patiently for Taliquant to join them.

"Sit. We have something to discuss that cannot leave this room." Zulien ran his fingers through his dark hair.

"The Debayluths had no business in this quadrant, and that story about the wizards is nonsense. That leaves only one alternative: someone on board one of the ships has been talking. I am sure Commander Ethram will agree that Ballion cannot be considered a threat. Although Minocs are greedy by nature, even at the offer of great boon they would kill themselves before they would dishonor their race. That leaves someone aboard the Quillant. The mates would not be able to operate the communication device without assistance, so that narrows it down to a warrior."

Letang and Taliquant eyed each other uncomfortably. Warriors became closer than natural brothers, and this was a crushing blow. "You know who it is," Taliquant stated.

Zulien nodded. "I think I do. The Debayluths have no reason to exterminate ancients, and their Commander made a curious comment. He said, 'The Magistrates would support their plan'. We all know the Magistrates would execute any pirate who dared to contact them directly. I am not sure how my mate could be a threat to the hierarchy, but I believe that is who ordered the attack. Only one warrior has direct contact with royalty." Zulien halted his summation to make sure they were following his thoughts.

"Berslan... his betrothed is the daughter of the Magistrate of Commerce." Taliquant put his head in his hands. Berslan had been on board the Quillant as part of their original crew and they had spent centuries in battles together.

He looked up at Zulien. "Do you think he knew they would order them destroyed? It is so hard for me to believe he could be a part of such a thing."

Zulien reached for a file on his desk and he pulled out a scroll with the gold edges of the Magistrates' decrees. "The Magistrates have ordered him off ship when we land on Latisqua for the ceremony. They would not risk his mate on a battleship. He was to be promoted within the hierarchy to strengthen the Magistrate's bloodlines."

"He never said a thing." Taliquant looked at Letang for confirmation.

"No, Commander," Letang agreed. "I never considered the consequences of his mating, and it makes sense now that he is so determined his true mate has decayed. I have never heard anyone so convinced. We all continue to hope until it is proven our mate is lost to us."

"I need to decide what to do. I am sure the Magistrates are waiting for Berslan to contact them, and I cannot keep the communication portal closed much longer without raising suspicions. If he tells them the two ancients survived, they are sure to make a stronger attempt." Zulien felt the twinge in his groin again. With his mate located, his protective instincts were becoming stronger and he knew it could interfere with rationality.

Letang smiled. "Perhaps they did not survive, Commander."

Zulien looked up at him. "What do you mean? Of course they did. The Debayluth vessel never got close to the Isotant."

"Please, hear me out, sir." The young man stood and began pacing. "This will not be a permanent solution, but it could keep them safe until we can decide what to do. Suppose we have Ethram communicate to the ship the two outer world mates have decayed. He could say they could not survive our atmosphere, or they contracted a strange virus that does not affect us, or something. He could deliver the mates to Shallistar while we deposit our traitor on Latisqua. We can skip Berslan's ceremony and head back to your home planet so you and Taliquant can properly mourn your loss. With the claiming and the ceremonies quickly concluded, the hierarchy would have a difficult time arranging another attempt on your mates."

Zulien thought it over. "That could work, Letang. What do you think, Taliquant? This concerns your mate, too."

"I feel like kicking Berslan's ass for delaying my claiming, but I see no other choice," Taliquant agreed. He had waited centuries for his mate, and now that she was found he was being denied.

His stomach soured.

"Letang, we need to keep this news between ourselves. Will Vasilla be able to maintain our confidence?" Zulien knew it would be impossible for Letang to keep the plan from his mate.

"I will tell her it could compromise my well-being if the plan were divulged. To protect me she would decay with it unspoken," Letang assured them.

"How do we keep Berslan from discovering our ruse? We have to tell Commander Ethram our plans." Taliquant was becoming agitated as he forced himself to accept the delay in meeting his mate.

Letang thought for a moment. "We will rendezvous with the Isotant as we planned, and the three of us will board and finalize the plan with the Commander at that time."

Zulien felt his cock quiver at the thought of being so close to Miranda.

"The crew will question why we are returning without our mates," Taliquant noted. He adjusted his breeches to accommodate the stirring in his groin.

Letang could not help himself. "Getting a little tough to think, huh?"

The Commander scowled at him. "I am fine."

"The feelings balance after the claiming, sirs. Might I suggest we return to the ship with the news the mates appear to decline, and until we learn what is wrong it is better to leave them with Commander Ethram as he is experienced in these matters?"

"By the stars, when did you become such a devious strategist, Letang?" Zulien knew the junior officer had great potential, but he had outdone himself with this matter.

"I have studied under a great teacher, Commander. You have yourself to blame," Letang laughed.

"I guess the plan is set. Letang, return to the bridge, make your apologies about the communication lock and arrange the rendezvous quickly. I want the news of our mates' decay to become known as soon as possible to divert another attempt on their lives." Zulien waited for Letang to leave.

"That warrior will have his own battleship one day," Taliquant commented.

"I've watched him. He is quiet and discreet, but misses very little, and I would not be surprised if he had figured out it was Berslan about the same time I did." Zulien poured them each a drink.

"Well, this sucks," Taliquant toasted.

"True. We wait centuries and then discover we have surviving mates who are friends, only to have to delay the claiming over some political crap. Why do you suppose the Magistrates want them destroyed?"

"I have no idea. I do not know the history of the ancients very well, but Celestials who have been living in the outer worlds could not pose that great a threat. It makes no sense." Taliquant shook his head in confusion.

"Mother says Miranda is Atlantian. I think they were the keepers of knowledge or something. I could not find much in the data banks, because they were thought to be extinct hundreds of centuries ago."

"I thought they were artists. That certainly would not cause any threat to the hierarchy. Maybe your mother can tell us more when we get back to Shallistar." Both men were shifting around stiff erections at the thought of their mates. "What a mess."

Zulien downed his drink. "You got that right."

"I wonder what they look like. I mean, the Ancient gene has been diluted with the primitive planet species for hundreds of thousands of years."

Zulien waved a frustrated hand at his charts. "I can not even locate the damn planet they were found on." Zulien ran his fingers through his wild hair in exasperation. "I know I will crave her anyway, but I keep hoping she does not have Minoc scales."

Taliquant rubbed his crotch. "Ouch."

Zulien was ready to burst. "Want to hang around a while? It is still my night with the Parina."

The rendezvous was set for late afternoon. With the exception of a brief conversation with Ethram concerning the docking procedure, Zulien avoided the bridge. He found it difficult to be around Berslan.

Ethram was still trying to figure out what was going on, but he cautiously avoided asking questions about the attack when Zulien neglected to bring it up. With a flash of insight, Ethram waited for the last communication before docking. "Commander, might I suggest you and the Major bring your joining gifts with you. Ballion has never seen the offering," he lied.

Ballion was across the bridge, out of communication range, and he raised an eye flap in question. He had seen several of the scarves. They were carefully embroidered with blessings from the warrior's mothers, and remained under the big men's pillows, sometimes for centuries, until their mate was found. Something else was going on, and he began nervously flitting around the ship getting things in order and generally driving Ethram crazy. "By the stars, Ballion, sit down someplace. They are warriors. They could not care less how the ship looks. They just want to claim their mates."

"Why did you tell them to bring the offerings? What else is happening?" The Minoc's nervous nature had him almost shaking at this point.

"It is nothing specific, Ballion. I just have a feeling we are not quite done with this mess."

Ballion secretly hoped the Ancient and her primitive friend would be transferred off the ship soon, so things could get back to normal.

Ethram had checked on the sleeping women at regular intervals. They should be peacefully unaware of all the conflict surrounding their procurement, and yet several times he had to brush deep sleep across Miranda's brow to stop her restlessness. She continually reached out, clasping her hand in the air. This was a new phenomenon he had never seen from a procured mate.

He inserted the small translation device under the skin behind their ears. The other three young women had not moved, other than an occasional unconscious smile at the prospect of meeting their new mates. Their men had communicated several times to find out when to expect them. Ethram did not mention the Ancient or the attack. He knew to be discreet until Zulien gave him more information.

In order for Ballion and him to collect the anticipated large boon and promotions for this procurement, the news would have to be logged eventually. He trusted the warrior to apprise him of his plans.

Ethram's musings were cut short by the sound of the transport lock engaging. "Well,

Ballion, I suggest we find out what this is all about."

Ballion ran his hands over his cheeks, smoothing his scales. There was nothing he could do about his nervous, wandering antennae. He followed Ethram to the transport room where the connecting doors had locked the ships together.

Ethram keyed in the code to unlock their door, and three warriors strode into the room. "Welcome aboard the Isotant, warriors."

"Thank you, Ethram. I believe you and I have met before." Zulien held out his hand.

"Yes, a few centuries ago at some Magistrate's rising or something." Ethram shrugged his shoulders.

Zulien was amused to find the procurer apparently had little regard for the pompous hierarchy. It would make the discussion of the attack and their plan easier to bring up. What they were going to suggest bordered on treason, and it would have been unthinkable if Ethram had been a radical procurer for the Magistrates. As fortune had it, he was an independent with a territory leased from the hierarchy. "This is Major Taliquant and Lieutenant Letang." The men shook hands.

"This is apprentice Ballion." Ethram introduced the short green Minoc, and Ballion held out a scaly paw.

Zulien smiled at him and said, "Thank you for caring for my Ancient while your Commander procured Taliquant's mate." After releasing Ballion's rough grip, Zulien thought again, *I hope she does not have scales.*

"Ethram, we have a lot to discuss." Zulien and his warriors followed the Commander towards the lounge and made it halfway down a corridor when Zulien and Taliquant stopped. Both men felt the uncomfortable sensation of stiff erections and a mental pulling to the right wall.

Ethram positioned himself between the wall and the warriors, and urged them forward. "My apologies, Commander. Your mate is two corridors over and I had not thought the effect would be as strong. I know you are anxious to meet her, but I think we had better get our talks over with first. You may be a little distracted when you see her until your claiming."

As the distance increased, Zulien felt himself returning to normal. "Is it always like that?"

Ethram chuckled. "Zulien, I have seen men try to claw through the corridor walls to get to their mates, so nothing surprises me anymore."

They reached the lounge and sat on the couches while Ballion handed out drinks. The warriors discussed their plan and waited for Ethram to decide if he would be their accomplice.

"Dammit, it would have to be the Magistrate of Commerce," Ethram said, exasperated. This was the Magistrate responsible for boons and for referring promotions to the Magistrate of Battle. "Well, it seems whether or not I go along with this, I will not be paid for her. The Magistrate wants her dead and you want her hidden."

"I cannot do anything about the promotions, but I will match whatever boon you think the Magistrate would have offered... before he decided to kill her," Zulien added, and Taliquant quickly agreed.

As was his habit, Ethram tented his fingers on his chin. "I have not been to Shallistar in over a century. It would be a nice place to take a break, and I think we can still push for the promotions. The mates were discovered off world, and we did survive the attack. You and I can figure out a boon when we meet up on planet."

"What will you tell the Magistrates when they turn up alive?" Zulien queried. It was the only part of their plan he had not figured out.

The tall man shrugged with indifference. "The same thing I will say about their decay. Apparently, outer world mates have a system that can shut down at will if they feel threatened. That would leave the Magistrates with some explaining to do, so I think they will drop it." Ethram rose.

"We had been keeping the two women together until after the attack, but now they are resting in adjoining procurement rooms. Ordinarily, I would wake them slowly at this point, but due to our current situation I think it is best we let them continue to sleep. They will still sense your presence and search for you when you leave, and that is why I suggested you bring your offerings. It should allow them some comfort. Shall we meet them?"

The warriors rose, and Taliquant asked uneasily, "What does she look like?"

Ethram smiled and said, "All mates are beautiful."

As they continued down the corridors, the warriors' pace increased. "We will introduce Taliquant to his mate first. Ballion, you will remain with the Major when I leave to present Miranda to the Commander."

Ballion's scaly green chest puffed out again. He had never been in charge of an introduction before, and his first was now to be a warrior, no less. His short legs moved quickly to keep up with the long strides of the group. Taliquant turned towards a door and Ethram produced his keys. He laid a hand on Zulien's arm and the warrior felt his anxiety subside a little at the delay of meeting his mate.

Ethram had worked hard on the introduction. It would be dicey informing the warrior that his mate was an outer world primitive, and he was fairly certain Taliquant had assumed he also would be mating with a Celestial. As he unlocked the door, Ethram said, "Tempest is the Ancient's closest friend." They walked into the room, and Taliquant found his legs were almost shaking. He felt himself pulled to the small sleeping form on the pallet in the center of the dimly lit chamber.

Ethram continued softly, "She is a primitive, Taliquant, and has a slightly wild nature. She will challenge and excite you. Her eyes are an emerald green."

Taliquant had stopped listening. He was looking down at the most beautiful creature he had ever seen.

"Ballion, inform me immediately if you sense any distress from Tempest. I think they will be fine."

"Yes, Commander." Ballion moved to the foot of the cot to afford Taliquant a little privacy with his mate.

Ethram, Letang and Zulien left the room and walked to the next door. "When we get to Shallistar, Commander, I would be most interested to hear how you discovered the forgotten mate." He opened the door.

Zulien went numb. Golden hair fell over the side of the sleeping pallet and skimmed the floor. Ethram spoke softly. "Her eyes are crystal blue, and she has a calm disposition and a reverence for nature. Your Ancient is a true treasure, Commander."

Zulien approached his sleeping mate. He knelt on the floor by her pillow and studied the serene face with her long lashes and full, red lips.

He reached a large hand out and gently brushed her cheek. She trembled slightly and moved towards his hand.

"Even in her deep sleep she recognizes her mate," Letang whispered.

Ethram took Letang by the arm and led him against a wall and said quietly, "I have a feeling something wondrous is to come of this mating. Letang, I am going to have to use a light tranquilizer to separate the warriors from their mates. It will be impossible otherwise. It is hard enough to pull two regular mates apart, and it would be dangerous with warriors. I will need your help to guide them back to the lounge where we can let it wear off."

Letang nodded in agreement. Zulien would be angry at the slight deception, but he would eventually realize there was no alternative.

Ethram continued, "This is part of the reason I think your plan will work. No one would except a warrior could be separated from his mate unless she had decayed. Your Commander and the Major are going to need a lot of support until they can be rejoined on planet."

"Yes, Commander. I have anticipated that perhaps more than they have." Letang thought about the separation. The warriors would be in rough shape.

"This is a bottle of the same thing I will be using shortly. Tell them to take one when things appear to be getting out of hand. Remember, they are supposed to be in mourning, not in a sexual mating frenzy."

Letang took the container and hid it in his pocket. He looked back at his Commander as he studied his mate, and he felt his own arousal. He needed to get back to Vasilla. He quietly left the room and waited outside the door.

Zulien stroked the soft golden hair. Her skin was alabaster, nothing like the bronze and golden hue of his people. He rested one hand on the cot by her chest and stroked her forehead with the other. Her breath shuddered, and a tiny hand reached out and gripped a finger on the hand he had rested on the pallet.

He lowered the sheet covering her, and she shivered slightly. Her breasts were full, with nipples the color of pink finisia flowers and tipped with buds that had tightened in the cool air. Being careful of the probe, Zulien lowered his mouth for one small taste.

His eyes traveled to the golden curls between her thighs as he suckled, and without conscious thought, his fingertips brushed though their softness. Her tiny fist tightened further around his finger as she moaned, and she pushed her hips towards the relief while she spasmed in empty frustration. Reluctantly, he pulled the sheet over her.

Zulien felt his arousal become painfully stiff as he smiled at his Celestial. Nothing, no one, would harm her. By the stars, gods and goddesses, he would die protecting his fragile mate. He leaned towards her and brushed a kiss across her lips. "Soon, Miranda, we will be joined soon, my mate." He tied his scarf around her wrist and whispered softly, "I give you the offering of the warriors. It has remained in my chambers for centuries, absorbing my dreams of our meeting. Know that from this day forward, I am always with you, my little Ancient."

Miranda brought her hand up towards her face, laying it on the pillow where she could sense his essence on the sash.

Ethram knew it was time to separate them. If they were together much longer, not even an arragon tranquilizer would work. He took the small dart from his pocket, drew his hand back, and released it. The small needle pierced Zulien's bicep and one hand dropped to his side. The other remained clenched in Miranda's grip.

Ethram gently pried her fingers loose and helped the dazed Commander stand. Miranda shuddered, reaching out blindly, and Ethram held her hand and lowered it to the pallet. He brushed her forehead. "Sleep and dream of your warrior, Miranda. You will be with your mate again soon."

Letang took Zulien's other arm as they led him back to the lounge. He felt a wave of sorrow for the Commander. He could not imagine being denied Vasilla for claiming once they had met. *Damn Berslan and his ambition.*

Letang stayed with Zulien while he reoriented himself, and Ethram left to collect Taliquant. The procurer entered the chamber and found Ballion still standing at the end of the pallet, his antennae almost beating his chin with emotion.

Taliquant's head rested on the pillow beside Tempest. His arm was wrapped around her, pulling her close, and the great warrior was crying silent tears as he watched his mate's peaceful face.

Ethram whispered, "He had given up, Ballion, and believed his mate to be decayed. Do you feel the importance of our chosen path? To save one man this torment is our true boon. This separation is going to be hardest on him." Ethram saw the emerald scarf on Tempest's wrist, and he threw his dart and helped the dazed warrior back to the lounge.

It took a few minutes for the warriors to regain their senses and straighten. After a few deep breaths, they were calmed. "I was not informed I was to be tranqued." Zulien narrowed his eyes at Ethram.

"Commander, there was no other safe way to extract you from the chamber. You would have ripped the room apart to keep from being separated, and my primary duty is to protect the procured mates. I act accordingly." Ethram waited to see if that would end the discussion.

Zulien glared a few moments longer as the reason for deception finally sank in. "I apologize, Ethram. For you to risk such an action to protect my mate gives me confidence she will arrive at Shallistar safely." He squirmed and said sheepishly, "I am not used to being out-maneuvered."

Ethram chuckled. "It is the effect of your young mates. They tend to unsettle even the most steadfast mind. I have given Letang a vial of a lighter dose of the same tranquilizer. It will keep you clear headed and calm enough to complete this task. Will you be announcing their decline when you return to the Quillant?"

"Yes. We will keep communicating for a few hours, and you can decide when to inform us they have decayed. I will make sure Berslan is within earshot. I trust we can all act properly shocked and saddened?" Zulien actually felt a twinge at the thought something could happen to his fragile mate.

Taliquant echoed his feelings. "Commander, all I have to do is think of losing her and I feel utter defeat."

"Ethram, my mother will be waiting for your instructions." Zulien stood to leave.

"You communicated over secure lines I take it?" Ethram had other mates on board to consider, and he certainly did not want to be scanning for pirates.

"I do not need to call her. Trust me, she is already making preparations," Zulien said.

Ethram raised an eyebrow as he looked at the warrior. "I do not understand."

Taliquant said, "He speaks the truth, Commander."

Ethram decided to take up the issue with the woman herself when he met her. "All is ready?"

"Let the ruse unfold," Zulien announced.

By the time the airlock doors sealed, the warriors had little trouble looking grief stricken. They felt the physical loss of leaving the other half of their souls behind.

CHAPTER IV

Miranda continued to wake in the darkness, only to once again settle into a deep sleep, quieting her fears. After one of her awakenings, she was aware she was not alone and she felt a comforting presence very close to her. She reached out, trying desperately to grasp the man. Yes, it was a man. She was sure of it. A vision of the large man with the long, untamed dark hair crossed her confused mind and the thoughts 'warrior' and 'protector' flashed with the vision... and the word 'mate'.

All this frightened her further, until she finally felt her hand clasped in a gentle large fist. A tugging at her breast was followed by a soft brushing through her sex, and she wanted the man to lie with her to relieve the constant sexual torment she was experiencing. Fingers stroked her forehead, and she leaned towards them for comfort. She knew this man would protect her and bring her back from the abyss. Something was tied to her wrist and she lifted her hand towards her head, inhaling the scent of the man. Lips brushed across hers and she shivered with fright when they retreated.

Stay with me, please, stay with me. I'm so scared, she sobbed and begged in her mind, and she thought she heard a deep voice say, 'I am always with you, my little Ancient'. The words brought comfort, but even more confusion. She sensed the man had gone away, and she panicked as she mourned his loss.

The warriors returned to the transport lock and prepared to go back to the Quillant. Taliquant was in clear distress and Zulien kept looking behind them towards the procurement vessel.

"Remember to take these when you feel yourselves losing rationality." Letang handed the warriors a few pills each and secured the remaining tranquilizers in his pocket. If either warrior displayed inappropriate behavior, he would risk mutiny by spiking their drink.

Zulien caught him palming the remaining pills. "I take it you are ready to act if we use poor judgment?"

"No, Commander. These are for Vasilla. She cannot keep her hands off me," Letang smiled as he told the obvious lie.

The young warrior heard the locks disengaging on the Quillant, and he glanced at his companions. Taliquant and the Commander had serene expressions on their faces, and Letang realized they were reminiscing about their meetings with their mates. Just before the doors opened, he said quietly, "I am sorry you could not bring them with you."

The two warriors gasped, and by the time the doors opened they had the honest cast of pain and sorrow in their eyes. Letang said, "I am sorry, warriors." He felt miserable dealing them a low blow like that, and it showed in his eyes.

The entire crew and their mates had entered the portal, waiting for their first glimpse of the new mates. Their smiles turned to concern as they heard Letang tell the warriors he was sorry, and the group exiting the air lock was empty handed and grief stricken.

With a feeling of dread, Seartock whispered, "What happened, Commander?"

Zulien cleared his throat and found he could not speak, and Taliquant was experiencing the same problem. They could not form the words to say their mates were decaying. The thought alone caused far too much distress.

Once again, Letang stepped in. "Commander, may I suggest you and the Major retire to your quarters for a while. I will inform the crew what is going on. We can meet on the bridge after you have had the chance to compose yourselves, and we can call the Isotant for an update."

The crew and mates silently parted, allowing the warriors to pass. When they were sure the men were out of earshot, they bombarded Letang with questions.

"They did get a chance to meet their mates and make their offerings. Apparently, something in our atmosphere or on the ship caused them to begin to decline. Ethram did not tell the Commander earlier because he did not want to upset him just before the impending Debayluth attack. He was hoping contact with their mates would revive them." Letang's eyes actually filled up with tears.

"We finally had to separate them, because Ethram was afraid the warriors would tear apart the ship as they watched their mates wither. He and Ballion are still trying to find something to stop the decay, but truthfully I do not see how they will last the day. They are small and fragile, and they do not have the immunities we are born with in the inner worlds." Letang looked up and noticed that, as with most of the people listening, Vasilla had tears of pain flowing down her dark cheeks. He wanted to throw his arms around her and comfort her, reminding her this was all a ruse, but it would have to wait.

The only one not distraught was Berslan. He was staring at his feet, trying to look devastated, but Letang saw through his guise as pure calculation and was almost sick as he flashed through memories of their years of camaraderie.

"Vasilla, my love, let us retire to our quarters for a moment. I apologize, friends, but until we hear from the Isotant I do not know any more than I have told you. We must be strong for the Commander and Taliquant. They need the support they have lent us on so many occasions."

He passed through a sea of oaths and promises, and guided Vasilla back to their quarters. As soon as their door closed, Vasilla threw herself into his arms. "The poor Commander... and Taliquant. He was so pleased to learn his mate was found. He confided to me years ago that he thought his mate was decayed."

Letang softly stroked the tall woman's back. "Vasilla, my love, remember this is an act. I can assure you the mates are fine. They are small and fragile as I stated, but otherwise they are healthy."

Vasilla stood back searching his eyes to see that it was the truth. "You are a good actor, Letang. I truly believed the mates were decaying."

"Let us hope Berslan is falling for the plan so completely. We have to keep up this pretense and continue to act distraught when we are outside of these quarters," Letang reminded her.

As was Vasilla's way, she changed the subject. The slender Armarzonian folded her legs under her on the sleeping pallet and looked up at him with her big brown eyes as she asked excitedly, "Did you really get to see them? What are they like?"

Letang sat next to her, pulling her head onto his shoulder and brushing his fingertips through her soft curls. He told her what he saw of Tempest and Miranda and of the great warriors' gentle way with their little mates. Vasilla's eyes filled with emotion as he whispered, "I thought of you when I saw the Commander kneel by

Miranda. His face was filled with disbelief and reverence, and I imagined I looked the same the first time I saw you. I could not imagine having to be separated like they are," Letang said. He held her tighter.

They sat in silence for a few moments while they composed themselves. Letang held his hand out to help her rise, and the couple masked their faces with compassion as they headed towards the bridge. The Commander and Taliquant appeared a short while later and there was an uncomfortable silence as Letang hailed the Isotant. None of the crew knew the words to express the grief they felt for their friends. Berslan hovered in the background, blending into the walls and waiting for news on the fate of the Ancients.

Ethram spaced out his reports of their decaying status and he kept Ballion out of sight, saying he was caring for the mates. Ballion was no actor, and in any case he had no control over the damning antennae that continued to stroke his chin in happiness that the warriors were pleased with their mates, and happiness of the impending large boon.

Ethram left the bridge to check on Tempest and Miranda. All the constant chatter with the Quillant about their withering was making him nervous and he wanted to make sure they really were all right. They continued to sleep, though Miranda would reach out, searching for her mate's hand. Ethram placed her wrist with the offering back on the pillow and waved a comforting aura towards her. She slept calmer.

He went back to the communications bridge. To summon up the proper countenance, he employed something he only did once a year on the anniversary of the discovery of his mate's decay. He envisioned coming across her withered body in the small home she had shared with her sister. Flowers, dried through time, were placed all around the faded rooms, and the possessions and decorations showed him she had been a gentle, kind woman. His own tears brimmed as he thought of his loss.

Ethram called the Quillant. He could see the devastated crew trying to stand back and give the anxious warriors room while hoping for good news. Ethram cleared his throat, "I am so sorry, Commander." He heard the groans from the crew, and watched as two of the warriors fled from the room before anyone could see their tears. "Nothing could be done. The outer world I found them on was polluted. The planet itself will be swallowed soon, and they did not have the strength to adapt to the inner worlds."

Taliquant began to panic, believing something had gone wrong and his Tempest was truly lost. "No!" he bellowed. "I want to see her. Commander, I need to return to the Isotant."

Zulien was barely holding it together himself as he stood up and threw an arm around Taliquant's shoulder and whispered in his ear, "She is fine, Taliquant. Take a chill pill." He turned back to the screen and said loudly enough for the crew to hear, "You are certain, Ethram? Maybe they are just in a deeper sleep."

"I am sorry, Zulien. Ballion remains with them, but there has been no breath or heartbeat for over an hour. They are decayed. Please, what can I do to ease your suffering?"

Taliquant had managed to discreetly swallow a pill and was better composed. "I wish my mate brought back to Shallistar. I want my mother to know I did have a mate and that I comforted her for the short time we had."

Zulien replied as though in a shocked state, "Yes, Taliquant. Ethram, that is my wish as well. My mother so wanted to meet my little Ancient, and I want her to know she received my offering before she decayed."

"Of course, Commander." Ethram appeared to be thinking something over, and he added the final line to his script... the line they all decided would seal the ruse. "I take it I will be compensated for this extra travel?"

Zulien exploded up from his chair, "By the stars, yes you will be compensated. My mate is decayed, but I will see to it you get your damn boon, Ethram. I trusted you to protect her." Zulien looked as though he was going to break through the communication screen, and Seartock tentatively walked forward and took his arm.

"Commander, let me escort you back to your quarters. Perhaps we can toast your mate's journey to the after worlds," Seartock said quietly.

Zulien needed to go back to his quarters and take his own little pill of sanity. For a brief moment he had believed Miranda to have decayed, and the overwhelming grief still had him weak. He allowed himself to be led off the bridge, and Letang followed with Taliquant. When they reached the Commander's quarters, Letang asked Seartock to get them some wine.

He took their time alone to make sure Zulien remembered his pill. "I promise you, your mates are fine."

Taliquant was panicking again. "How can you be so sure?"

"Ethram has been very careful to keep Ballion off screen. He has made continuous excuses all day because the Minoc cannot control his emotions. His antennae were waving with joy like a flag when we left them earlier. There is no acceptable protocol for him not to have been seconding his Commander when he gave us this news," Letang reasoned.

The warriors looked at each other. Letang was right. It was an unforgivable breach of protocol for the Commander to stand alone while admitting failure in his mission. "I hope Berslan does not think of that," Zulien commented.

"Check your communications log. He has already sent two messages back to the Magistrates, so I think our plan is working." Letang shook his head in sadness. The ambitious warrior's betrayal was complete.

Taliquant gave a nervous laugh. "By the stars, Zule, I thought you were going to dive through the screen when Ethram asked for compensation to return our mates to Shallistar."

The Parina's head was being shoved down on Taliquant, and Zulien was standing behind her unlacing his breaches. Tomorrow would be Berslan's day with her, and they were not sure how they would relieve their pressure.

"That was close," Zulien admitted. "We all have a future on the stages of Valeridon if we ever want to stop this warrior nonsense." He quickly entered the android from behind.

The two men pumped to frenzied relief, just as they heard Seartock approaching. They shoved the android into the closet and got back into the form of grieving mates. Seartock was weighted down with the pressure in the room, and made excuses to check the bridge. He almost slipped and said he needed the comforting arms of his mate.

Zulien had the feeling he was forgetting something, and he had half convinced himself it was another side effect of being separated from Miranda or of the tranquilizers. All of a sudden, it hit him. "Letang, we need to disengage from the Isotant. Now," he ordered.

"What is wrong?" Taliquant asked.

"The Magistrates may order the body of an Ancient be returned to Latisqua under the guise of ceremony but perhaps to make sure she is really decayed. We need to get Ethram underway to Shallistar. He knows we have to deliver Berslan on planet before we can meet him, so he will deliver the other three mates first. They are bound for Perith Three. The hierarchy there is on silent communication until the world divisions are decided. They would not be able to hail him down and ask him to return."

"I am on it." Letang dashed from the room and ran to the transport portal. He quickly unlatched the outside locks, knowing the Commander or Ballion would see they were no longer docked. Hopefully, Ethram would figure out it meant to leave.

Ethram noticed the red docking light go out and the green light come on, and at the same instant it occurred to him the Magistrates might call him in with the Ancient. To have her found alive would be treason. "Ballion, by the polluted planets of the outer worlds, get us out of here. Now."

Ballion quickly set the navigation screens for Perith Three, and they were more than a quadrant away before anyone else on the Quillant knew they had disengaged.

Zulien was sitting at the helm, gazing blankly at the stars through the bridge view port. The crew did not disturb the brooding man. They could not fathom the grief he must be suffering. In reality, Zulien was scanning the stars and imagining his Celestial bound for the safety of

Shallistar. He was anticipating her waking and how he would show her the beauty of his home. He could picture her overwhelming delight after leaving the polluted planet in the outer worlds. When a small smile would crease his eyes, those that saw him thought it was caused by the short, bittersweet moments of his meeting with his mate.

Taliquant had sequestered himself in his quarters over his loss. In truth, the tranquilizers made the warrior nervous and he only took them when he had to move among the crew. For now, he was taking out his frustrations and release with the Parina. He had tied her, not that he needed to, over a chair with her naked ass facing the ceiling, legs spread wide. He looked at the android and thought, *By the stars, I need my mate.* When he did leave his quarters, he avoided Berslan as much as he could, because even with the 'chill pill' he wanted to throttle him.

Taliquant reluctantly released the Parina, and she made her way to Berslan's room.

Zulien and Taliquant met back in the Commander's quarters. "I hate having no communication with the Isotant," Taliquant complained.

"I am convinced our mates are fine. I feel as though a fire has been lit inside me, and if something happened to her I think the flame would extinguish as well." Zulien's hand rubbed absently over his heart. "It bothered me the Magistrates have not called for her body."

"Now it does not? It could mean they are after the Isotant." Taliquant rose and began to pace.

"Berslan has been in his quarters with the Parina, and Letang informs me he does not even know we have disengaged. Perhaps he is having a fit of conscience." Zulien shrugged in indifference. Berslan had chosen his path. "The Magistrates have not called because they would show their hand and expose their spy. How else would they have even known Ethram had procured an Ancient? He has not logged a boon for her." Zulien lifted his wrist and tapped a number on the band. "Letang, come to my quarters."

Letang arrived within minutes. "How are you feeling?"

"Like I have a crater the size of Josarin where my heart should be. How are you?" Zulien waved him to a chair.

"I wish the rest of the crew knew the sacrifice you are both making." Letang watched Taliquant drop into a chair. "Major, you look like you are going to be sick."

"Thanks for reminding me, Letang. I hate the pills. I feel like I am standing beside myself watching a robot take over." Taliquant let out an exasperated breath.

Zulien nodded in agreement. "At least they allow us to function." A look of concentration came over his face. "Letang, how difficult would it be to spread a rumor we have the decayed mates on board? We could secure the hatch in the hold and no one would dare disturb our mates. The rumor would have to be something vague, so we could deny it when we get to Latisqua."

"I think the easiest method would be through the mates. They live for gossip. I could tell Vasilla, and by the time the news spread to the warriors no one would be able to track its source." Letang smiled. "Berslan will hear about it by dinner."

"It would keep the Magistrates from

considering the Isotant, and it may give Ethram extra time to get them secured on Shallistar. When will we be arriving at Latisqua?" Zulien rubbed his crotch. The infernal need was driving him crazy. No wonder they did the claiming so soon after the mates were joined, because an ordinary man would go crazy if he had to wait for the ceremony.

"I told Nemiste to drift in that direction an hour ago, because I was not sure whether you would want to drag it out. We could be there in a little more than three days if we push it. No one will question the orders, and if they think they are unusual, they will attribute it to your mourning."

"I will go up and issue the order myself. I cannot keep hiding in here, and if I do not keep occupied I will lose it. Have Vasilla start the rumor among the mates, and let me know when Berslan communicates with the Magistrates."

"Yes, Commander." Letang headed for his quarters where Vasilla was napping after a serious round of sex. Letang found his urges constant with all that was happening.

Vasilla was pleased to be of assistance with the ruse. She was an excellent actress, and the entire ship had heard the rumor before late afternoon. Everyone believed that the decayed mates had been secretly transferred to the hold before the ships had disengaged.

Berslan made the call before dinner, and he actually looked relieved when he showed up on the bridge. Letang whispered to Zulien, "I think our spy is off the hook until we reach Latisqua. He probably thinks we do not suspect a thing."

"I am sure he has no idea. He has been so caught up in his duplicity that he has not had time to digest what has been happening. It will be a pleasure watching his expression when the Magistrates ask for the body of an Ancient they are not supposed to know about and that we do not have."

"What a nice way for the Magistrate's future son-in-law to begin his career." Letang wandered over to check the ship's progress.

Three hours before they docked at Latisqua, Vasilla approached Letang in the lounge where he was pretending to commiserate with the Commander and Taliquant. "Letang, mother sent a message she received our packages. She says she really likes them and will keep them protected."

Letang looked a little confused. *Packages? What packages?*

Vasilla laughed, "The way our mothers gossip and pass information to each other, the other mates better get busy sending gifts as well."

Now the message was clear. Tempest and Miranda were safe on Shallistar, and Zulien's mother had sent word through Vasilla so that the communication would not be intercepted. Naturally, she would have been concerned with her son's distress.

Taliquant kicked him under the table and Zulien noticed the brief flash of relief on his face. The strain was taking its toll on both of them.

A few hours later, the crew and their mates disembarked onto Latisqua. The sky was lit up by the major and minor suns that sparkling off the gold roofs of the mirrored buildings. "Honestly, every time I come here I think of the waste. No less than twenty planets are destitute of resources, and still the taxes go up," Vasilla whispered to her mate.

Zulien overheard her. "Think of the cost of labor to polish the sidewalks," he replied sarcastically.

They were ushered into the outer rooms where they expected a long wait. The Magistrates always pretended to be busy. Berslan stood close to the door, eyes wide and looking as though he either wanted to bolt or drop through the floor. "Anxious to see your betrothed?" Seartock asked. "I remember the wait for Ebonisia."

"Ebonisia is your mate, Seartock. This is not the same," Berslan muttered.

Seartock looked confused. "You're not having doubts, are you? No one will question you if you back out of a convenience commitment."

Berslan knew he was in too deep. He had no experience in the subterfuge of the hierarchy. It was not that he minded being used. The mission the royals charged him with was for the protection of the inner worlds, although he was sure Zulien would never understand. It still confused him why the haughty daughter of the Magistrate approached him for the joining commitment. He looked around the lavish chambers and shivered. Berslan felt as though he was the one being duped.

The Magistrate of Commerce finally entered the chamber with his daughter. She held her head high in her thin embroidered shift, and she gave a slight nod towards Berslan while looking down her nose at everyone else in the room. "It looks like Berslan is going to have a lifetime to pay," Taliquant whispered.

The Magistrate of the Old Ways also entered. It was a bit of a surprise to see the two Magistrates working together. None of them generally got along with each other, all vying for leadership and causing constant turmoil in the hierarchy. Letang was standing behind Zulien. "What the dremont is he doing here?"

"I guess we will find out," Zulien whispered. "They are going to have to admit Berslan told them about the Ancient, and it will be interesting to see if anything is mentioned about the attack."

The Magistrate of Commerce raised his staff to thump the required three times to begin the audition. The Magistrate of the Old Ways, not to be bested, managed a quick tap with his own before the loud boom landed.

Taliquant whispered, "I wonder if they will begin beating their chests."

Zulien bit back the laugh. "Shut up, Tali. We are in mourning."

"Commander Zulien," the Magistrate of Commerce called. The Magistrate of the Old Ways seemed to constantly be a step behind.

Zulien stepped forward, and he nodded to the Magistrate of Commerce. "Magistrate." He turned and nodded to the Magistrate of the Old Ways. "Magistrate." It did seem to appease the old man somewhat.

"It has come to our attention that you and Major Taliquant are in mourning. Our condolences on your loss."

It reminded Zulien to put the appropriate expression on his face. He wanted to ask how it had managed to come to their attention, but waited to see where the audition was leading before he planned his attack. "Thank you, Magistrates." He decided to bait them a little. "We would like to collect the boon for the Debayluth battle and return to Shallistar as soon as possible."

The Magistrate realized what Zulien was trying to do and decided to slow the proceedings down. "Was there nothing Ethram could do for your mates?"

"He assured us there was not. He said the

pollution of the outer worlds had weakened them, and they were fragile and their bloodlines had been thinned for centuries. He had no understanding of their species," Zulien replied.

The Magistrate of Commerce arrogantly ran his hand down his robe. "As Celestial Ancients, I am sure their bloodline had thinned far too much to survive our advanced worlds." He waited for the warriors' reaction to the news that he was aware the mates were ancients. The Commander would not know how much information the Magistrate had obtained, and he smiled confidently at Zulien.

Berslan did not know that Taliquant's mate was a primitive. He told the Magistrates they were both ancients. Zulien made the first tear in Berslan's information. "Apparently the source of your information is inaccurate, Magistrate."

The Magistrate of Commerce's eyes darted to Berslan, and then returned to fix on the Commander. Zulien enjoyed his unease. The path of the audition was definitely shifting.

"That is impossible, Commander. Explain the inaccuracy."

Zulien could almost feel Berslan squirming under the royal's scrutiny. "Only my mate was an Ancient. The Major's mate was a primitive." *This should make them reconsider the rest of the information Berslan has passed on to them.*

The Magistrate of Commerce looked a little rattled. "The women were bonded on the outer world, were they not?"

"That is our understanding. Ethram found them together," Zulien admitted.

The Magistrate of the Old Ways spoke up. "Do you mean for us to believe a Celestial Ancient had bonded with an outer world primitive? Preposterous," he declared.

The Old Ways leaders never mixed with ordinary subjects, believing it lessened their power and credentials. The fanatic religious order had separated from the citizens for so many centuries, they had convinced themselves it was a decree from the Old Religion scrolls.

"Perhaps Miranda was not a Celestial, Magistrate." Zulien was backing him into a corner.

The Magistrate of the Old Ways sneered, "Perhaps it was this bonding with a primitive that weakened her so much she decayed."

Zulien grabbed Taliquant's arm to silence him from responding to the insult against his mate. "Stand down, Major." He glared at the pompous royal. "Magistrate, I ask your compassion and permission to send the Major back to the Quillant. He is in mourning and cannot be held responsible for his actions if you continue to insult his mate." The anger was clear in Zulien's voice.

The Magistrate of the Old Ways saw the murderous glare in Taliquant's eyes, but word had not gotten back to them and it would be a disaster if any of the crew returned to the battleship. He shifted uncomfortably under the Magistrate of Commerce's stare as he tried to figure out how to retract his words and still save face.

Zulien did not give him the opportunity. He turned and whispered quickly, "Let me know if they have begun searching the ship." He said louder, "Major Taliquant, wait in your quarters for our return."

The Magistrate of the Old Ways squeaked out, "The Major has not been released from the audition."

Taliquant ignored the Magistrate completely.

"As you wish, Commander." He stormed out of the chamber without asking leave from the Magistrate of Commerce either.

"A primitive would have suited him," the royal sneered.

The audition was definitely breaking down. Zulien persisted, "If there is nothing further, Magistrate, we would like to collect our boon and take our leave. Our mates are decayed. We are in mourning, and any discussion about what we might have learned from the Ancient is best left to the Magistrate of the Old Ways."

There were a few gasps behind him as the crew realized Zulien had effectively dismissed the Magistrates. He could not have insulted the Magistrate of Commerce more, short of slapping him. His daughter's mouth was flopping open and shut like a trelang, and the worst part, the Magistrates conceded, was that Zulien was right. The Magistrates were showing incredible breach of inner world protocol by keeping the warriors from their mourning rites, and they knew it.

Taliquant came bursting back into the chamber.

"You were ordered to quarters." The Magistrate of Commerce banged his staff and paled slightly.

"Commander, the hierarchy guard is crawling through the Quillant. There must be thirty soldiers, and they are even going through our private quarters," Taliquant exclaimed.

Several of the mates began crying, and Zulien was outraged. "Warriors, back to the ship and secure."

"You have not been released," the Magistrate bellowed. "No one is granted leave." He began thumping his staff wildly.

Zulien spun back around and glared at the

royals. "Magistrates, your breach of protocol will be reported to the hierarchy commission." The Magistrate of the Old Ways almost fainted at being implicated in this mess. "My warriors are returning to the ship and removing your guards, physically if necessary."

The warriors and mates left the chamber. Berslan remained. He had no idea what to do.

"Explain this," Zulien thundered.

The Magistrate of Commerce stalled. "We do not explain ourselves to warriors."

"Then you will be explaining this outrage to the commission," Zulien said evenly.

A member of the guard ran into the chamber and approached the Magistrates. "We have been forcibly escorted off the ship, Magistrates. We did have time to check the holds, and except for supplies they are empty." The Magistrates were almost shaking with confusion. The guard had done as instructed and reported back to them, but they had neglected to tell him to wait until they were alone. The breach was undeniable now. If the guards had been able to secure the Ancient, the commission might have overlooked the means to obtain her. They were perilously close to losing their position in the hierarchy at this point.

"What the dremont are you looking for?" Zulien demanded.

The Magistrate of Commerce stuttered, "We were told the Ancients were being transported on the Quillant and we wished to honor them." His lie rang thin.

"Honor them how? By distressing their mates and keeping them from their rites? Who told you they were on the Quillant?" Zulien slowly turned to face Berslan, and he managed to look shocked as if he had just learned of the warrior's deceit.

"Berslan. We have been warriors together since we boarded the Quillant centuries ago. Why would you do us this dishonor?"

Berslan had nothing left but a small vestige of pride, and he stood as straight as he could manage. "Why did you choose Taliquant as second in command?"

Zulien shook his head sadly. "Because he would never have chosen a path such as this." Zulien stared back at the Magistrates. "This breach of protocol will be reported to the upper rank commission when we reach Shallistar. The commission will be told the seriousness of the breach, and that we have been kept from mourning rites by this audition and the filing of the report."

The Magistrate of Commerce straightened. "You have proof of nothing, warrior."

"Then you would not mind explaining the tape of communications between the Debayluths stating you ordered the attack on my mate." Zulien tensed a little. That was not the exact transmission, and he counted on Berslan's memory faltering and that he had correctly guessed the source of the attack.

Berslan slumped in defeat, and the Magistrate of Commerce glared at him. His daughter realized the damage her betrothed had done and screamed at Zulien. "Dremont! You are a dremont, Commander. Secrets of the ancients are dangerous. They can undermine the entire hierarchy," Sharpina screeched.

Zulien laughed at the shrew. "You say that as if it is a bad thing." He turned back to the Magistrate of Commerce. "I expect my boon for the attack of your Debayluths on my mate, and Commander Ethram is expecting a healthy boon for traveling to the outer worlds and discovering an Ancient. If the funds are not credited by the time the Quillant reaches Shallistar, I will demand your removal when I file my charges of protocol against both of you."

The Magistrate of the Old Ways fell back on his throne in shock. The Magistrate of Commerce had promised him an Ancient. Decayed or not, she would have furthered the religious order, and instead he was close to a humiliated dismissal. He had had no idea what the other Magistrate had been up to.

Zulien turned to leave, and he made one last comment before he left the chambers. "Major Berslan, you are stripped of your duties aboard the Quillant. I will be forwarding a formal request to the Magistrate of Battle to strip you of your rank. You are dismissed." Zulien left the chamber as Berslan blinked back tears.

The Magistrate's daughter realized she was now betrothed to a disgraced warrior. As a female, she was not in a position to break the commitment. She was already making plans to talk to her father about an assassination.

Zulien hurried back to the Quillant and ran to the bridge. "Nemiste, disengage from the docking portal." He turned and saw most of the crew had hurried after him for news when they saw him return.

"Letang, take the helm and head full speed for Shallistar. Maintain alert and call me immediately if any ships follow. Everyone else, crew and mates, meet in the lounge in ten minutes. It is time for you to learn what is really going on." Zulien heard the excited conjectures of the warriors as they ran towards their quarters to collect their mates.

Zulien and Letang were alone on the bridge, and the Commander stared at the stars. "I called them out. They will either back down or make an attempt to eradicate us."

"Do they think you have the communication tape?" Letang asked.

"No, you were right. Berlsan was not sure if the Debayluths had said the Magistrates 'will' support the attack or 'did' support the attack on my Ancient." Zulien was trying to calm down. He had never stood up to the hierarchy before, much less insulted and threatened them.

He began to think out loud. "I am giving the tape to my father, and we will make sure the Magistrates understand that should anything happen to the Quillant, the tape will be turned over to the Magistrate of Battle."

Letang was silent for a while, and then spoke up quietly. "Commander, why are they so afraid of your mate?"

Zulien had touched on that question several times, and came up with nothing but frustration. His little mate and her Atlantian gene had been raised on the primitive outer world planet for centuries. What could she possibly do to harm them? "I do not know, Letang. By the stars, I wish I did, so I would know how to protect her."

"You have the crew behind you, Zulien. We are a family and we will all support you."

"Thank you, Letang. I had better go face my loyal crew and tell them how I have lied to them." Zulien headed towards the lounge.

On his way past Taliquant's door he knocked. "Go away."

"Taliquant, come with me to the lounge. I have called an assembly. It is time to let them know what is going on. Come with me so we can properly celebrate returning to our mates," Zulien lured.

Taliquant opened the door. "What happened

to Berslan?"

"I think the proper question is 'What will happen to Berslan?'. If the look on the face of his betrothed is any indication, Sharpina will be holding her own mourning rites soon."

Taliquant shook his head in sadness. "Why would he choose such a path of dishonor? I would never have believed it from him."

Zulien did not want his friend to feel any worse about the situation, and decided to be evasive instead of telling him it was the choice of making him second in command. "Who knows why a man follows a given path?"

When they entered the lounge, the mates looked scared and the warriors looked determined. "Calm down, crew. At this time, I do not know what the Magistrates plan to do, but we are not on high alert."

"Why did the guard search the ship, Commander? They ransacked our quarters... our private quarters, sir. They broke a vase Seartock had given me on our century celebration." Ebonisha's syrupy brown eyes were red from crying.

"I am so sorry, Ebonisha. All of you, list the damages the guard did and I will send the inventory in with the charges," Zulien assured them. The crew looked confused. "I will be filing breach of protocol charges against the Magistrate of Commerce and the Magistrate of the Old Ways when we are on planet. In answer to your question, Ebonisha, the guards were looking for the Ancients."

Seartock spoke up. "The first thing we did was check the hold when we returned to the ship, and they had already secured the Ancients. It was empty. If they already had them, why did they go through our quarters?"

"The Ancient and Taliquant's mate were never on the Quillant. They were transported to Shallistar on the Isotant." Zulien waited for the information to set in. "Taliquant's mate is an outer world primitive, not Celestial. It was obvious someone wanted my Ancient destroyed, and I am afraid I have let you believe a mistruth to keep our mates safe. They are sleeping on planet, waiting for us."

Vasilla reached her arms out to Ebonisha. "I am so sorry for avoiding you. I knew you would know something was up and I was not allowed to tell anyone. Please forgive me."

"You have known all along? It must have been horrible for you." Ebonisha looked at the Commander. "How have you and Taliquant been able to bear the separation? Your hearts must be aching."

Taliquant rubbed his crotch. "Among other things," he laughed. The relief was etched on his face finally to be able to receive the support of his friends. What he had not expected was the admiration.

The crew and mates celebrated with them and decreed it would become legend, the sacrifice they had made to protect their mates. Zulien filled them in on everything from his initial discovery after the attack through the part of the audition they had missed. Berslan received little sympathy on his assumed pending assassination, and the ladies teased Vasilla about starting the rumor. It was nice to see everyone in a jovial state once again.

CHAPTER V

Miranda tucked her hand close to her face, and she had sobbed until she had no more tears. An eternity of darkness was all that was left for her. That, and the comforting scent of the man who promised to return and protect her. Her hand fisted the sash, and she inhaled and felt the tight clench as she spasmed towards a climax that was just out of reach. The torment went on and on. Where was the man?

She was obsessed with him and waited anxiously. She felt he was waiting just beyond the vastness of this frightening place, and she saw his proud face, dark eyes flashing. Bronze, no, golden skin stretched across tightly corded muscles. His black hair flew wildly around his face and shoulders in anger as he tried to reach her. *Please, please find me soon.*

She felt herself lifted and moved to a place of serenity, and once in a while a hand brushed across her forehead and she felt calmed. Her heart felt something coming closer. No, it was someone. It was the man who would take care of her. He was coming back to her.

While Miranda slept in her deep sleep, the Quillant docked on Shallistar. Early in the morning, Zulien turned the ship over to the Port Commander for repairs and supplies, and he released the crew and told them he would be issuing orders after the mating ceremonies, which they all planned to attend.

As Letang disembarked, Zulien pulled him aside. "I am putting in orders for a commission for you, and before we leave planet you should have your Captain grade. Letang, there is no way for us to express our gratitude for the discreet assistance you and your mate provided."

Taliquant stepped forward with his hand outstretched. "We are having a joint mating ceremony, and we would be honored if you would second."

Vasilla tried to stifle her cry, and Letang's mouth dropped open. This was the highest honor a man could offer. In the event something happened to either one of the warriors, it would be his responsibility to aid his bereaved mate through mourning until, and if, a mating of convenience was made. To entrust a man with your mate's protection was the highest tribute one man could give another. "I am honored, sirs. I will pray to the stars daily for your continued well-being. This small experience protecting your mates leads me to believe this would be no easy task."

"Your comportment through this exercise leads me to believe you are the only one we would approach," Zulien smiled. "Now, take off, you two. I imagine your mother is most anxious to hear of this escapade, Vasilla."

"Yes, Commander. All the on-planet mates have been conjecturing the wildest of tales," Vasilla laughed. "Perhaps another rumor is in order."

"Do not even think about it," Letang joked, and they headed towards their shuttle.

"Tali, I am filing the reports before I join Miranda. I want the Magistrates distracted with the mess they have made so I am not disturbed later. We have waited a long time to be joined, and I will not have it interrupted. We will have to find out where they are being chambered, but I see no reason for you to delay your claiming."

"Zule, we have always jumped in together. I will wait to collect my mate." Taliquant shifted his stance around the erection that had been thickening as they approached Shallistar.

"Then, I suggest we get the filing done quickly," Zulien laughed as he rubbed his own bulging breeches.

The warriors commandeered a shuttle to Zulien's home where their parents were waiting outside. Zulien's mother's hands were on her hips. "By the stars, what have you two been up to? Word has reached us from Latisqua that two Magistrates are panicked beyond the suns, and packing treasures from their apartments and secreting them away. Your names are in every transmission. We even heard you," she pointed at Zulien, "dismissed the Magistrates during an audition."

"A fine welcome home, mother, considering we arrive in one piece with mates," Zulien chuckled. "Can you manage to feed these warriors while we discuss it?"

Her eyes narrowed. "Zulien, you did not really dismiss them, did you?"

"What did your visions tell you?"

"As if I could calm myself to have a vision with all that has been happening. Come, your feast awaits."

The warriors embraced their parents and turned as another shuttle glided to a stop. Ethram climbed out, untangling his cloak from the seat. "You would think they could design these contraptions better," he muttered.

"You could have just 'cloaked' here," Taliquant suggested.

"I am on vacation. I like to see the surroundings."

Zulien's mother stepped forward and offered her hand. "We were just preparing to feast, Ethram. Please join us."

"Thank you, Zalana."

"How are the mates this morning?" she asked.

"Sleeping peacefully." He nodded to the warriors. "I take it the immediate crisis has passed?"

"We will discuss it over feasting. There are a few things we need to take care of before our joining," Zulien explained.

Ethram studied the warriors a moment. They should be tearing through the village to get to their mates by now. "You are tranqued?"

"To a zelang's gills," Zulien admitted. "We each took our last two. We have to settle a few matters so we can join uninterrupted."

"You have drugged yourselves?" Terena, Taliquant's mother, looked at her son disapprovingly.

"Mother, I would have been decayed in a shariver's suit by now, three quadrants away in space trying to get to my mate if not for Ethram's magic."

Ethram had told Terena about Taliquant's meeting with Tempest, and how he had cried as he laid his head on her pillow. She quickly embraced him. "I am sorry, Tali. This must have been unbearable, son."

Half way through feast, Zibula called the Draft Commissioner to draw up the breach of protocol papers and the Magistrate of Battle chambers for Letang's commission request. The Magistrate of Battle was already headed to Shallistar for a meeting with the Quillant officers, and he was hoping to arrive before their mourning rites began.

Obviously, he saw this as an opportunity to raise his place in the hierarchy, as the Old Ways and Commerce royalty would be questioned and presumably demoted after the protocol papers were filed. Zulien could not care less what shuffling the royals did, but he knew it would be in his best interest to keep the Magistrate of Battle on his side. Even with his lower ranking in the hierarchy, no one pushed the Magistrate controlling the battleships too far.

The Magistrate said he would be arriving within the hour and appreciated the warriors' sacrifice. Ethram fished in his pocket and handed the warriors another pill. "Just in case he is as long-winded as the rest of those pompous dremonts."

When the Magistrate of Battle arrived, he reluctantly agreed it would be best not to push the issue over the attack by the Debayluths after listening to the tape. They all knew the Magistrates were responsible, but the proof was thin. He settled the boons with the Quillant and Isotant without consulting the Magistrate of Commerce. "He would not dare deny the request. Ethram, we will discuss your promotions when things have settled down."

Ethram seemed appeased, and was very pleased with the amount offered for the boon. It was much larger than he had prepared to request. Ballion would preen.

The group had a good laugh when the Magistrate of Battle confirmed the apartments were being cleared of treasures. "Fortunately, they commissioned a battleship to move their wealth. They wanted it protected. I assure you, everything is in a secure location. Of my choosing, of course," he added.

"What is on your mind, Commander Zulien? I can see you want to ask me something." The Magistrate sat back in his chair.

Zulien was uneasy, still deciding who to trust

within the hierarchy. His father, former Commander Zibula, assured him, "Zule, I am honored to be friends with the Magistrate. We fought together for centuries when he was known as Commander Vesario. I believe he can be trusted, son."

The Magistrate smiled at Zibula and sighed, "Aah, Zib. They do not have battles like that any more. Zulien, I am not without the flaw of ambition. My ambition is perhaps misplaced, as I believe all Magistrates design to be of the highest importance, but I was not that far removed from the Battles of Chaos. I know what can happen if the hierarchy is manipulated for personal gain, and I desire the Battle Chambers risen for our citizens' protection."

Zulien glanced at his mother. She nodded, an indication she sensed no deception. He turned to his friend. "Tali? This concerns you as well."

The Magistrate realized something important had not been revealed. He was curious. "I cannot imagine you have done anything worse than dismiss the Magistrates, Zulien."

"We have to trust someone, Zule. As for protection, who better than the Magistrate of Battle?" Taliquant was nervous, but he knew they needed aid.

Zulien altered course. "Magistrate, why did they want my mate destroyed? What effect or damage could an Ancient raised in the outer worlds present to them?"

The Magistrate smiled a little. "They live, don't they?" He sat back again and slapped his knee. "Of course they do. There is no possible way the gods would have let them be discovered only to be taken. How have you managed this subterfuge? The separation while all this nonsense has been going on must have been excruciating."

Zulien's shoulders sagged. "Yes, Magistrate, they live. Miranda is the Celestial Ancient, and Taliquant's mate is her bonded friend, a primitive from the outer world planet they were procured from."

The Magistrate's smile broadened. "By the stars, warriors, congratulations." He was rather pleased with himself for figuring out what the Magistrate of the Old Ways and Magistrate of Commerce did not. "Do we know the Ancient's lineage?"

"Mother says she is Atlantian," Zulien replied.

"I have never known Zalana's visions to be wrong. Atlantian? This is unbelievably good news. Oh, I must plan. We must keep her protected at all costs."

Zulien was relieved he was getting at least that much. He persisted, "Why is she a threat?"

"Your mate holds the secrets of the Old Religion, the true Old Ways, within her genes. With guidance, all the knowledge destroyed during the Battles of Chaos can be revealed again. The hierarchy would crumble. It has been based on a foundation of lies, and they know it. The Magistrates have been worried for centuries that an Ancient would be found."

Zulien looked at him suspiciously. "Then it would affect you as well?"

"Rubbish. It does not matter if I am the Magistrate of Battle or what title is decided. The inner worlds will always need peacekeepers and a leader. I should think my protection and encouragement of the Ancient would set me in good standing for the position. What the inner worlds do not need are these pompous, self-serving Magistrates.

"We have a wealthy Magistrate of the Old Ways preaching false doctrine, a Magistrate of Commerce taxing the citizens into destitution, a Magistrate of Law creating policies and punishments according to his beliefs and not for the good of the citizenry, and a Magistrate of Building who tears down centuries old structures on a whim to build his newest designs. We have Twelve Magistrates, obscenely wealthy on the backs of the citizens, and each clawing for top position. I know what I speak is treason, Zulien, but I am not the only Magistrate who feels this way and has managed to position himself to help when the opportunity presented itself."

"You think the discovery of my Ancient will be that opportunity?" Zulien had a queasy feeling.

"She is precisely what we have been waiting for. Zalana, when the mating ceremonies have ended, you can aid her in remembering. She has the information locked inside her and you can be the key."

"Magistrate, of course I want to help, but I remember very little of the Old Religion," Zalana worried.

"You remember enough to have visions. Very few have accomplished that. What knowledge you have will build within her. New secrets will come to light that you can help her decipher. It may take a long time, but I believe it will happen. It must."

"How will I be able to protect her against the other Magistrates?" Zulien was beginning to panic. The thought of his little Celestial against all that power and greed was frightening.

"I am going to speak with those that believe as I do. I am afraid you will not like what I have to say next." The Magistrate glanced at Taliquant. "You will be grounded, effective immediately. There is no way these mates can be on a battleship."

Zulien and Taliquant were stunned. They had not considered this, and Zulien whispered in shock, "You're resigning my commission, sir?"

"By the stars, no. You will be promoted to Admiral. You are getting a desk job, and you as well, Taliquant. If you would have taken that ship I offered you, you would have been a Commander for a century by now."

Zulien looked at Taliquant in confusion. The Magistrate continued, "He would not let you know he had turned the commission down. I believe the reason he gave was that you could not command without his help," the Magistrate chuckled.

"I never knew," Zulien admitted, overwhelmed at the sacrifice his friend had made so they could fight together.

"As far as being grounded, well, as you young warriors say, it sucks. There is no alternative. I am suggesting to our group that we find a lesser planet to place you on. We will regulate the people who can transfer according to requirements your mate designs, when she is ready. Of course, we will arrange the finances so you have what you need, and I will rotate a schedule of battleships to guard the planet and the quadrant until you and Taliquant are settled enough to take over."

Zulien shook his head, clearing it. "We are getting our own planet?"

Taliquant smiled. "That is way better than a royalty apartment. I so want the Magistrates of the Old Ways and Commerce to hear about it... and Berslan, if the dremont is still alive."

"Taliquant, we are getting a planet," Zulien repeated. This was too much with all that was happening.

"I take it we will be moving as well, Magistrate?" Zalana was already planning.

"Yes, you will need to be with the Ancient. Communicate any visions you have concerning this, and if you see a suitable location then let me know that as well. I have a few in mind." The Magistrate turned his attention back to Zulien. "Now, the matter of Lieutenant Letang's commission. I have read the logs, and after hearing how he reacted throughout this situation, I take it you have confidence in this young man."

"Magistrate, we would not have succeeded without him. He has incredible control and wisdom for one so young, and we have named him second in our mating ceremonies," Zulien said.

"Both of you? You have that much confidence in this young man that he would second for both of these valuable mates?" The Magistrate was astounded.

"Absolutely, Magistrate. Much of the planning of this ruse was his," Zulien admitted.

The Magistrate sat back, stroking his beard in thought. "I have seen old fools and young wizards. Age is truly in the mind, experience and beliefs and how you choose to use them. If you are that confident in this man's abilities, I trust you. I am promoting him to Commander of the Quillant. It needs a commander now anyway, and it can be the first ship on rotation to protect your planet."

Zulien's jaw dropped. "Can you do that? He would be skipping four commission grades."

"I am the Magistrate of Battle. I can do whatever the dremont I please with my ships," he chuckled. "Any thoughts on a second? Taliquant's position needs to be filled."

Zulien answered immediately, "Captain Seartock, Magistrate. The two men work well together. Seartock's strength is with weapons, and Letang will not hesitate to refer to him."

"Will this cause discourse among the crew?" The Magistrate had seen it before.

"No, sir. Three junior officers will have to join the ship, so the rest will move up a commission. They all know how Letang risked charges of treason to help us. A few of them might have faltered if put in that situation. It should be a respected and commendable solution." Zulien pictured Letang's face when he told him. He was sure Vasilla would faint.

The Magistrate stood. "Well, I have planning to do, a planet to find, and you men have a claiming that has waited far too long. I will be forwarding gifts for the ceremonies."

"What, a couple moons and suns? You are already giving us a planet," Taliquant laughed.

"The planet is an honorary gift from the inner worlds for the Ancient, Taliquant. She will be our salvation." The Magistrate gathered his cloak and staff, tapped the floor lightly three times signifying the end of the audition, and walked to his shuttle.

"Was it this hectic when you met your mate, father?" Zulien watched the Magistrate's shuttle shoot towards the docking portal.

"Your mother had a vision when you were born that you were destined to be a great protector. At the time, I thought she meant you would be a warrior, like me." He put an arm around his son's shoulders. "I wish the dremonia she would be more damned specific about things."

Ethram cleared his throat. "Can we get this joining underway so Ballion and I can begin a proper vacation?"

"Can I see her first?" Zalana's eyes were begging to Zulien.

The mates had been on planet for days. "You have not seen her?"

"No, Ethram has not let anyone near them. We do not even know where he has secured them," Taliquant's mother complained.

"I have had the foresight to sequester them in a place they will not have to be moved for the joining. The last thing I need is a mishap during a joining transport." Ethram picked up his cloak.

As the group moved towards their shuttles, two new vehicles approached, and as they pulled closer, Zulien saw they were filled with warriors. A Major stepped out of the nearest shuttle and walked up to him.

"Commander, the Magistrate of Battle has commissioned us to protect you and your mates during joining and ceremony. There are three battleships already in quadrant to circle Shallistar. We would like to congratulate you and Major Taliquant." He offered his hand.

"Thank you, Major. How much is known?"

"We do not think the news has left Shallistar yet, but we feel fairly certain that someone on planet will know of your joining and communicate with Laquista before the day is out. It will probably start as mere gossip, but it will reach the hierarchy by nightfall. The Magistrate of Battle is already communicating with his allies, and he is deciding if he wants to issue the news of the Ancient's discovery himself. Fear not, warriors. You and your mates will be well protected."

Zulien's father chuckled. "No, son, it was not quite this hectic when I joined with your mother."

The group followed Ethram's shuttle to an

abandoned temple in a valley of the Shalliton Mountains. Three small buildings were arranged around a decaying stone altar, and Zalana stared in wonderment. "It is a temple of the Old Religion. How in the goddess' name did you find it?"

Ethram smiled. "I could tell you it was a vision, Zalana, but in truth, my father told me of its existence when I communicated news of the Celestial. The locations of a few remaining temples have been passed down through our family for centuries."

"I forget you inherited the Isotant from your grandfather. Why did your father not follow the path of procurement?" she asked curiously.

Ethram looked at the mountains, weighing the decision to tell them. "There is so much that is not known about the Old Religion. Our power to cloak and to feel the mate beacons skips a generation. My father did not have the abilities, and felt he could not bear the responsibility of commanding a vessel and relying solely on a scanner.

"For the most part, the independent procurers not commissioned by the hierarchy are forgotten once they find the mate. We purposely appear to be a greedy lot. The hierarchy prefers to ignore us that way, and it has enabled us to keep our own secrets. We follow the teachings of the Old Religion, as best we can remember. Those in the generations without the abilities have made it their life's vocation to search for information on the rituals and places such as these, the old temples, since the Battles of Chaos.

"If the hierarchy ever discovered all that we have learned, they would destroy us. My father has already spread the news of the Celestial's procurement, and you will be able to count on them for assistance with the Ancient's remembrance. When they hear she is Atlantian, there will be a huge celebration. I would like to discuss this with you further after we initiate the joining. We are most interested in your ability of visions."

Zalana was ecstatic. Their combined research would be a huge help, and she had already planned to call the few women she knew who possessed the power of visions.

The warriors spread out through the valley, prepared to defend the Ancient if the need arose. It was finally time to wake the mates.

Ethram turned to Zulien and Taliquant. "This is going to be confusing for them. Women born in the inner world dream of the day their old life will disappear and they will wake with their mates beside them. These women have no knowledge of our existence, much less our ways. I have been issuing calming thoughts and insinuating a little of the inner worlds in their dreams along with enhancing them with your genetic profiles. They may wake completely satisfied with the changes.

"My guess, however, is they will wake disoriented and panicked, stripped of their world and all that they know after the prolonged emptiness. They do not know to expect their mates when they are re-awoken, so you must be patient with them. Try to calm them while you explain. They will feel the physical bond, but they may think it is a trick. Eventually, the bond will overcome their fear, but it could take time.

"This could be harder than the separation, warriors, to have them within arm's reach and still have to hold back. Remember, the joining is a time of introduction and acclimation. The mothers and fathers may enter the chambers, but must leave when the mates begin to wake. This will be unsettling enough without a crowd around them, and their focus must be on learning to trust their mates," Ethram finished.

The parents nodded in agreement. Taliquant voiced Zulien's thoughts. "What if she wakes so fearful she will not let me comfort her?"

"Be persistent and calm, and eventually, the physical draw and the instinct of your protection should wear through their distress. They will learn to rely on your wisdom. We will visit Tempest first. Ballion will remain outside the door if your mate requires anything, or you need him. Remember, Taliquant, she is primitive and she may present an even greater challenge than the Ancient. For some reason, the two women have bonded, and we need to discover her importance to the Atlantian."

Ballion stood in the archway to the door of the temple with his antennae waving madly, and he looked exhausted from the strain. Ethram had left him in charge of preparing the mates. He was afraid he would leave bruises when he bathed the fragile creatures and it had taken him hours to choose the caftans he draped over them. He finally remembered Ethram's advice and matched the color he was told their eyes were, which happened to match the warriors' offering sashes.

He spent another hour brushing Miranda's hair, and was at a loss over Tempest's. He was unsure whether the flat side or the spiked side was correct, and in frustration, he ran his claws through the short mass and it separated into clumpy spikes. He decided it was a sign and left it. *By the stars, I hope that was the right decision.* He smoothed his scales one last time as the group approached.

Taliquant smiled down at the distraught Minoc. "Thank you for preparing my mate, Ballion. I can see you have been judicious in your planning, and I am sure you will be welcoming your break."

"Thank you, Major." Then, Ballion confided, "These have been most unusual procurements, and this has been my first independent preparation." He hoped that would earn forgiveness if he had miscalculated the hair.

The group entered the chamber where Tempest lay sleeping in an emerald caftan with gold embroidery, and Taliquant moved towards her without realizing his motion.

Zelana whispered to Taliquant's mother, "She is lovely, Terena. She has the look of nature's wild beauty."

Terena's eyes were filled with tears over the joy she felt for her son. She was to have a daughter. "She truly is nature's child, Zalana, is she not?"

Even the fathers cleared their throats of emotion as they thought of their own joining. Taliquant was staring at his mate silently. He was suddenly terrified she would reject him.

Ethram sensed his distress and sent a slight aura of calmness. "Be persistent, Taliquant, and nature will bind you. Ease her stress." Ethram brushed his fingers over Tempest's forehead and she inhaled a deep breath.

"It is time to leave the chamber to the mates. Ballion, you remember your instructions?"

"Yes, Commander. Major, I will be just outside if you need assistance calming her." It had not occurred to anyone that the mere sight of Ballion would cause the primitive hysterics.

As the group quietly left the room, Terena turned around for one more glimpse of Tempest.

Her eyes were still closed but she had stretched her little arms high over her head, and as she brought them back down, she clasped onto Taliquant. Terena smiled and closed the door.

Zalana began running her hands through her hair and smoothing her long shift. Zibula chuckled, "You look beautiful, mate. Her eyes will not even be open to see you."

"You do not understand, Zibula. My daughter-in-law is an Ancient. By the stars, I never hoped to be so blessed. How do I honor her? There is no remembered ritual or protocol. Suppose she is displeased to find she is to be mated with a family with only a visionary?" Zalana was practically shaking.

Zibula pulled his golden beauty to him. "Zulien, you may be calm with your mate. Your mother is certainly nervous enough for all of us," he chuckled. In truth, he was also wondering what role he was supposed to play with a Celestial. He had secretly gone through the banks of knowledge and found nothing.

"Wait until you see her, mother. Merely being in her radiant presence is calming," Zulien smiled.

Ethram led them to the chamber, and Zalana gazed in stunned silence as she approached the vision on the pallet. She wore a pale blue caftan with moons and stars embroidered in silver. Tears filled Zalana's eyes as she saw the matching sash she had embroidered for her son's mate so many centuries before tied to her wrist and tucked up by her chin. Her golden hair surrounded her with the rays of the suns, and pale, delicate skin stretched across high cheekbones.

As Zulien approached her, one small hand reached out, searching. Zulien clasped it gently and brought it back to her side as he knelt, and Ethram whispered, "Your bond is strong, Zulien. Several times I have had to issue a wave of peace towards your little mate, yet she continues to search for you. Are you ready, warrior?"

"Yes, Ethram. I have been waiting centuries for this moment. I never dreamed it would arrive."

Ethram pulled Zalana back from the pallet where she stood almost in a trance as she gazed at Miranda. "Zalana," he said gently, "this is your son's time. You will have a lifetime with her."

Zalana leaned down and brushed her fingers through her warrior son's long dark hair. "I love you, Zulien, and I do not need a vision to know all will be well."

"Thank you, mother. I can feel the peace she emits also."

Ethram brushed his fingers across Miranda's forehead, and she sighed and reached her other hand over to Zulien's comforting grasp. Zulien smiled and began stroking her head as she slowly awoke.

Ethram escorted the parents out of the chambers. "I will, of course, be remaining here. I will have one of the guards inform the Magistrate of Battle when the joining has ended."

Zalana and Terena were hugging each other and crying. Zibula glanced over at them, then looked back at Ethram and rolled his eyes.

Ethram laughed quietly. "Mothers." The women turned to him. "I suggest you get busy. Planning ceremonies for a Celestial Ancient and her bonded friend will be quite a task."

Zibula's mind flashed on the uproar the house would be in while his mate panicked over the preparations and said, "Thanks a lot. I will be lucky to have another joining of my own until this is over."

Zalana and Terena were already discussing the location for the joint ceremonies, and whether it was a breach of the Ancient's protocol to even hold the ceremonies together.

Ethram chuckled, "I thought you wanted them to stop their tears."

The parents returned to their shuttle and headed back home to begin the preparations for the ceremonies. In the inner worlds, the son's mother always arranged the ceremonies. It was an honor given to welcome the new mate to her family, and Zalana and Terena were petrified of failing.

Zulien continued to stroke Miranda's forehead until she gasped a little and her eyes began to open. They were a crystal blue and watery, and as she focused, she looked up at him with alarm. "Wake slowly, Miranda. You have been in deep sleep for a long time," he said softly.

Zulien was encouraged. At least she had not screamed. He thought of how he must look to her. He was large, even for a warrior, with dark hair that fell well below his shoulders in a thick, wild mane. His ebony eyes were completely the opposite of the light blue pair gazing suspiciously at him, and he wondered if the people of her planet even had his coloring. The golden bronze skin was unique to the people of Shallistar, so he was sure she would find that as unusual as he found her luminescence. He hoped she would be as pleased.

She had not released his hands as she continued to calmly stare at him, and then she spoke in a soft voice, and said the last thing he expected to hear. "I know you."

Zulien thought she meant the unique knowing of the mate's gene bonding, until she said, "I've seen you in my visions."

Zulien was confused as to what to do. He was prepared to comfort her, but she appeared to be completely calm. "When did you have these visions, Miranda?" He loved the feel of her name as it rolled off his lips.

She released his hand and struggled to sit up. A wave of dizziness washed over, her and Zulien quickly placed his strong arm behind her for support.

"Thank you. I guess I am a little weak. Was I in an accident?" She took in her unusual surroundings. The last thing she remembered was going to bed in her cabin.

"May I get you something? Perhaps a drink to strengthen you?" he offered.

"A little juice would be nice, if you have any. I am a little parched." She had steadied enough for him to stand, and she continued to look around in confusion. She certainly was not in a hospital room, and the giant in tight black leather was no doctor.

Zulien looked around the room. There was nothing other than her sleeping pallet, a joining pallet and a chaise. Generally, when mates awoke, it was a constant sexual interlude and they did not consider libation. He was distressing over not being able to provide for her first request, and he reluctantly walked to the door. "Ethram?"

Ethram stiffened. No way was the joining completed. He calmed himself, prepared to match whatever crisis had occurred. "How may I assist you, Zulien?"

"My mate would like some juice. She says she is parched."

"I will be right back, wait here." Ethram cloaked to the third temple where he and Ballion had set up quarters. He quickly poured a glass of nintine juice and cloaked back. "I have returned."

Zulien opened the door. Ethram inadvertently glanced into the room and saw Miranda. "You're the man from the shop," she exclaimed. "I remember your cloak." She was a little confused as his words came back to her. "Is this who you meant?" She nodded towards Zulien, and Ethram looked bewildered. "When you spoke to me in the shop, you said, 'He will be so pleased'. I was going to ask you who you were talking about." The beautiful face frowned. "I'm sorry, I don't remember anything else about our conversation."

Ethram was shocked she had remembered him at all. He had pushed a strong wave towards her so she would forget their meeting. The joining was taking an unusual path, and for the first time Ethram was at a loss.

Zulien broke the silence. "Ethram, you may as well come in. As you can see, my Ancient has questions and you may be able to answer better than I can. I am not forcing a joining until she is prepared."

The big man's words made no sense to Miranda at all, and she studied the room again. It seemed to be nothing more than a large bedroom. She swung her legs over the side of the sleeping pallet and used it to steady herself as she stood. She coughed a little, and Zulien grabbed the juice from Ethram and ran to her. "I am sorry, Miranda."

She took a sip of the juice and smiled up at him over the rim of the glass. "This is delicious. What is it?"

Zulien had actually been a little nervous Ethram had not returned with at least pallachi juice. "It is called nintine juice. It is very common." Zulien looked down with embarrassment at the poor offering.

He felt her stiffen, and he was terrified he had offended her. She walked slowly over to the window and looked out. Lavender skies with light blue clouds were adorned with two suns and a crescent moon. Unusual trees edged a valley with a thick blue carpet of grass, and she began to fall as she turned back to the men. Zulien rushed to catch her, and frightened blue eyes looked up at him. "Where am I?"

"You are on Shallistar," Zulien replied weakly. He was totally unprepared for this. Actually, he did not know what was going to happen when she awoke, but he certainly had not expected this calm Celestial vision to be asking questions. Any answer he gave could panic her.

He guided her back to the chaise. "Am I dreaming?" She shook her head and laughed, and the sound reminded Zulien of his mother's musical laughter. "That's silly. Whenever you're dreaming and you ask, it's always denied."

Ethram remained by the door, entranced by the Celestial's behavior. Shrieking in fear, attacking Zulien with lust, or uncontrollable sobbing were what he had prepared for. Not this calm, questioning creature.

Suddenly, the silence was broken by a shriek, but not from Miranda. It was Tempest. "Where in hell am I, and who the hell are you?" she screamed.

"Tempest!" Miranda dashed past Zulien and Ethram before they registered she was moving, and they quickly followed after her.

Miranda ran towards the building she had heard Tempest's scream coming from, ignoring the blue grass. She could not ignore the large lizard-type thing outside the door, and she stopped abruptly. Ballion and Miranda stared at each other with their mouths gaping open.

Ballion quickly bowed his head and stuttered, "It is a pleasure to meet you, Celestial. I am the apprentice procurer, Ballion."

Zulien managed to catch her as she fainted. Ballion began pacing, his antenna waving furiously in terror at having upset the Ancient mate, while Tempest continued to shriek at Taliquant behind the door. Ethram lowered his head. *What a disaster!*

"Zulien, take your mate back to your joining room. I am going to calm Tempest and I will be right back." He waved an aura of calmness to Ballion. "You did nothing wrong, Ballion. This entire joining is new territory."

Ethram entered the room and quickly took in the scene. Tempest was standing in the corner on the chaise staring wild eyed at a very distraught warrior. "You." Tempest pointed her finger and glared at Ethram. "What have you done with Miranda?"

Taliquant used Ethram's distraction to edge closer to her, and she narrowed her eyes at him. "I told you to back off, big guy, or I will kick you again."

"Miranda is fine, Tempest, and I will take you to her shortly. Taliquant, I think you should sit over there. Tempest and I have a few things to discuss."

Taliquant reluctantly sat on the joining pallet. He was still trying to figure out how to comfort his mate. He watched his beautiful wild primitive climb off the chaise and sit down, green eyes flashing. "Start explaining, Mister."

Ethram decide to try what had worked before, and held out his hand. "Ethram, my name is

Ethram."

Once again, Tempest reached out her hand in automatic response, and once again, she fell instantly asleep. "This is a huge mess, Taliquant. Let me get back to Zulien and put Miranda back to rest, and then we need to get together and discuss this."

CHAPTER VI

After the mates were once again sleeping, the men sat outside in the clearing. "Either being off planet has not registered yet, or they do not have a problem with that. We know they do not have a problem, at least from a bonding aspect, of recognizing you as their mates. The reason they are reluctant for the joining is the mystery." Ethram was speaking his thoughts out loud.

"Tempest became extremely agitated when she did not recognize her surroundings. At first, she was fine, and just lay there with her eyes closed while I comforted her. As soon as she opened her eyes, she looked surprised and ran away from me." Taliquant lowered his head in misery.

"Miranda was just the opposite. The first thing she said was that she knew me, and she was completely calm and asking questions until she heard Tempest scream." Zulien was upset and confused.

Ballion cleared his throat for recognition. "Yes, Ballion. Do you have any thoughts about this?" Ethram asked.

Ballion began to slowly pace, his hands clasped behind his back while his antennae slowly stroked his chin in thought. "My studies, as you know, were in procurement, but as a Minoc I realized my chances of getting picked for a procurement vessel were slim. I am not blind to the fact my emotions and greed can overshadow good judgment, and it is a constant battle to control those limitations. Because of this, I have the second education of Minocs' in Ancient civilization." Ballion noticed their surprise. "Oh, yes. Minocania has researched and observed the cultures for generations. We know it is treason, but really, who pays any attention to us? We could not be of much assistance when the temples fell, but we are determined to help them rise again. Now, of course, none of our resources go back as far as the Atlantian era, but still there was quite a diversification of peoples in the inner worlds."

The three men looked at the Minoc curiously. Even Ethram had never heard him speak with such eloquence. Ballion continued, "My observations lead me to believe the world these women were raised in was perhaps a little more evenly divided on authority. In other words, they do not consider a male superior and, if anything, they are a bit of a threat."

Taliquant blanched. "My Tempest thinks I mean to harm her?"

"No, no. I think she does not know what to expect. Her species is not able to transfer all their well-being and judgment based on the exclusivity of the mating bond."

What he was saying was making sense, based on the women's reactions. They seemed to want to talk and have explanations before their joining. "Do you have any suggestions?" Ethram asked.

"I do, but I do not think you are going to like it because it will once again delay your joining. I think anything short of force is going to delay it at this point," Ballion stated.

His antennae had been calmly stroking his chin since he had begun speaking, and all three men had noticed that Ballion was not the least bit nervous as he discussed their predicament. "What is it you think needs to be done?" Zulien asked.

"I think you need to get your mothers back here, and I think the four women need to sit down together and talk. It will be easier to have the joining explained, and they are more apt to accept what is said by a member of their own sex."

"There is no protocol for that," Ethram interjected.

"We have never tried to introduce mates from the outer world before," Ballion reminded his Commander. "Add to that, we are working with an Ancient, so there is no protocol for any of this. It is up to us to design the protocol," Ballion declared.

Ethram sat back. "My little green apprentice is right. I do not have to refer to my ship's logs, and they go back centuries and generations, to know this has never been attempted. Do you really think this will help?"

Ballion smiled, "Well it sure in dremonia cannot hurt."

Ethram called for a member of the guard to send word the mothers were to return, and the warriors returned to their mates. In their deep sleep, they once again reached out to them and were comforted by their touch. Both men felt much better at the sign of acceptance.

The fathers returned as well, and with Ballion's assistance Ethram explained what was happening. "I guess the men can lounge in our quarters while the women speak. I have no idea how long this will take." Ethram pointed to his quarters and sent Ballion to retrieve Taliquant while he went to Zulien.

Zalana followed. She watched her son rise from his mate's side. "I am so sorry this is such a trial for you, Zule. You should be safely wrapped in each other's arms by now."

Zulien smiled. "I have the rest of my life for that. She knew me, mother. The first words she spoke were that she knew me from her visions, and if her adjustment takes time, then she will have it."

Zalana stretched and kissed his cheek. "You are a wise warrior, and I see now you will be a wise mate."

"Zulien, would you carry the Ancient to Tempest's joining quarters. I think that would be a good place for their talks. Ballion, get a pitcher of nintine juice. The Celestial enjoyed it, and Tempest may wake with a thirst after all that shrieking."

Zulien and Ballion left, and Ethram waved the mates awake. They were sleeping side by side on the joining pallet. He left before they opened their eyes, and Zalana and Terena waited as the young woman woke up.

Tempest opened her eyes and was facing Miranda. The two girls stared at each other, and then Tempest broke out in a huge smile. "Cripes, Miranda, where have you been? I looked everywhere for you. When you transferred the cabin to me, I thought maybe you went to find your grandmother." She hugged her tightly.

Miranda frowned. "Transferred the cabin? I don't remember doing that."

Zalana and Terena remained silent, waiting to be recognized. Tempest noticed them first. "We've got company."

Miranda turned around to see two women with the golden skin of the large men, sitting on the chaise in the corner. Miranda felt a twinge of despair. "Where is he?"

Zalana was nervous to the second sun, but managed to reply calmly, "Where is who, Miranda?"

"The golden man. He was with me when I woke up before, and he promised he would never leave me." She was becoming visibly agitated and could not understand why. "Where did he go?"

At the mention of the man, Tempest's eyes roamed the room and she began to actually panic. "Where is he? Where did the big guy go?" She stood up and searched the empty space. "He could not keep his hands off me. Where the hell is he?" she demanded.

The mothers realized the bonding was going to keep any meaningful discussion from occurring. "Would you like me to send for them? They are waiting close by," Zalana offered.

Terena was amused with Tempest's outrage that her son was absent, and she watched her search impossibly small places around the room for him.

Miranda tried to calm down and absently stroked her sash. She could not think of anything else but the man. "Please, I just want to know he is all right." She had no idea why she had said that.

Terena spoke up. "Tempest, would you like me to send for Taliquant?"

"Tali what?" Tempest asked. She was still frantically searching, double-checking places she had already been.

"My son, Taliquant," Terena replied.

"If that is the big guy that was here before, then yes. I wasn't done yelling at him." She nervously plopped down beside Miranda on the pallet. "Coward," she added.

Terena laughed. "He is certainly going to have his hands full with you."

"He's already tried to have his hands full of me, and I am not done with him yet," Tempest declared.

Zalana walked to the door. "I will go get

them."

Terena was pleased by the girls' obvious discomfort over the separation. When the warriors returned and the agitation subsided, they would begin to understand the bonding.

The anxious men looked up, surprised when Zalana entered. "How are they? Did they tell you to leave?" Zulien asked.

"Quite the contrary. Your mates have not even asked our names or why we are there. They awoke in a state of extreme agitation wanting their mates. Tempest even checked under the joining pallet for you, Taliquant... three times," Zalana laughed.

Taliquant beamed. "I knew she would miss me."

"At any rate, we are not going to be able to discuss anything with them until you are near them. Zule, Miranda wanted to know if you are all right. I think you should sit away from them and let Terena and me see if we can get them to talk. They will approach you when they are ready."

The warriors strode behind Zalana, relieved at the prospect of seeing their mates again. When they walked through the door, Tempest walked over, put her hands on her hips and glared up at Taliquant. "Where the hell did you go? I wake up with your hands all over me and then you just disappear? What is that about?"

Taliquant was facing the same angry woman from before. "I thought you wanted me to go. You said to leave you alone," he explained.

"Well you don't just paw a girl and disappear with no explanation, big guy. At least, not this girl." Tempest poked her finger into his chest for emphasis.

Terena was laughing out loud at this point.

The primitive barely reached her son's chest, and was berating him like a farong. "Tali, she is a challenge for you."

Taliquant looked over at his mother in distress. He had no idea what his mate wanted from him, and it seemed whether he stayed or left, she was unhappy. "What do you wish me to do, Tempest?"

Tempest looked around the room, and pointed to the sleeping pallet. "Go sit over there until I figure out what is going on."

Taliquant looked at Zulien, shrugged, and did as she had asked. Miranda was still standing by the joining pallet. When Zulien had entered the room, she smiled at him, and then closed her eyes, breathing deeply.

Zalana watched her. "Do you know what she is doing?" Zulien asked.

"She is grounding herself. With you away, she was very upset, and she is bringing herself back into balance. In a way, Tempest was doing the same thing by expressing her frustrations."

"I think I like Miranda's way much better," Zulien observed.

Tempest glanced away from Taliquant just long enough to glare at Zulien.

"Me too," his mother laughed. "Zule, I think you should join Tali? Miranda will speak to you when she is ready."

Zulien did as his mother suggested. Tempest was standing near Miranda, waiting for her to open her eyes, and continuing to glare at Taliquant. Miranda finally opened her eyes and again smiled at Zulien. "Did a really cute little green lizard man really speak to me?"

Zulien smiled back. "That was Ballion. You scared the dremonia out of him when you fainted. He thought he had hurt you."

Miranda scoffed. "He would not hurt anyone. He has a very gentle nature. It just surprised me."

"What are you talking about?" Tempest was torn between following the conversation, and scowling at Taliquant, making sure he did not leave her sight.

"Tempest, you know we're not home any more, right?" Miranda asked.

"Well, yes, Miranda. I did notice this was not the cabin," she replied irritably.

"That is not what I mean. Come here a minute." Miranda took her friend's arm.

Before she could be pulled away, she pointed at Taliquant. "You. Stay."

Taliquant continued to watch his feisty mate in fascinated silence as Miranda led her to the window. "What do you see?"

"I don't see anything, Miranda. It's night time." Tempest glanced back at Taliquant to make sure he had not moved.

"Tempest, try to pay attention. Look at the sky." Miranda pointed at the midnight blue sky, scattered stars and three moons.

Tempest was about to ask her what she was supposed to be looking at when she caught sight of moon number two, and by the time she spotted number three, her mouth was hanging open.

"Like I said, we're not home any more." Miranda led her shocked friend back to the joining pallet and sat down next to her. "Now, these people don't seem to want to hurt us, so I think we need to find out what is going on. It appears if we get all crazy, they're just going to make us go to sleep again."

Zulien interrupted, "Actually, Ethram's the only one who can do that."

"That is the man with the cloak?" Miranda confirmed.

Zulien nodded. "Is she all right? Tali is getting a little nervous over here. It might help if he held her," Zulien suggested.

"Only if he wants his arm broken," Tempest shot back.

"She is fine," Miranda laughed. "Tempest, calm down a little bit. He has not moved since you asked him to sit down." Tempest glanced over at him to make sure.

Miranda guided Tempest over by where the women sat, and she placed them where they could see the men sitting on the table in the middle of the room. It made no sense to her why this was important, but she realized it was hard to concentrate when he was out of sight. She looked at the woman who had brought the men back. Miranda was on eye level as she stood by the tall, sitting woman, and she held out a small hand. "I am Miranda and this is Tempest."

Zalana beamed and wrapped the small offering in both her large, slender hands. "It is so good to meet you, Miranda. I have waited a long time for this. You as well, Tempest."

Tempest glanced at her and gave her a quick nod of acknowledgement, before her eyes fixed on Taliquant again. The big guy sat there grinning at her, and it was beginning to piss her off.

The golden woman continued, "I am Zalana. Zulien is my son. This is Terena. Taliquant is her son."

Tempest looked at Terena, who was smiling at her in an extremely amused way. "You should teach the big guy some manners."

"He does not mean to dishonor you, Tempest. We do not understand your ways. He will learn," Terena said. "Of this, I am quite certain."

"Miranda, you have already figured out you are no longer in the outer worlds, and I am sure you have a lot of questions. I promise you, all of them will be answered in time. You are correct that we will not harm you. That is positively the last thing we want to happen. There are those who would, though, and it is important for you to understand these dangers."

Tempest turned and stared evenly at the woman. "Lady, no one is hurting Miranda. They would have to get by me first."

Zalana smiled at Terena. "I believe I am beginning to figure out why they have bonded, though it is unusual for a woman to be a protector."

"Miranda, we need to get out of here." Tempest was still studying Taliquant.

Miranda sighed. "Where do you suggest we go, Tempest?"

"If ever there was a time to use your magic, this would be it, don't ya' think?"

The Shallistarians tensed at Tempest's words. They had no idea if the Celestial could actually transport them back to the outer worlds, and the warriors gripped the pallet to keep from running to them.

Miranda laughed softly. "Tempest, we are here for a reason. The goddesses showed me visions of Zule or whatever he's called. I'm sorry, what did you say your son's name was again?"

Zulien closed his eyes as he heard his mate say his name. He felt a peace he could not remember since he was a boy and his mother held him to ease his fears.

"Zulien, but Zule is fine if it is easier for you. It is our nickname for him." Zalana straightened and said proudly, "I have visions as well."

"Have you seen me? Can you tell us why we

were brought here?" Miranda asked with a tinge of anticipation. She had never met anyone else who had visions like she did, and the thought of meeting someone else like her was exciting.

"When Zulien was a child, I had a vision of him standing before the moons and the suns with his arms across his chest. I immediately thought it looked like he was guarding and protecting them, and here you are with the golden hair of the suns and the luminescent skin of the moons. I did not see your face back then, but I recognized you immediately."

Miranda frowned. "Then you believe I am here for a reason too?" Miranda's hand trembled a little in the woman's grasp.

"Oh, yes, Miranda, there are so many reasons for you to be here. I have been asked to help you." Zalana bowed her head, a little embarrassed that she should have the task of guiding an Ancient.

"I've waited so long for a teacher to help me understand why I am so different. Whatever the reasons we were brought here, thank you, Zalana."

Zalana was shocked that the Celestial had reached the conclusion that she was to be the teacher. It was Miranda's destiny to teach the people of the inner worlds, and Zalana chose her words carefully. "We will learn from each other, I think."

Tempest was confused by the constant feeling she needed to watch the golden man. "So what is the deal with the big guys? Are they going to teach us to fight or something?"

Terena said, "No, they are going to protect and comfort you."

Tempest turned on her. "Protect and comfort me? That big guy," she turned to point at the warrior, trying to remember his name.

"Taliquant," Terena reminded her.

"Whatever. That big guy was running his hands all over me. We do not call that protection where I come from," Tempest replied indignantly.

"No, that was meant for comfort, Tempest. He thought you would be afraid when you woke up in strange surroundings. Obviously, very little scares you, and for a primitive you are adjusting well." Terena smiled at the opportunity to compliment her.

"Primitive? Who the hell are you calling a primitive? You don't even have a television in this room."

Terena experienced some of the distress her son had been feeling, realizing she had insulted her prospective daughter unintentionally. She was afraid to say anything else, and she looked at her son with an apologetic expression for upsetting his mate further. Taliquant was still grinning at Tempest.

Miranda stepped in. "Tempest, I think to them we are primitives. Goddess knows, on Earth we were still trying to figure out if there even were other civilizations in the galaxy. I expect they either discovered long ago what a waste of time the trash on television was, or they have something far more advanced."

"Miranda, we're in a stone room with no electrical outlets, radios or anything. How advanced can they be?" Tempest reasoned.

"Then how do you explain the light?" Miranda responded.

Tempest searched for lamps, and her expression softened to wonder as she realized the light was coming from the stone walls and ceiling themselves. She looked at Terena. "Can you turn them off?"

Terena smiled. "Those in the room merely wish them dimmed, and it happens. Not all worlds have the Shallistones. They are a major export for us, and our family owns one of the largest mines," she said proudly. It was important her son's mate knew his family had a strong heritage, even if they were only merchants.

"Okay," Tempest admitted. "That's pretty cool." She looked over at the warrior. "Stop staring at me," she demanded.

Taliquant continued to grin. "That is the one thing I cannot do, Tempest. My eyes are drawn to your beauty, and I have no control over them."

Tempest knew she looked all right, in a weird sort of way, but no one had ever mistaken her for a beauty. "Bullshit. Stop staring at me like I'm weird or something."

"Your green eyes are the color of veruch, a very rare Shallistone. Your skin is the color of palliston, even rarer. Never has such beauty walked our planet," he said reverently.

Tempest studied his face to determine if he was making fun of her. She had to admit, he did look sincere and totally entranced by her, and now she began to feel uncomfortable because she started to think the big lug actually liked her. "Well, you shouldn't stare anyway. It's impolite."

"And you've been displaying such good manners yourself," Miranda chided.

Tempest turned to her. "Well what do you expect? I am talking to the dude in the cloak in my flower shop, and the next thing I know I wake up in this crypt with a Neanderthal feeling me up?"

Terena's mouth dropped open. "Tempest, you have the magic of the plants?" she asked in awe.

Tempest straightened. "I will have you know, I have a degree in botany." All right, maybe it was only a two-year degree from the community college, but she had always had a green thumb.

Terena was delighted. "You have studied the magic of the growing things. We were not told. I cannot wait to tell my friends."

Tempest was surprised by the woman's obvious respect for her chosen field. Cripes... it was just a little flower shop. "Miranda and I liked to grow our own herbs and vegetables. That way, we know there's not any poisonous junk sprayed on them. They always tasted better, too, don't you think, Miranda?"

Miranda agreed. "Tempest can grow anything. I'm not quite as handy. I did manage to keep from killing the plants," Miranda laughed. "But Tempest really cared for our garden. She supplied the herbs for my soaps and candles."

Terena was almost bursting with pride. "You supply the Celestial's ritual herbs?"

Zalana's mouth dropped open. Terena realized her mistake immediately and shrank back, miserably staring at the folded hands in her lap, and she whispered, "By the stars, Zalana, I am sorry."

Miranda searched Zalana's eyes as Tempest asked, "What the heck is a Celestial?"

"I think Zalana has a little more to explain to me," Miranda said quietly.

"I did mention there were many reasons you were brought here," Zalana weakly offered.

"I do not shock easily, Zalana, and even when I do, I sort it out and recover quickly, just as I did when I realized I had been kidnapped by what we refer to as aliens, brought to another planet which is obviously not even in our solar system, and met a little green lizard that could speak. What do you possibly think you could say to me that would come as more of a surprise?"

Zalana felt now as though she had insulted the Ancient and deceived her. To save face, she decided to admit the truth. "Miranda, you are a Celestial Ancient. You are the last of the Atlantians and most of the inner worlds will be hoping you can bring back the Old Religion. You are also Zulien's destined mate." There... she had gotten it all out. It was now up to the Ancient to either forgive her or to chastise her. She had released Miranda's hand and was clasping hers so tightly together that her knuckles were a pale yellow. She squeezed her eyes shut.

Miranda realized the poor woman's distress, even as her words banged through her mind. Ancient, Atlantian, Old Religion, mate. Mate? Her head swiveled around to the big man on the table. He was sitting in stunned silence at his mother's admission. "I think you had better come take care of your mother. I need to sit down for a moment."

Zulien rose to walk over to his mother as Miranda started drifting towards the joining pallet to sit down. Her knees buckled half way there, and Zulien caught her before she hit the ground. Terena and Zalana gasped and rushed over to her as Zulien laid her down. "By the stars, is she all right? Zulien, I am so sorry. I have made such a mess of this, and I was supposed to be helping," Zalana cried.

Tempest had walked up behind them. She had seen Miranda faint before over a weird vision, like in high school when the lab blew up. She figured her friend's brain just kind of overloaded and needed to cool down. "She'll be fine. She just needs to get this figured out."

Zalana looked up at Tempest with tears in her eyes. "Are you sure? Is there anything we can do to help her?"

Tempest realized the woman really was upset. "Hey, it's okay. I've seen her do this lotsa' times. It's like when she was standing earlier with her eyes closed. She tells me it puts her back in balance. She taught me to meditate, also. I tend to get somewhat irrational about things. I don't actually collapse like she does, though. Just back off a little so she can get some air. She'll be back with us in a few minutes," Tempest assured them.

Zulien was holding Miranda's hand, with his face close to hers and speaking softly.

"Hey, big guy, give her a little room."

Zulien moved back mere inches, and never looked back at Tempest. "He's really stuck on her, isn't he?"

"They are destined mates. It is why she was so nervous when he was not in the room earlier, and even if she does not acknowledge it yet, the mating genes do." Zalana was holding her hand over her son and Miranda's.

Tempest thought about what the woman had said, and it began to dawn on her about the agitation she felt when the 'Tali' guy was gone. She slowly turned to look at him. He was still sitting on the sleeping pallet and grinning at her. "Oh, no." His grin broadened. "You can get that thought right out of your head, big guy."

"It is not anything we have control over, Tempest. You are my mate. Our gene is matched." His big hand rubbed over his heart. "You are my other half, and I devote myself to you."

"Cripes!" Tempest exclaimed, and she sagged to the floor. Zalana ran for Ethram, and all the men came rushing back into the room.

Taliquant had laid Tempest on the sleeping pallet, and the warriors were fussing over their fainted mates. "Well, this is certainly going well," Zibula chuckled.

Ballion was dashing between the women, making sure they were all right. "How much did you tell them?"

"Everything," Zalana admitted.

"I said to explain things to them slowly. No wonder they retreated." Ballion shook his scaly head in admonishment while his antenna wandered around in distress.

"It just sort of came out." Zalana began to cry.

Terena spoke up, "It was my fault. I slipped up. Really, Zalana, they did not seem that upset."

"Not that upset?" Ballion shrieked. "They have retreated into deep sleep."

Terena continued, "I think Tempest is right. Miranda gets overwhelmed, probably because she is so sensitive. Tempest was fine with everything until Taliquant expressed his devotion, and it is the first time she has not glared at him. I think all this is a good sign."

Everyone in the room stared at her. Ethram gritted his teeth. "I have two mates passed out in one joining chamber. How, by the stars, do you think that is a good sign?"

Zalana realized what Terena was saying. "Ethram, neither one of the young women has become hysterical, and they have been told everything. I think things are going to go much better," she glanced at the pale women, "once they revive."

Miranda opened her eyes first, and found herself looking into the worried brown eyes of Zulien. He smiled and asked quietly, "Would you like some more juice?"

She smiled back at him. "Yes, please. Can I have some of that nin...?"

"Nintine juice," he supplied. "Mother, can you get Miranda a glass of juice, please."

Zalana rushed back with the juice. "I am so sorry, Miranda. It was unforgivable for me to throw all that at you at once. I did not want you to think I was being deceptive."

"You were kind of caught between a rock and a hard place, Zalana. It just overwhelmed me a bit." She sat up. "I am afraid you're mistaken about a few things. There is not any way I am leading anyone in an Old Religion. I could not even manage to find a group to be with on my planet. As far as the other stuff, I guess we will have to talk some more about it. I don't understand most of what you said."

"You do know me though, right? You told me you saw me in your visions." Zulien needed the reassurance.

"Yes, once on Earth several years ago, and several times while I was in some kind of blackness. I couldn't find my way out, and you came to me. You said you would protect me and never leave." Zulien was pacified and awed that she remembered his words of offering.

She looked bewildered. "I just don't know what it means." Miranda thought about the wild dark hair on the man in the vision she had during the one and only time she had sex, when she was with Johnny. Was that a sign? She got up and walked over to where Tempest lay gripping Taliquant's hand. She knew she was all right and began to laugh. "I never saw her pass out over anything before. What happened?"

Terena said, "I think it dawned on her that Taliquant, the big guy, is her mate."

"That would do it. She must have freaked.

Tempest is kind of a 'take charge' type of person."
Miranda swept her fingers through Tempest's
bangs.

"No kidding?" Taliquant grinned. "I was
beginning to take it personally."

"Oh, I am sure it's personal."

Tempest began to shudder awake. She
immediately released Taliquant's hand and
shoved him away. "Stop pawing at me," she
ordered. She looked at Miranda as she sat up. "I
told them you were all right," she muttered. Her
eyes roamed the room anxiously, until she found
Taliquant standing near a large lizard. She
pointed, "What the hell is that? Your icky pet?"

"Tempest," Miranda admonished. "That is..."
she looked at Zulien.

He whispered in her ear, "Ballion."

"Ballion," she said. "He is incredibly sensitive
and kind, so please be nice."

Ballion had begun shaking, and his antennae
went haywire. To have the primitive afraid of him
and the Ancient honor him in such a short span
of time was unnerving. "Thank you, Miranda," he
said quietly.

Tempest screamed. "Did that thing just
talk?"

Miranda rushed over to Ballion and knelt.
She took his scaly claw. "I am so sorry. She
sometimes handles strange situations without the
best control."

"It is all right, Ancient, she is primitive. We
expected this to be a little more difficult for her."
Ballion was puffed out with the attention and
concern from the Ancient. He could not wait to
tell his mother. What pride she would have that
her son, a mere Minoc, had received concern from
the Ancient.

Tempest watched the unusual beast and could see he was obviously enthralled with Miranda. "I guess he is kinda' cute. He sorta' grows on you."

"He is not a pet, Tempest. He is an apprentice of something."

"Procurement," Ballion said proudly. "Only two other Minocs have ever been so honored."

"Then that is quite an accomplishment. I am sure your teacher is proud of you." Miranda stood up.

"That I am, Miranda. Ballion also has studied Ancient civilization, and has been quite helpful to us in trying to figure out the best way to introduce you to the inner worlds." Ethram walked over to her.

She eyed him suspiciously. "You're not going to put me to sleep again, are you?"

Ethram laughed. "No, I think you have slept long enough. Actually, I just wanted to shake your hand and welcome you to our worlds."

Miranda took his hand. "Thank you. How do you work your magic?"

"We will discuss it at a later time. There is plenty you should become accustomed to first, and as it looks as though things are as under control as they are likely to be. I would like to gather my 'icky pet' and begin our long overdue vacation."

Tempest shrugged in slight embarrassment. "Sorry, Ballion. I keep forgetting we're not in Kansas any more."

Terena was intrigued. "Is that the name of your world? Kansas?"

"Apparently, there's a lot we'll be getting you guys accustomed to, also," Tempest smirked. "Hey, big guy. How about a glass of that juice?"

Taliquant ran to fulfill her request. He proudly handed her the glass, thrilled he had finally been able to comfort her.

Tempest took the glass. "Ya', ya'. This does not mean you can start pawing me again. Got it?"

"I've got it, Tempest." He lifted a big hand and studied it. Perhaps they called them paws on 'Kansas'.

Cripes, he looks like a big lap dog. Tempest began to feel a little guilty about the way she was treating the big guy. It was obvious, for whatever reason, the guy adored her. "Hey, Tali, can you take me outside for some fresh air? It's getting kinda' crowded in here."

Taliquant looked at his mother. "She is your mate, son. The guards are out there to watch over you if you get... distracted."

Taliquant was so confused. Never had a joining been described to him this way. To leave the chambers before it was completed was never done before. Then, he remembered hearing her speak his name for the first time. He walked over and nervously took her arm, and Tempest rolled her eyes, resigned. He was not going to stop touching her. Taliquant proudly announced, as if everyone in the room had not already heard it, "My mate wishes for me to escort her outside. I shall describe the Shalliton Mountains, the soft grass, the..."

Tempest interrupted. "You will be describing the damn sunrise if we don't get on with it."

Everyone burst out laughing, and Terena whispered to her husband, "She is a wild one. I think she will be good for him. I cannot wait to tell you of her special gifts and knowledge."

"Miranda, would you like to go outside, as well?" Zulien asked.

"If you don't mind, I think I would like to talk with your mother again. I'm still a little rattled."

"Perhaps we should go back to our own joining room. I would not want to interfere with Taliquant and Tempest when they return from their walk," he said.

Miranda looked around. She had not really noticed she was not in the same room she woke up in before. "Yes, of course. Zalana, would you mind coming with us?"

Zalana was relieved she had not disgraced herself with the Ancient. "I would be pleased to come with you and answer any questions that you may have."

The remaining group wandered back to Ethram's quarters. Terena looked out into the clearing and saw Taliquant pointing at the mountains with Tempest by his side, her wild hair outlined by the light of the second moon.

CHAPTER VII

Miranda sat facing Zalana with her back to Zulien on the chaise in the other building. Once in a while, she would feel the light brush of his fingers trailing through her hair, and she realized it calmed her.

"Please explain why you think I am this Celestial?" Miranda asked.

"Oh, you most definitely are, Miranda. Even without the physical Atlantian attributes, there is no mistaking an Ancient gene." She took Miranda's hands. "You have no idea how long we have waited for someone like you. The believers have never given up hope that the gods would send us a messenger, someone to remind us of all we have lost." Zalana could tell the Celestial was uncomfortable and still did not believe she was the one.

"The best guess we have been able to come up with is that a few Atlantians must have escaped during the Battles of Chaos." Zalana saw the confusion on Miranda's face. "The Battles of Chaos were many, many centuries ago. There is not anyone alive who actually fought in them. Zulien's father was a boy when his grandfather was a warrior.

"It was a war between the political hierarchy and the Temples of Knowledge. The Atlantians were the primary race for the temples. They kept the scrolls, and from what we have in our data, people in our worlds traveled to their planet for learning. All the inner worlds were based on the Old Religion. The politicians, on the other hand, had been strategizing and building war ships for a generation to overthrow them. The temples never really had a chance." Zalana looked down and shook her head in sadness.

"Shallistar was caught in the middle. Our warriors, and those of a few other planets willing to fight against the hierarchy, sided with the temples. The politicians were smart enough to promise those that stood with them power and riches. They destroyed Atlantia first, knowing it would undermine the Ancients' support, and the destruction of the temples drained the Celestials' powers," she said sadly.

"Ethram said his grandfather had come across a ship on the edge of the inner worlds, with one Ancient barely alive. He had spoken of placing his gene on an outer world planet, but Ethram's discovery of you was almost an accident. Thank the stars he took the chance to travel there. People of our inner world have a mating link with only one other person. My son would have never found you."

Miranda shifted, still uncomfortable with that bit of news. "So, you think I am a descendant of the temple people?"

"As I said, you are. There is no doubt about that."

"But I don't know anything. No one ever taught me any great secrets of knowledge. I don't have any secret scrolls, or anything. Even if I am related to these people, it seems I don't have anything useful to show for it." Miranda shrugged, but she thought of her obvious differences, the abilities that had made her always feel like an outcast.

"We think it is locked away inside you, and we are hoping, with the little I know of the Old Religion and help from others, we can prompt you to re-discover some of the forgotten knowledge."

"Wouldn't that just start another war?"

"We are better prepared this time. We have

strong allies that reach deep into the hierarchy, and the politicians' abuse of power has lost them most of their support."

Miranda paled, panicking again. She could not bear to be the reason for a war, and did not understand why her beliefs could be so important.

"Let us not talk about wars and battles right now." Zalana had already upset the Ancient once, and decided to change the subject. "I would like to know more about you. I confess, I am curious. A woman does not find out she is to have a daughter who is a Celestial Ancient and from the outer worlds, everyday."

"I guess you've had to make a few adjustments lately, too." Without realizing it, Miranda settled back against Zulien's chest. He smiled at his mother and slowly wrapped his arms around her as she began to speak. "I was born in upstate New York."

"Is that a province of 'Kansas'?" Zulien asked.

Miranda smiled. "No, I will explain that one to you later. My world was called 'Earth'. I moved to West Virginia, that is a state like New York, and grew up there. My grandmother had my gifts also, but she went away when I was a little girl so I never got to ask her about them. They say they skipped a generation for as long as we could trace back."

Zalana thought of Ethram's magic. She would mention this to him later.

"I can sometimes forecast when something bad is going to happen." Miranda thought about that for a moment. She seemed to only forecast tragedy, and she had had no warning about her 'procurement'. It must not be a 'bad' thing. "You already know I have visions. Some come on unexpectedly, like the one I had about Zulien.

Others are brought on when I meditate, or when I am in a trance. I honor the goddess on full moons and observe the sabbat rituals... mostly everyone thought Tempest and I were weird and avoided us.

"We've been on our own for quite a few years. We tried to find a group to join who we thought believed like we did, and it was a disaster. The woman in charge thought I was trying to steal her followers and asked us not to return. Tempest and I just made our own way."

"Does Tempest have powers, too?" Zalana knew Terena wanted to know what her daughter-in-law's gifts were.

"Tempest has... something. We've never been able to figure it out. I sense some kind of power within her, not as strong as yours, though."

Zalana's mouth dropped open. "You sense power within me?"

"Besides what I can feel in Tempest, you and Terena are the only people I've ever had this sense about. Yours is stronger than Terena's, and hers is stronger than Tempest's." Miranda frowned. "Tempest's feels different, though. I'm sorry, I guess I'm not explaining it very well."

"Maybe we will discover more about this." Zalana was bursting with pride. It must be why she had the power of visions.

"As far as leaving our planet, I guess it worked out pretty well, under the circumstances. Both our parents are gone, so we're not really leaving anyone behind to miss."

Zalana was relieved. "I was concerned about that. Being uprooted into this unusual situation is difficult enough."

Zalana was also relieved to see Miranda had placed her pale hand over her son's as it rested in her lap. She was so proud of his restraint. For his part, Zulien hoped his mate did not notice the stiff erection resting along her spine.

Miranda surprised herself with a yawn.

"Mother, perhaps we should continue this discussion tomorrow." Zulien stroked his thumb over her hand.

"I'm sorry," Miranda said. "I don't know why I should be so tired. Apparently I've been sleeping for days."

"It is not a true sleep," Zalana explained. "At least, not a regenerating one, from what I understand. Ethram's magic puts you in a kind of holding pattern. From what I can remember, it is a time of dreams, waiting to wake in your mate's arms." Her voice was wistful. "We do not know who our genes were matched with. He could be a tradesman, royalty or a great warrior." She smiled at her son. "When we were finally procured, we only knew we would wake to a life with our mate and protector."

Zalana cleared her head. "When you are released from deep sleep, it is like you had never closed your eyes."

Miranda's brow creased in thought. "I think he took me from my cabin after I had gone to bed. I guess that would explain it."

Zalana stood up. "You get some rest, Miranda. We can talk more in the morning if you would like." She leaned down and kissed her on the cheek. "Zulien, take care of our little Ancient."

As Zalana reached the door, Tempest began yelling. "Miranda, where are you? I am telling you, Tali, if you guys have taken off with her again, you're going to wish you had left me on that primitive planet."

"We did not take her away the first time, Tempest. The Procurer secured her." Tali were still trying to figure out how to deal with his unpredictable mate.

Miranda sighed. "I had better let her know I'm all right before she rips this place apart." Zulien followed her to the door. "Tempest, we're over here."

"Humph." She strode quickly over to her friend with Tali following close behind. "Have you seen the grass? It's blue," she said with astonishment.

"I saw it this afternoon. It's beautiful in the sunlight; sapphire and turquoise." Miranda looked around and she moved towards the remains of the stone alter in the middle of the clearing. "Tempest, this looks like a miniature Stonehenge, like the one we made near the orchard."

Tempest frowned. "Some of the pillars are a little out of place, but I bet they could be put back."

Miranda studied the sky. "Zulien, do you think you and Taliquant could help us fix it tomorrow? It looks like there will be a full moon, and I could really use a cleansing ritual."

Zalana almost fell over. "You know the placement of the altar stones?"

"I think so. We had a place with pillars like these, only much bigger. No one knew who put them there, but there wasn't any rock with the same composition anywhere near them. We used to wonder if they were placed there as an altar. Tempest, you remember, don't you?"

"Heck ya'. You had me clearing the rocks out of the edge of the clearing for a week, and then chiseling them so they would fit together. I will never forget that project." Tempest automatically reached to her back, remembering how much it ached after the first day.

"Tali and I would be honored to help you re-build the altar." Zulien looked over at Taliquant. His friend actually looked a little disappointed. He was planning on having his joining well underway by then.

"This is going to be so cool, Miranda. What do you think will happen with three moons in the ritual?" Tempest was giddy with excitement.

"I don't know. The one in the middle will be full, and the two on either side will be crescents. It's going to be interesting, for sure." She turned to Zalana, "Would you like to join us?"

Zalana actually did slide towards a rock this time. "By the stars, I would be honored."

"Terena too, of course." Miranda laughed nervously. "With all these moons I may need the extra bodies for grounding. It is quite a liberating experience."

Tempest nodded. "I can't wait."

Zalana had to tell Terena. Their value in the community would go up exponentially. "What should we wear? Should we bring anything? Do you need a robe?"

"This shift I have on is lovely, and no, you don't need anything special. Heck, I've done the blessing in jeans before. The goddesses look inside, and I don't think they care about the wrapper."

Zalana planned on wearing what she considered her ceremonial robe, just in case. By the stars, how would she ever be able to sleep tonight?

"If you have some bread and a little wine, that would be nice. Juice will work if not. I like to leave an offering." Miranda ran her hand over one of the standing pillars. "This is so strange."

"Ethram said his people knew of several ruins of the old temples. We thought they were all destroyed and were amazed when he brought us to you here. He could not have picked a better place for the joining," Zalana smiled.

"Okay, but what the heck is a joining?" Tempest glared up at Taliquant, feet spread and hands on her hips in challenge. "It better not be what I think it is, big guy."

Taliquant was once again distressed. He wanted to do the joining, not talk about it. Zulien was standing behind Miranda and put his hands on her shoulders. Again, the calm feeling spread through her. "Tempest, this has been a most unusual mating. Sometime, Tali will tell you what was involved to bring you here safely. There was quite literally a battle, with three battleships destroyed and an almost a treasonable audition with the Magistrates over your procurement. Look around the edge of the glade."

Tempest squinted and saw there were guards spaced at the foot of the hills.

Zulien continued, "Those are the Magistrate of Battle's personal warriors. He has left them to guard us so the joining could proceed uninterrupted. There is still a lot of danger for you both. By now, the royals will know you are on Shallistar, and by morning they will be searching for you. If you are not joined, we have no claim to you, even if we are your mates. Because you are from the outer worlds, I am sure the Magistrates are hastily drawing up some new edict declaring you belong to all citizens of the inner worlds. They will demand your return to Latisqua, and most probably arrange your assassinations so you cannot spread teachings of the Old Religion."

Tempest let it sink in. He was saying they must have sex to be protected from the politicians. Cripes! She glanced at Tali. He was a foot and a half taller than her. Someone's math was seriously off. "Are you sure that's not a load of bullshit to get me in the sack, big guy?"

Taliquant tried to work his way through his mate's question. "It is no kind of excrement, and I will not put you in a sack... unless that is what you desire, my mate." He was quite pleased with his response.

Miranda burst out laughing and Taliquant was exasperated, thinking he had further disgraced himself. "Tempest, I think you've met your match," Miranda smiled. "Taliquant, it might be safer to bag her anyway."

"Very funny, Miranda. In case you're not following their little story, we have to have sex with these guys or risk being killed by a bunch of paranoid aliens, so excuse me for wanting to see if it was a bunch of crap," Tempest scowled.

"Three Debayluth battleships sent by the hierarchy to intercept you, were destroyed. We had to pretend your decay in front of royalty, and one of my finest warriors has been completely disgraced. This is not 'crap', Tempest. They are after the Ancient, and they will use you to get to her, if they can. I do not even trust my mother is safe until the joining and ceremonies are completed. The hierarchy cannot interfere with bonded mates, though they may still attempt an assassination." Zulien felt Miranda begin to quiver, and pulled her close. "Taliquant and I have been warriors for many centuries, Miranda. Along with the guards, we will keep you protected. The Magistrate is reassigning my ship, the Quillant, and permanently grounding the two of us."

Miranda gasped. "I am so sorry, Zule. Please don't let him do that to you. I'm sure there must be some other way to keep us safe."

Taliquant grinned down at Tempest. "They gave us a planet."

She looked up at him. "What?"

"The Magistrate of Battle has promoted Zule and me, and he is giving us our own planet. We are going to coordinate the security, but he wants Miranda to be safe enough to re-build the Temples of Knowledge. You have to admit, my mate, having your own planet is going to be pretty cool." Taliquant was quite proud of himself.

"This story gets weirder by the minute. I am about to go searching for a rabbit hole." Tempest could see the question in Taliquant's face. "Don't ask."

Miranda turned to Zulien. "They're giving us a planet?"

Zulien leaned down so Tempest could not hear, and whispered, "The Magistrate did say it would be a lesser one."

Zalana had drifted towards Ethram's quarters. This would be in her son's hands now, and she also could not wait to talk with Terena.

"It is difficult for Tali and me to understand your reluctance to the joining." Zulien glanced at Taliquant, who gave him a nod. He had certainly had no luck trying to explain things to Tempest.

"We know you feel the mating gene, because even in your sleep you move towards our protection. In the inner worlds, as mother explained, it is the time young women dream of. They wait for the day the Procurer comes for them, delivering them to the arms of their mate. We want to be sensitive to your ways, but our own ways make it impossible to do anything but protect you. It must be done."

Miranda looked at her feet. "So, if we agree to this joining, what happens next?"

"The hierarchy will have to back off on their

insistence to acquire you. They may try to insist we move to Latisqua, but I think the Magistrate of Battle is dealing with that. Our mothers are preparing the mating ceremonies. They will be held together and quickly after the joining. After that, no one can tell you what to do, other than your mate," Zulien explained.

Tempest thumped Taliquant on the chest. "I knew there was more to this. If you think you're going to start ordering me around, you've got another thing coming."

"I will only offer advice to keep you safe, my mate," Tali assured her. "It would be nice to keep you of even temper," he added.

The Major of the guards came running up to Zulien. "I apologize for interrupting your joining, Commander," the nervous man looked at the group. They should have been locked in their quarters instead of roaming around the grounds.

"Yes, Major, what is it?" Zulien asked.

"The Magistrate of Battle has informed us that the Magistrates of the Old Ways and Commerce have called an emergency commission of the royals. They have stated that they were responsible for locating and procuring the Ancient, and due to her heritage they are demanding she be returned to Latisqua for her safety."

"Has the edict been drawn?" Taliquant asked.

"Not yet, sir. The Magistrate of Battle is arguing that you have proven your capability to protect them, and he is using the Debayluth attack as proof. He does not want to expose his allies. He is trying to find Ethram and Ballion. He wants a transmission of the log proving they acted on your behalf to locate your mate. He also wants to warn them that the Magistrates may have sent the royal guard to find them to make sure this does not happen. Some of the Quistar's warriors are moving the procurement ship back off planet to throw them off."

"No one wants a war, yet. The Magistrate of Battle has cracked the hierarchy armor, questioning the illegal search of the Quillant, but even if the two Magistrates are asked to step down, the damage has been done. The hierarchy will still try to obtain her unless you have claim."

"Thank you, Major. Keep me posted." As the Major wandered back to his post, Zulien said to Taliquant, "I was hoping those two pompous fools would have followed their stolen treasures and been off planet in hiding by now."

"They're planning a war?" Miranda asked nervously. "Over me? Zulien, you have to stop them. This is insane. Maybe if I explain to them that I don't know any information that can hurt them, they'll leave us alone."

"Miranda, you have already told us you know how to rebuild the altars. You hold knowledge you are unaware of. Make no mistake: there will be war. We would just like to control the timing of it." Zulien stroked her shoulders, waving calmness into her.

She turned and looked up at him. "Zulien, I need to speak with Tempest alone for a few minutes." Miranda placed her hand on his muscled forearm. "Please. You can stand on the edge of the clearing watching us," she smiled. "I would like that."

He could drown in her smile. "Of course, Miranda. Tali, we need to give our mates a chance to talk." The warriors moved away.

"I wish they would say girlfriend or fiancé," Tempest griped. "I can only think of one thing when they keep calling us mates."

"That is what we are, Tempest. For so many

years I've asked the goddess to help me find a place and people who would welcome us. I think we never found it back home because it was not there. This is her answer."

Tempest stroked her sash and glanced for Tali. Confident he was close, she turned her attention back to Miranda. "You feel it too, Tempest. I don't care how upset you act, I know you do. You can't stop searching for him, and I feel the same way about Zulien. All he has to do is be near me, and I feel safe. And, why aren't we scared? We've been abducted by aliens, for goddess' sake?"

Tempest began to really think about what Miranda was saying. "It's because we belong here. It feels right, somehow. Even that talking lizard guy didn't freak me out for long."

Miranda laughed. "I fainted the first time he spoke to me," she confided.

"So, you think we should go along with this joining stuff?" Tempest asked.

"Ask yourself this: would you rather be sleeping alone tonight, or safe beside him?"

Tempest visibly trembled and searched for Taliquant again.

Miranda touched her arm to get her attention. "I think that is your answer. To be truthful, the thought of being with Zulien has not been far from my mind since I was in that sleep."

"I dreamt Tali was with me. At least, I thought it was a dream."

"No, they saw us for a short time when we were on Ethram's ship." Miranda held up her arm. "They gave us these scarves so we would remember they were thinking of us. I think it was really difficult for them to let us go, and they've made sacrifices to try to adjust to our ways. It is never going to happen. With these feelings we're having, even we can't do it our way."

Tempest kicked her foot in the grass. "To be honest, I've wanted to jump the big guy since I laid eyes on him."

"Then I think that is what you should do. He adores you, Tempest. If you could see how hard he is trying to please you. You're driving him nuts," Miranda laughed quietly.

"And it's going to stay that way. I don't like that Once we're joined, I have to take orders from him? Crap," Tempest muttered.

"No one thinks that will happen. You've made quite an impression. Let's just go back to our little suites and let what happens, happen. We can decide in the morning where to go from there," Miranda suggested.

"Well, I guess we can't spend all night out here and I'll just wake up with the big guy pawing me anyway," Tempest conceded.

Miranda walked over to Zulien. "I think I would like to lie down now." They walked arm in arm back to their building.

Tempest strode towards her chamber and looked over her shoulder. "You coming, big guy?" Tali ran to catch up with her.

Miranda walked over to the joining pallet and anxiously sat down. "Show me how the light thing works."

Zulien sat next to her. "Think about how you want the room to look, and push that energy towards them. Take my hand." Miranda did as he asked. "Now, think of the light dimming. Think of the shadows and look at the walls and the ceiling."

The light slowly dimmed to a faint lavender glow. "Dimmer?" he asked.

"Maybe a little bit," she replied nervously.

The lights dimmed further.

Zulien put his arm around her and she laid her head on his chest, relaxing until she heard Tempest screaming.

"Tali, it looks like the strobe lights of a disco in here. I want the damn walls off."

"But I want to look at you. Your eyes flash fire. Your skin is the color of the moon."

"And your butt is going to be kicked, if you don't shut them off. Now."

Miranda sighed, and Zulien kissed the top of her head and whispered, "I am glad you are mine. I do not like that you are afraid of me, Miranda. What can I do?" he whispered.

"It is all right, Zule. There have just been a lot of things to get used to. Where I come from, people get to know each other, and they do things together, before they... join. I'm just nervous, but I'll be fine."

Zulien tilted her chin and looked into the liquid pools of her blue eyes, lit by the moon. His mouth came down on hers and the Atlantian ancestry she tried to deny took over. The sensation of his tongue sliding into her mouth caused instant desire to flood from her.

Zulien smelled her arousal and groaned into her mouth as her arms tried to circle his broad back and pull him closer. His hands were buried in her long, wavy tresses.

He pulled back and looked at her. Her eyes were filled with anticipation and her bottom lip trembled. She stood and lifted the caftan over her head. Zulien quickly removed his clothes and pulled her on top of him, thrusting his tongue back into the warmth of her mouth.

The sparse curls on his chest tickled her nipples and sent more throbbing heat through her, causing violent, tight contractions at the emptiness. Miranda felt as though she was going to explode and thought, *Cripes! All he's done is kiss me.* His tongue skated across her teeth and left her mouth.

He laid her back on the pallet and leaned over her, his dark mane forming a curtain around his face as his mouth lowered to her breast. She balled her fists in his hair as his teeth nipped and proceded to suckle and tickle her nipple with his tongue.

She gritted her teeth, sucking gulps of air in a light hiss. His hand traveled down her stomach to the soft, damp curls of her sex. A finger slipped along her warmth and wetness, and she reached blindly to stop the agony.

"I can't. Zulien, please, I can't."

It was far too late for that. The denial and sacrifice that had been building for days erupted in him, and he took the small wrist with the scarf and raised it over her head. After circling the bedpost with the sash, he grabbed her other wrist and secured it to the other end.

Miranda began crying. "Please, Zulien, I can't do this. I thought I could, but I can't."

He whispered in her ear, "Shh, my mate. You are safe."

She whimpered as his kisses trailed down her body. On the first stroke of his tongue, her hips rose off the bed and she gasped. He wrapped his strong arms under her thighs, while she continued to shudder and cry softly as his tongue lapped her warmth.

Instinctively, he knew she was all right. The passion boiling to the surface of his little mate frightened her, but she was all right. Zulien was ecstatic. At first, he was nervous at the thought of pleasing the Celestial, but their mating gene was strong, and the room was permeated with their musk.

Miranda twisted her useless arms and turned her head into the pillow. His tongue found her centers of pleasure and she gasped as her muscles tightened with need. She had not wanted to do this, but how badly she needed it now. She felt herself strain at the emptiness and her mind exploded.

A vision of her standing in front of a great glass pyramid with her warrior at her side threw her into a trance. She was wearing a sapphire robe, and their hair was moving with the wind. There was a crescent and a full moon lighting the darkness.

She felt him enter her with a lunging thrust and she wrapped her legs around him. He was her warrior, her protector, her mate, and her mind cleared enough for her to feel him inside her, his long length filling her.

Her muscles grabbed tightly at him, but his strength was great enough that he could pull and plunge, satisfying his claim on her. He held her hips and thrust deep, swearing oaths as she gripped him. Never was there a woman such as this, and he knew his climax was near and unstoppable. As it hit him and the heat of it spilled into her, he yelled his triumph.

Miranda screamed at the same moment, and then his bucking hips caused her to climax again. The vision this time was of an infant lying in a cradle with the phases of the moon, suns and stars carved into it. Whether it was a boy child or a girl she did not know, but when she came out of the trance Miranda knew she was pregnant.

Zulien collapsed to the side of her. He stopped shuddering as she came out of her trance, and after quickly untying her wrists he pulled her up to him and rested her head on his slick, bronze chest. He stroked her side until she calmed.

He finally whispered, "You are all right?"

She turned her head and kissed the sweat on his chest. "I am all right, my mate."

CHAPTER VIII

There were smiles and celebratory toasts in Ethram's quarters. The warriors' triumphant yells left no doubt the joining was completed, and the Major and guards in the field glanced at each other, grinning. Their worlds would be saved.

The weary parents made their way back to the shuttle. Zibula asked the Major to contact him when the mates left their joining chambers, and he wrapped his arm around Zalana. "This is a happy occasion, my mate. I am so proud of our son."

Miranda woke to sunlight, curled into Zulien's side with his strong arm holding her close. She felt at peace, and her small hand worked its way between them and rested over her womb.

Zulien shifted awake with her movement. "Are you okay, Miranda?"

"I am fine, Zule." She looked up at his handsome face. "We will be fine. I know I belong here, and I understand some of what I am supposed to do."

"You had a vision?" he asked in awe.

"Yes, and you were standing beside me. It is all right, now. You are where I am supposed to be."

Zulien blinked rapidly. It would not do for his mate to see her protector weep with joy. She snuggled into him, running her fingers over his chest. They lay in silence for a long time, until Tempest's predictable shriek pierced the dawn.

"I don't care, big guy. I'm hungry. Maybe on your world you don't eat, but this girl wants food. Now."

"Please do not rise," Tali begged. "We are warriors, and the joining can last for days if we want."

"Then you will be joining with a decayed corpse. I'm starving."

Zulien bounded off the pallet. "Miranda, this is true? You will decay if you do not feast now?"

Miranda shook her head. "I suspect no faster than you would, Zule. Tempest is ruled by her stomach."

Zulien was unconvinced and would not take the chance. He picked up her caftan, pulled her to her feet and dressed her. "We will feast now."

"Well, I guess I would like some more juice." She took his hand and they wandered over to Tempest's chamber. "Tempest, Zule and I are going to the other building to get some breakfast. We'll see you there."

"At least someone knows how to treat their mate," Tempest huffed.

Tali quickly dressed and pulled her in the direction of Ethram's quarters.

The Major saw the couples as they walked across the yard. *What the dremont are they leaving the joining chambers so soon for?* He placed the promised call to Zibula.

"Did you see all of them?" Zibula shook Zalana awake as he hastily got dressed. "No one looked ill? We are on our way."

Zalana rose and yawned. "What is wrong?"

"They have left the joining chambers." Zibula knocked on the guest room door. "We need to get back."

As the shuttle sped towards the temple, Zibula assured them the mates were all right. "The Major has no idea what happened. He said Zule and Miranda were holding hands and

Tempest was not shrieking at Tali. They just left the chambers and wandered over to the procurer's quarters."

On approaching Ethram's quarters and as Zibula prepared to knock, they heard Tempest. "Tali, sit still. You look like a stray dog. Yes, I know, my eyes flash with fire. My fist will flash with thunder if you do not sit still."

Zibula looked at Terena, then knocked, and Zulien opened the door. "Good morning, father, mother."

Miranda peaked under his arm. "Good morning. I was just making breakfast. Come on in. Have you eaten yet?"

Whatever the anxious parents expected to see, it was not Tempest trying to comb the knots out of Taliquant's thick curls while the Celestial prepared a feast on the morning of her joining.

At first, the mothers were too shocked to move. Zalana finally sprung into action. "Miranda, please sit. Terena and I will prepare the feast." Maybe a feast on joining morning was a ritual that had been forgotten. Maybe it was a feast prepared by the mate in honor of their joining. Zalana did not know what to do.

"It's cool. I am just making pancakes. I found some sweet, sticky stuff that makes good syrup."

Zulien looked up from a stack of flat bread covered in pillachi juice and shrugged. "It is delicious. I wonder why we never thought of it."

Taliquant held up a dripping forkful and Tempest leaned over, devouring it. "I can't imagine drinking this syrup like juice, can you, Miranda?" She smacked Tali on the head when he tried to follow her sweet voice. "Sit still."

"No, I like the nintine juice much better. It makes good pancake syrup, though." Miranda had braided her hair in a rope and tied it with the offering sash.

She placed a plate of the feast in front of Zibula. "Don't forget the syrup." She flipped another pancake.

Zalana was mystified. Now, the Celestial offered her mate's father the feast. She finally had to ask. "Miranda, if I am not following protocol, I apologize. This has been forgotten."

Miranda spun around. "What are you talking about, Zalana?"

"Were we supposed to prepare a ritual feast on your joining morning?" Zalana looked down at her lap, completely embarrassed.

"Ritual feast? Oh, for goddess sake. It's just breakfast, Zalana. Tempest and I were hungry. We've only had a little nintine juice since our procurement."

"Then you will be going back to the joining chambers?" she asked.

Tempest laughed. "I am sure we'll be going back to the joining chambers." Tali beamed. "But not until after we get that altar set up. I want to make sure it's ready for tonight's ritual." Tali's face fell again.

"I can't wait. If ever there was a time to bless the goddess, it would be now," Miranda agreed.

Miranda placed a stack of pancakes in the center of the table, and place settings in front of Taliquant's parents, Zalana and herself. "Dig in, guys," Miranda said as she plopped onto Zulien's lap. They each took a flat bread, and Terena gulped as she poured a small amount of pillachi juice on it. After one bite, she reached for more juice and another flat bread.

Miranda sat comfortably on Zulien's lap while she ate. She was sipping some of the unusual juice while the group talked and got to know each other.

Zulien nuzzled his mate's neck. "Miranda had visions at our joining pinnacle," he announced proudly.

Miranda coughed up her nintine juice and blushed furiously.

"More info than we needed there, Zule," Tempest laughed.

Zalana and Terena bowed their heads. Zalana whispered, "Is it a vision you will share?"

Miranda finally managed to compose herself enough to relay the vision of her and Zulien. They all agreed what she told them was a positive sign. For some reason, she felt it was important to keep the vision of her pregnancy a secret.

Zalana said, "Miranda, and Tempest this concerns you too, we have arranged your ceremony for tomorrow. Usually, we have more time to prepare, but the Magistrate of Battle said it was important to have these completed quickly. Is there anything special you would like us to add?"

"I never really thought about my wedding before," Tempest mused.

"Well, I certainly never thought about one," Miranda said. "I think I would like to carry a bouquet. I'm sure you don't throw them here, but I could keep them to remember the ceremony."

"Who do you throw them at?" Zulien envisioned a bunch of fesinia flowers aimed at his head.

"The bride tosses the bouquet into a group of single... unmated, women. Whoever catches it is supposed to be the next one married," Miranda explained. "I would like to keep mine. When they dry, we can hang them over our bed for good luck."

Tempest agreed. "That sounds good."

The young women did not ask for anything else. The mothers were beginning to look exhausted from everything that happened, and Miranda reached over for Zalana's hand. "We appreciate all that you and Terena have done to welcome us and make the ceremony a special day. Why don't you rest for a while in one of the chambers?"

Zalana gasped. "I cannot lie down in your chamber. Suppose you wish to return?"

"Nonsense. We will be busy with the altar for quite a while. You should feel more refreshed after the ritual tonight."

Tempest added, "Mom, you really need to lie down. I can see how tired you are. Go on. I'll wake you up if the big guy gets cranky." Tempest was finally satisfied with Taliquant's hair, and she moved his arm to sit in his lap.

Terena was confused and not sure if she had been insulted. Miranda caught her blank stare. "Mom is short for mother where we're from."

"You called me mother?" Terena was shocked.

"It's not official until tomorrow, I guess. My own mom never really wanted the role. You wouldn't mind filling in for me, would you?"

"My heart has yearned to have a daughter. It sings with joy. Never has its heavy weight been lightened so."

Tempest laughed and looked up at Taliquant. "Well, big guy. I guess I know where you get it."

Taliquant and Terena looked at each other in bewilderment. *Get what?*

They finally convinced the mothers to try to rest. Miranda sat on the edge of the clearing, watching Tempest order the warriors around.

The fathers pitched in and the altar was beginning to take shape.

The Major came up and announced the guard was changing. He took off in the shuttle that brought the replacements, and the new guard took their positions by the hills. Miranda became bored and began walking barefoot through the soft blue grass. Wild flowers in bright hues sprouted in haphazard pockets and she began gathering some, thinking she could ease the extra burden on the mothers if she made the bouquets for her and Tempest.

She had not noticed how far she had wandered, and when she looked up she saw she was close to one of the perimeter guards. "Thank you for guarding us," she said, as she stooped to pick a pretty red flower with yellow and green spots.

"It has been a pleasure, Ancient."

As he spoke, Miranda backed away from him, a really bad feeling starting in her stomach. The guard reached for her, grabbing her braid as she turned to run. "Zule," she screamed. The guard to his right ran towards a tree.

Miranda was kicking and screaming as the man returned with a small shuttle, and she dug her little feet in the grass and tried to claw the big warrior. "Perhaps I have misjudged, and you are the primitive," he laughed.

Miranda drew a swatch of blood down his cheek, and he placed a beefy hand around her throat and lifted her. She kicked frantically at him as his grip closed her windpipe, and then she went limp. The guard dropped her to turn and open the shuttle door, and immediately she was on her feet and running as fast as she could.

Zulien and Taliquant passed her with looks of outrage on their faces that froze her blood. She stopped and turned around as Tempest caught up to her, gasping for breath. Zibula whizzed by in the shuttle and blocked the smaller craft's escape.

The other guards had joined the foray and were trying to pull the mates off the imposters before they killed them. By the time Miranda and Tempest walked back, two guard warriors held each of the men. "Miranda!" Zulien ripped free from the guards that were restraining him. He ran to her and clutched her to his chest.

The guards whispered something to Taliquant. He nodded, and they let him go to Tempest. The guards who had been holding the warriors made a quick scan of the trees. They came back a few minutes later and the Major walked up to Zulien. He looked sick at his failure.

"The guards... the real guards... have been drugged. They have been pulled beyond the tree line. They must have been lured there." He would lose his commission over this. "Ancient, I hope you have not been injured. Commander, I will of course sign any document you wish to log and have it delivered to the Magistrate."

"Do you recognize the imposters, Major?" Even with his mate's foiled kidnapping, Zulien was patient and fair. He continued to hold her close, stroking his comfort into her.

"It was my fault, Zule," she was still hitching frightened sobs. "I should not have wandered so far away."

"Shh, Miranda. It is all right now," he said calmly. "Major?"

The Major walked over to get a better look at the beaten men. Zulien and Taliquant had torn them up pretty badly before the guards could pull them off. "Yes, Commander. They are from the royal guard."

"Bring them to the quarters, Major. Perhaps the cowards have information to trade for their lives."

Miranda's tear filled eyes looked up at him. "You would not really kill them, Zule?"

"I would if they had hurt you."

Miranda managed to discreetly untie the sash from her hair and place it around her neck, hiding the bruising before it began to show too much. She took Zulien's hand as the group headed back to the buildings. "What is going to happen to them?"

"After we question them, they will be quartered on a battleship and shuttled to Latisqua to stand charges," Zulien said without emotion. He could not lie to her, and that is what was supposed to happen. He knew the traitors would be released in space without the benefit of shariver suit before they left the quadrant. Unofficially, the war had begun.

It did not take long for the beaten men to confess their plan. The royal guard was the weakest of warriors. They were men not suited for the battleships, demoted or with no future. Two more Magistrates had joined with the Old Ways and Commerce to secure the Ancient. Zulien was somewhat relieved to learn they wanted her alive.

The information was communicated to the Magistrate of Battle. "Have the Major and another guard bring them in."

"Magistrate," Zulien said. "I would like the Major to remain on guard. It was his perception that led us to find the guards in the trees. If it were not for him, we would be left with the understanding the security in charge of the guard rotation itself had been compromised. At least we know the correct warriors are arriving. The Major and I have discussed it, and he feels, and I agree, it would be wiser to pull the guard closer to the temple away from the tree line."

The Major looked at Zulien with disbelief. He had never heard the plan, much less designed it. The Magistrate recognized one of Zulien's strategies. For whatever reason, he did not want the Major to suffer consequences for the situation. "Very well. Have the Major send two other warriors with the prisoners. We need to move you. The valley has been compromised."

Miranda overheard the transmission. "Absolutely not. We're not going anywhere until after my ritual. Zulien if we start running now, it is never going to stop. I will not spend the rest of my life in hiding. I agree, for the safety of our families, to move after the ritual."

The Magistrate's voice came over the line. "Zulien, the Celestial is to perform a ritual?"

"We have been reconstructing the altar. Miranda and Tempest remembered the design from their world, and they were planning to hold the ritual tonight."

"By the stars, Zulien. I will send two more regiments to guard the valley. We need the Ancient's rituals to strengthen us again."

Miranda whispered to Tempest, "Cripes, it's only a cleansing ritual."

"The joining has occurred?" the Magistrate asked.

"Yes, Magistrate. We have had our joining," Zulien smiled.

Now, it was Tempest's turn. "Does everyone in the galaxy have to know we did the deed?"

Miranda whispered to Zulien, "If you tell him I have visions when I... you know, you will not have another joining for a long time."

"Miranda, I am proud to bring you visions. Why do you not want others to celebrate?" Zulien decided he would never learn her ways.

The Magistrate's voice boomed, "The Ancient had a vision? I need to be advised. Her visions are of great importance."

Tempest laughed quietly and whispered, "Next, he will be ordering you to bed until you predict the outcome of the damn war."

"This is not funny, Tempest. In case you haven't noticed, they have some pretty strange ideas about me."

Zulien relayed the vision and the Magistrate smiled. Zulien asked, "Do you know what the vision means?"

"Not all of it, but she has predicted her planet."

Zulien, Taliquant and Tempest stared at her. "Don't ask me. I have no idea what he is talking about."

When the communication signed off, the Major approached Zulien. "Commander?" The man was flustered. "Why?"

"Major, four Magistrates planned against us. You stood your ground and accepted responsibility for your men and the failure of the regiment. In my eyes, you are a man of honor and the kind of warrior I want on our side." Zulien shook the man's hand.

"Thank you, Commander. You and your mate have my complete support. My life is yours."

The other two regiments arrived by late afternoon, along with replacements for the original missing guard warriors. Twenty-seven large warriors stood nine feet apart around the clearing and the altar. By dusk, everyone from the Quillant and their mates was there. They had heard about the ritual.

Zulien began getting nervous while Miranda, Tempest, Zalana and Terena were in their joining chamber getting ready. Vasilla and Ebonisha slipped by the guard at the door and, after introductions, Miranda invited them to join the ritual as well. Ebonisha could not keep the secret, and soon all six mates from the Quillant were busy fixing hair and smoothing shifts.

Miranda and Tempest were getting more excited as their group grew. Zulien was watching lights from shuttles begin to shine through the trees. Soon, mothers of the warriors' mates arrived, husbands in tow, to proudly watch their daughters in the first moon ritual performed by a Celestial Ancient of the Old Religion since the Battles of Chaos.

The Major walked up to Zulien. "Any suggestions, Commander?"

"We should have built bleachers." Zulien put his head in his hands. At least he had his crew from the Quillant if there were problems.

Zalana came up to him. "Miranda would like you to light the fire now. Are you all right, Zulien?"

"I never expected all this. I always thought my mate and I would be living on the Quillant."

"Are you disappointed?"

"By the stars, no. I would not trade one minute of this circus for a life without her. It is just... an adjustment."

"The ceremony will be over tomorrow and we will have our own private place in the worlds soon, Zule."

"I know, mother. She belongs to all the inner worlds. It does not mean I can not wish her for myself."

"You have the part of her that no one else can hold, Zule. It shines in her eyes when she looks at you."

Zulien smiled and stretched. He leaned down to kiss his mother on the cheek. "Thank you, mother. You always know what to say." He left to find Tali and light the bonfire.

The guards and visitors formed a circle around the altar. As Miranda left the chamber, she looked at the crowd and whispered again to Tempest, "Cripes, it's just a cleansing ritual."

Tempest looked up at the three moons. "So, let's hit a triple tonight."

The crowd parted to let the women pass. Miranda approached the altar, the fire mirroring off her golden hair. Everyone was silent. Miranda had a touch of stage fright until Tempest whispered, "Hey, girl. Just do it the way we do back home."

Miranda remembered the time in the glade and calmed down. She held out her hands, closed her eyes and breathed deeply until she felt herself in balance. In a few moments, she opened her eyes and took Tempest's hand. "Everyone take the hand of the woman standing next you. Tempest reached out for Zalana who reached out for Terena and so on, around the circle. Vasilla was on the end with no one to hold her other hand. "Vasilla, if you feel disoriented or ungrounded, I will come to you at the end of the ritual. Nothing is going to harm you." Vasilla nodded, nervously.

Miranda raised her hand to the full moon. "Blessings, goddess. I am happy to be joined by believers who have yearned for your cleansing light. Thank you for bringing Tempest and me to this place of love and acceptance. Our hearts are filled with gratitude that you showed us the way to our new families and friends, and our mates. We are confident with the protection and comfort they offer. Your wisdom shines around and through us."

There were quiet gasps as the beam from the center full moon narrowed to her small hand. "May the crone and maiden share our joy and our gratitude." The crescents' beams joined the other.

It reminded Taliquant of the lasers on the battle crafts focusing on the view port of the Debayluth vessel, and he stared, as they all did, mesmerized.

"I seek, with thanks, only the blessings of your wisdom." Miranda closed her eyes. The beams strengthened, and her pale skin took on a glow that passed to Tempest. All the women in the circle closed their eyes as the light passed through their hands, and they felt a euphoric lightening of their spirit and a calming, renewing energy.

They remained that way for several minutes, until Miranda opened her eyes again. "Thank you, goddesses, mother, maiden and crone. May your light continue to shine upon your children." Miranda slowly lowered her arm and the moonbeams broadened to their natural aspects. "Tempest, are you all right?"

"I'm fine, Miranda. I just need to stand here for a moment."

"I need to let go of you and check Vasilla."

"I'll be all right. Zalana's pretty good at grounding me."

"I sensed she had power. I'll be back in a minute."

Miranda walked over to Vasilla. She still had her eyes closed, and Miranda could see tears leaking out the corners of the tall woman's cheeks. She took her free hand in both of hers. "Valsilla, honey, are you all right?"

Vasilla opened her liquid brown eyes. "It is beautiful, Celestial. I never knew it would be like that."

"It's that way for me, too. I love the esbat rituals. You're welcome to join me for them until you learn to do it yourself."

"Do you think I can?"

"It might not be as intense at first, but, yes, you can do this. It's natural, and the more you believe, the more intense it becomes. Letang, I think your mate could use your strong arms to hold her for a while."

Letang rushed to his mate, and the other warriors took it as a sign and went to theirs.

Miranda walked back to the altar. "We give thanks to the gods and goddesses for joining us tonight." She nibbled a piece of pancake she had saved from breakfast. "We give nourishment to Shallistar for the gifts she gives us." She crumbled the rest and let it drop to the ground. "We toast your blessings and wisdom." She sipped some wine. "We toast Shallistar for the blessings she gives us." And she spilled the rest of the wine on the ground.

Miranda left the altar to stand by Zulien. "I feel much better. Isn't that a kick? Tempest adores the esbats." She realized Zulien had not spoken, and only a mechanical arm reached around her. "Zulien, are you all right?" He looked completely panicstricken, and Miranda was becoming concerned. "Zulien, talk to me."

He finally managed, "I am mated to a goddess."

Miranda groaned. "Zule, I am no goddess. Stop that, or rumors are going to fly out of this valley. If the hierarchy wants me assassinated for being an outer world Ancient, imagine what they would do if they think I am an inner world goddess. Chill out a little. You are *so* not coming to the sabbat rituals."

"Miranda," Tempest called out. She was still standing by the altar with all the excited woman.

"Zule, I am the same woman whose hands you tied to the bedpost last night, and hopefully the same one you will do that to again. I am no goddess. Think about the danger of such a rumor, please." She stretched up on tiptoe, and still had to pull his hair to bend him down enough to kiss. She walked over to Tempest.

Zalana was beaming, and Miranda's heart skipped at being in the center of such a group. "How do you feel? I mean, isn't it the best? I told you it would rejuvenate you and clear out the old cobwebs."

"Miranda, this will be the first of the new scrolls," Zalana said excitedly. "Until we get a scribe, I guess I will have to write it down, and you will have to remind me of some of the words."

Miranda's face went blank.

"Oh man, a vision in the middle of our party. Get ready to grab her if she decides to deep six on us again." Tempest got behind her.

The cloistered women could not have moved if an ibila was attacking. The Celestial was having a vision. On top of the ritual... they were in shock. Miranda's eyes began to refocus. "Terena."

Terena stuttered, "Yes, what do you need, Miranda?"

"No Terena, it is you. I saw you. You were in this big crystal library thingy, and there were a lot of people writing like crazy, but you were the one with the originals they were copying. You have a photogenic memory."

Terena looked confused, "A what?"

"It means you can remember exactly. What you see and what is said, you remember all of it. It's true, isn't it? You remember all the blessings."

"Of course I do. No one could forget what happened here tonight."

"But, they do not remember it exactly, and you do. You are the one to write them down. I knew I sensed a power in you. Tempest, maybe I'll finally figure out what you're supposed to do." Miranda was thrilled as her abilities were beginning to have meaning for her.

"By the stars, Zalana." Terena was still in shock. "I am to be scribe to the new scrolls as decreed by the Ancient herself."

"I am so happy for you. Personally, I am scared witless. How am I to guide the Ancient when she can do things like this? It is like asking a child to teach its mother."

The circle began to disperse. Mothers proudly hugged their daughters and begged for information on their experience. The gossip of the ritual would hit Laquista before dawn.

It was agreed the parents should stay in Ethram's quarters for the night. There was no way to properly guard the house and the valley the night before the ceremony. With so many people witnessing the ritual, the Majors from all three regiments tripped over communication lines reaching the Magistrate of Battle. He insisted on lengthy descriptions of the ritual and the Celestial's trance as he shuffled papers, deciding how to best protect her.

He was not the only Magistrate making plans. The enemy Magistrates learned their kidnapping attempt had failed and, worse, the Magistrate of Battle already had a signed confession implicating them. All they could do was tell the commission the word of men with dubious character could not be trusted, and if that did not work they were going to say Zulien tortured the renegade soldiers until they lied. They knew the men would never reach Latisqua to refute whatever story they devised.

Now the Ancient had begun holding rituals and trances... in public. With over thirty warriors in attendance, there would be no way to lessen the impact. They had to make the commission agree to order the Ancient brought to Latisqua... for her own protection, of course.

Miranda entered the joining chamber and stretched. She turned to her mate sitting on the sleeping pallet in the middle of the room. "Zule, will you stop staring at me like I have three eyes or something."

"I would love you if you had three eyes, my mate." He frowned, and added, "I might have a problem with scales, though."

"So, it's just this touchy feely I have going on with the moons that upsets you?"

"I am not upset, Miranda." Her handsome warrior looked at his feet. "I just do not understand why a warrior, with no real knowledge of the Old Religion, would be mated to you."

Miranda felt as though she had been punched in the stomach, and tears welled up in her eyes as she whispered, "You wish you were not mated to me, Zule?"

"No, oh gods, no. That is not at all what I mean." Zule rushed over and pulled her against him, a feeling of loss crushing his chest. He could feel her trembling, and felt guilty after the happiness she was feeling earlier. "I want you to teach me the Old Religion," he confessed. "I want to feel the joy and passion I saw on your face tonight. I am a warrior, and I do not know if it is possible."

Miranda was astonished. "But your mother... I don't understand."

Zule guided her over to the joining pallet. "My mother had a vision when she was very young. She is convinced it came from an Ancient, and most of the women of visions she knows say the same thing happened to them. They believe it is the Old Religion, but nobody knows for sure. It was lost long before they were born. She does not know any rituals or blessings, and we only have vague knowledge to honor the moons, suns and our worlds."

A far away look shone in his dark eyes, "We do know that the time of the Old Religion was a time of enlightenment. No one knows if there was ever a war before the Battles of Chaos." Zule looked down at her. "This is what the inner worlds want back, peace and harmony. Mother watched what you did tonight, and she is questioning herself. She is afraid you are going to think she is a fraud," he admitted.

"Zule, your mother lives the life of the Old Religion. It is not just a series of rituals. It is a way of life." Miranda shook her head. "She must hate me and the pressure I've put her under. I feel terrible about this. I could be undermining her whole belief system. This has to stop. I'm no leader. I simply believe the way I believe, and I don't want to mess with what works for other people."

"Do you not see, Miranda? You are what works. Even if you do not think you are a leader, the people do. I heard Tempest whisper, 'Just do it the way we do back home'. That is all you have to do, Miranda. That is living the life of the Old Religion, and it is what the inner worlds want back."

Miranda gazed across the chamber, willing the light to dim. She pulled her caftan off, lay down on the pallet and held her arms out to her warrior. This was all so overwhelming. "Hold me, Zule. I need you to hold me."

He quickly shucked his clothes and drew her close. The warmth of his strong bronze body felt comforting. "What does it feel like when the moon joins with you?"

"Light, like you do not even realized how heavy all the junk inside you is until its weight is being held up. When the beam pulls back, it feels as though it takes all the ugly stuff, things that are wrong or troubling, back with it. That is why I call it my cleansing ritual. I feel so clean and free when it is finished." Miranda began tracing her finger on his chest. A slight pulse twitched inside her.

"Can a man share this ritual?" Zule's fingers traced lightly down her back. He felt his arousal grow in time with her pulse.

"I really don't know, but I don't see why not." Miranda tried to think. She realized it was becoming more difficult with each brush of his hand and smell of his scent. "There was a man in the disastrous esbat in the glade."

She felt the vibration of a growl rumble through his chest. "You will not share this cleansing with another man, Miranda."

"Calm down, Zule. Cripes, the guy is on another planet." Secretly, she was pleased he was jealous.

Zule felt much better. The man would be swallowed with that world soon. "Would you teach me?"

Miranda scooted up and leaned over him. In the dim lights, she could see his sincerity. "Of course I will. I should have had you by my side tonight." She leaned down and kissed him as his arms circled around her, pulling her close.

She lifted her head and he brushed her long shining hair away from her face. Her azure eyes were wide and he looked deep into their depths, feeling her power, wisdom and love. "Never has a mate been as beautiful as you, Miranda. By the stars, I know this is true. You have made the centuries of my yearning seem but an instant, and I would gladly wait twice as long for your discovery, knowing your arms would be held open to me."

Miranda wiggled her hips as they resting on his stomach. Their arousal was building and she felt the weight of his shaft on her bottom. "I'm sure glad you didn't have to wait twice as long."

His hand tangled in her hair and he pulled her lips to his again, opening and devouring her mouth. Her hands rested on the pillow on either side of his head, and her fingertips stroked his wild mane as he lowered his hands and lightly kneaded her bottom, pulling her into him. Involuntarily, she rubbed her dampening sex against his flat stomach. She felt empty, longing for him to join with her.

Desire mounted, and she could not understand how her nipples became so sensitive when he touched her. As her passion grew, she quivered with anticipation, and as she felt one large hand stroke the length of her side, her nails dug deep into his shoulders. The warrior groaned into her mouth.

Her lips left his and kissed their way down his chin and onto his chest. She found the tight peak of a darkened nipple and bit lightly. "By the stars, Miranda. I am in such need." Her tongue licked the trapped peak. Hands circled her waist, squeezing in time to the rhythmic pulse of their sex.

Miranda abandoned the nipple and continued to leave kisses along the corded muscles of his abdomen. His hands found their way to her silken hair as she traveled lower. Miranda was curious. She had never been this close to a man's shaft, and she decided to take her time discovering its wonders.

Her sex spasmed wildly at the first inhale of his scent. Zulien felt her little fingers brushing the thick curls surrounding his manhood, and when they ran up the length of his shaft, he gasped. Miranda studied him intently, and then a tentative tongue reached out to taste him. One hand gripped him to hold him still while the other searched under and around, exploring everywhere.

Zulien gritted his teeth and clenched his jaw tightly. By all the stars of the inner worlds, he needed to have her now. Her mouth came down on him and her tongue swirled, causing his nerves to fire and shoot through him like sparks. Her grip tightened as the object of her attention jerked in her fist.

Her other fingers continued to travel around, tracing and then gently squeezing one side, rolling and discovering in wonder. She sucked at the velvet smoothness in her mouth and he reached under her arms, pulling her away. He pushed her on her back and kneed her thighs apart.

"I wasn't finished," she whispered her complaint.

The warrior braced himself over her, his dark hair hanging almost to her chest. "I can stand no more of your torture for fear I will split my little Ancient open with my spear. It needs satisfying.

Now."

He lunged forward and into her with one deep thrust. His shaking arms buckled and he dropped to his elbows. "Aaargh." His scream of passion echoed off the walls, and Miranda was lost.

She scored his back in mindless passion as she thrust her hips to meet him. "Oh goddess of the moon, what is happening to me?" she cried. With all his agonizing size, she needed him deeper, and on each of his retreats she demanded his return to her.

Zulien's teeth chattered with the force of his desire. He felt himself building towards eruption, and thrust with a frenzy. As Miranda sensed his approaching climax, she was suddenly holding an open palm to the moon behind the crystal pyramid. Her other hand reached out to the blackness of space, and a white line left her fingertips focusing on a point in the distance, concentrating its light until a new star appeared.

When she came out of her trance, Zulien was holding her quivering body. Tears spilled down her face and onto his chest, mixing with the sweat from their exertions. His mouth was buried in her hair, lips whispering tender words. "Your mate holds you, little Ancient. No one will harm you, my mate." She balled her fist on his chest and he realized she was coming back to him.

He had seen her face mirror his passion, and then her expression went blank, and he thrilled with her vision until fear passed into her features. It frightened him, and he held her close. It was several minutes before her eyes began to clear. "My stars, little one, you gave me a bit of a fright that time."

She brushed a kiss on his chin and he laid

her down. Melting her body beside him, she held the strong arm of her protector around her until she could finally settle down enough to sleep. Her last conscious thought was, *Cripes, I'm getting married tomorrow.*

CHAPTER IX

Zalana had been up for an hour, nervously pacing Ethram's quarters with Terena. "This whole joining has been unpredictable."

"Yes, but Zalana, what you are suggesting." Terena shook her head. "To interrupt the mates in their joining chamber? I do not know."

Wringing her hands, Zalana replied, "We must wake them. If the Ancient wants a morning feast again, we will be late for the ceremonies." She turned to her mate. "Zibula, what do you think?"

"If I were answering for Zule and Tali, I would say lock the door and throw away the keys. The boys finally seem to have them settled down and accepting things, and I only heard Tempest shriek once last night."

"No, she did it again right before I nodded off," Terena admitted.

Zibula continued, "Why not prepare the feast? Then you can wake them, and if she is not hungry we can give it to the guards."

The mothers agreed this was the best course. Zalana made a stack of the flatbreads she had carefully watched Miranda make. She was pleased she remembered the recipe, as it was used in the blessing the night before. Terena sent one of the guards after more pallachi juice.

When everything was ready, the mothers smoothed their dresses, ran their hands through their curls, straightened with as much courage as they could muster, and headed towards the joining chambers.

Zule heard the soft knocking on the door and woke Miranda as he bounded out of bed. Not knowing if the Major was bringing him a warning for his mate, he threw the door open. "Mother, is anything wrong?"

"No, Zule. I just wanted to let you and Miranda know a feast is prepared if you are hungry." Now Zalana felt miserable for disturbing them. "If you desire to feast, we must do it soon or risk being late for the ceremonies."

"Thank you, Zalana," Miranda called from across the room. "We'll be right over. I'm starving."

Zalana beamed. "I have made the ritual flatbreads."

Miranda smiled at yet another misconception. Was everything she did to be attributed to ritual? "I hope we have enough of the syrup, er, pallachi juice left."

"Terena sent the guard to get more," Zalana assured her.

"Okay, see you in a few." Miranda reached for her caftan.

Zalana met Terena as she was leaving Tali's chamber. "As I expected, my son was not thrilled by the interruption, but my daughter was already dressing before I finished speaking."

"You answered the door butt naked, Zule." Miranda handed him his breeches.

"I was butt naked when the door was knocked upon," he explained.

"Yes, but you answered the door to your mother... naked," Miranda emphasized.

A confused look passed over the big man's face. "My mother has seen me naked before, mate. I was not born wearing aaragon breeches."

"I hope to imagine you've changed some since you were an infant."

His mate's ways were difficult to understand, he decided.

Tempest caught up to them as they passed the altar, and she grabbed Miranda's arm and pulled her off to the side, whispering, "Is your guy as incredible in the sack as Tali?"

Miranda leaned in with a conspiring closeness. "I don't know. I've never been in the sack with Tali."

Tempest punched her lightly in the arm. "You know what I mean."

"Yes, Zule is undoubtedly the most incredible man I could have ever imagined. I feel so safe when he holds me, Tempest. It is like nothing can hurt me, and the sex... let's just say it is a good thing shallistones are not flammable."

"Tali is so in love with me it freaks me out. Heck, even when I'm snippy with him, he doesn't get angry. The thing is, I think I do that because I am afraid I've fallen for him too." Tempest glanced over to Taliquant. He was over by Zulien and grinning at her, and when he saw her look over, he waved.

"Well, that would be helpful. We are getting married today. I think we're going to be all right now, Tempest. Like your mom would say, I think we've 'found' ourselves."

The young women walked over to their waiting mates and continued on to the feast. After breakfast, the parents got into their shuttle and the Major loaded up the guards and mates in two others. They sped to Zulien's home to prepare for the ceremonies.

It was a one-story building made of light blue shallistone, and when she passed under the entry arch into the foyer, Miranda stopped and stared. On every built-in shelf, there were bouquets of all different kinds of unusual flowers.

Zalana looked around warily. "You said you would each like a bouquet, and we were not sure which flowers would be right for the ritual."

Tempest's mouth was hanging open. "Great goddess, mom, are there any flowers left on Shallistar."

Terena straightened with pride when her wild new daughter called her mother again. "We have beautiful flowers on planet. Many of these bouquets came from the growers when they heard it was the only request from the Ancient for the ritual. Their importance in the Merchant Chambers has already risen, and they are anxiously waiting to see whose gift the Celestial and Provider of Ritual Growing Things will choose to adorn their robes."

"No wonder you look tired. Zalana, I am so sorry. I was trying to suggest something easy." Miranda gazed around the walls in embarrassment. "Did you say whichever bouquet I picked would make a difference?"

"Oh, yes." Zalana swept her arm around the room. "To be the grower of the flowers the Celestial picks for her ceremonial bouquet... every new mate will need the ritual flowers for their ceremony."

"Cripes, I just wanted a little bouquet," Miranda muttered.

As usual, Tempest took it in stride. "Imagine the sales for pancakes and pallachi juice when it comes out that is the official joining ritual feast."

"Stop it, Tempest. I'm afraid to ask for anything at this point."

Zulien recognized his mate's distress, and placed his big comforting hands on her shoulders. He bent down and whispered, "Why are you upset, Miranda? The growers are trying to honor you and Tempest."

"The flowers are not for ritual, Zule. It was just something I wanted to carry to remind me of weddings back home. I could tell your mother wanted to do something to make me more comfortable. It would not be right for one grower to flourish on my whim."

Zulien studied the foyer with all the brightly colored arrangements. "I know what to do, my mate. Do not let this distress you any further."

Sagging against his chest she looked up, strained with all that was happening. "Are you sure? I don't want to insult anybody."

"I am sure, my little Ancient. Go prepare for the ceremony." A quick kiss brushed her temple, and Zalana led the women down the hall to her bedroom where they would get ready.

The mates from the Quillant showed up and insisted on helping. They could see Zalana and Terena were exhausted with the hurried preparations for the important event.

Vasilla was brushing Miranda's drying hair, and Tempest was screaming from the bathing chamber, "Cripes, Ebonisha, I can wash myself. Oooh... Oooh. Women don't touch each other there." Terena rubbed her temples.

"I wish I had some chamomile tea for you. It would make you feel so much calmer." Truthfully, Miranda wished she had some for herself.

"Is this a plant magic?" Terena was interested in anything that had to do with her Tempest's power over growing things.

"I guess it is. Tempest had to plant two pots for us back home, because it helped me get to sleep," Miranda confessed.

Tempest came out of the bathing chamber wrapped in Terena's robe with it dragging behind her and her hair sticking out at crazy angles.

There was a knock on the door and she strode angrily over to answer it. "What now?" She swung the door open to find Tali standing on the other side. He was missing his mate and wanted to make sure she was okay.

"Cripes, Tali, get away from here. You're not allowed to see me." She tried to push him back to close the door.

Tali persisted. "Why, my mate? Why am I not allowed to see you?"

"Because it's my wedding day, you big oaf. You're not supposed to see the bride."

Tali was devastated. "Ever? How do we join again?"

"Oh goddess, Tali. You're not supposed to see me until the ceremony. It's supposed to be a surprise."

The warrior took in his wild mate's appearance with the sleeves of the robe bunched up on her arms and pooling around her feet. He could not begin to figure out how she got her short hair to poke out like it did. "I am surprised, Tempest."

Both her small hands shoved against his chest, and pushed him into the hall so she could slam the door. "Surprised at the ceremony, big guy."

"Zalana, I have an idea for some of those flowers. Could you ask Zulien to send us some with small petals and different colors?"

"I will get them myself, Miranda. I can use a little walk."

She returned a short while later, a mysterious smile in her eyes as she laid the flowers on the sleeping pallet. "You look lovely, Miranda."

Her ceremonial robe was the usual caftan in some shimmery sapphire material Miranda could not discern, cut in a vee to her waist in the front and back. Tempest's was the same in a shimmery emerald green.

It was obvious the mothers wanted their new daughters' unusual eye color to be noticed. Everyone else they had seen, with the exception of Ethram and Ballion, had the chocolate eyes of the Shallistarians or Amarazonians.

Miranda's robe was edged in silver, Tempest's in gold, and the only other adornment on the caftans were tiny bells trailing down the front from the waist to the floor. Naturally, Miranda's bells were silver, Tempest's were gold, and every time the girls moved the bells chimed softly. It was driving Tempest crazy. "Okay, what's the deal with the bells?"

"They are a symbol for your mate that he can always find you and protect you." Terena thought Tempest shone like the brantola trees.

"Like he can't find me. I practically trip over the big guy every time I move," she said to no one in particular.

Miranda sat on the bed, breaking the flowers off the bouquets and leaving one-inch stems. Vasilla and Ebonisia joined her in the task, wondering if it was another ritual, and afraid to show their ignorance. When they had a pile of brightly colored flowers, Miranda instructed them how to weave them through her long hair.

She took what was left and braided two haloed crowns for her and Tempest. It was a bit of a task to arrange the crown over her friend's spikes, and when Miranda finally looked up from her task, all eight women in the room were staring at them and silently crying. "Cripes, I wonder what I did now?" she whispered to Tempest.

"Have I broken some..." Miranda searched for

the word, "oh yeah, protocol?"

"Miranda," Zalana gasped. "You have shown the people of Shallistar the most respect. To adorn your head with the natural flowers of our planet, will show them you wish to share your wisdom, and for Tempest, the Provider of Ritual Growing Things for the Ancient's rituals, to also honor us..." She was so overcome, she could not finish.

Tempest leaned in, "I guess veils would have been less complicated. Provider of Ritual Growing Things, hrrumph. I think I've finally had a vision. I see myself spending my life on a tractor or with a shovel in my hand."

Miranda giggled, then sobered. She had not told anyone of the vision she had last night. Zulien did not ask her because it had shaken her up so badly. "Zalana, can we speak privately for a moment?"

The tall woman licked her lips in apprehension as she followed Miranda to the bathing chamber, wondering what mother's wisdom she would ask.

"I am supposed to tell you my visions so you can help me figure out what they mean. Well, last night I had a doozy." Miranda told her about the pyramid, the beam of light and the star. "Any thoughts?"

Zalana paled a little. "I think I need to talk to the Magistrate of Battle as soon as the ceremonies have ended." She would not explain anything else.

The time had come to proceed to the ceremony. The men had already gone, leaving a regiment of guards and the Quillant warriors to escort the women.

When they reached the foyer, two small bouquets lay on a shelf with a note, and all the other bouquets were gone. Miranda picked up the sheet. "Miranda, I think I have read your distress correctly. Tali and I have picked the smallest stem from every vase and my mother helped us arrange the bouquets you wish to hold. No grower should reap more significance than another to prosper on our day, so the remaining flowers have been brought to the ceremony and scattered on the aisle that will lead you to me. I hope this eases your stress and is in accordance with your wishes, my mate." She wordlessly handed the note to Tempest.

A look of wonder flashed in her eyes. "I can't imagine the big guy going through flowers for me." She picked up the bouquet of predominately green petals, held it to her face and inhaled the sweet fragrance. Terena noticed the moisture pooled in her eyes.

Zalana and Terena were nervously fidgeting in the shuttle seat across from the mates. Tempest was quivering a bit at Miranda's side as the enormity of what was happening today began to sink in. To Miranda, it appeared she was the calmest of the group, and she could not stand the silence any longer. "I understand why Tempest is nervous, but Zalana, please calm down. I am sure whatever preparations you and Terena have organized are going to be perfect."

"I fear you will be disappointed, Celestial." Zalana was ready to cry.

"Zalana, if I had less than a week to put together two weddings with aliens, one of whom you think is going to save your race, surrounded by guards because you're afraid the brides will be kidnapped or killed... cripes, I would have had a nervous breakdown by now." She took the woman's hands and held them until their eyes met. "Anything, absolutely anything, you have arranged is going to be perfect."

"It is in the valley," Terena blurted out.

"What?" Tempest asked.

"The ceremony. It is in the valley," Zalana repeated anxiously. "It is the only place with a ritual altar, and we thought it might be necessary for you."

Miranda's mouth dropped open as Terena continued, "We tried to remember the placement of the stones to build one by the Zabilla, but we could not. We even tried drawing it when you sent us to lie down in the joining chambers, but when we compared pictures, they were completely different," she said miserably.

Miranda smiled. "That is perfect. It is where I met all of you, and Zulien. It will make me so much more comfortable to be in familiar surroundings." At the mention of Zule, Miranda lifted her wrist with the offering scarf and brushed it down her cheek. She had been away from him for too long.

"Oh, mom, thanks. I was afraid we were going to end up in some huge Shallistone cathedral or something. The valley is much nicer. It is exactly the spot I would have picked." Tempest squeezed the woman's hand.

Zalana and Terena studied the mates closely to see if they were merely hiding their disappointment, but both prospective daughters looked genuinely pleased, and they began to relax. "We hope the ceremony is to your liking. Terena and I agree that most of it must come from the Old Religion. They could not have taken everything away from us."

Now Miranda was nervous. It had not occurred to her that she had absolutely no idea what the 'ceremony' entailed. In a regular wedding, there were rehearsals, and everyone knew what to expect on the big day. She was getting ready to ask when the shuttle pulled into the valley.

"By the polluted planets of the outer worlds," one of the guards in the shuttle exclaimed.

At least five hundred people had crammed into the small clearing, half of them warriors. "I thought this was supposed to be a small affair," Miranda whispered, her eyes wide as she took in the crowd.

Seartock met the shuttle and overheard a shocked Zalana say, "Terena and I only invited our closest friends."

The warrior rolled his eyes. "Who invited their closest friends, who invited their closest friends... ladies, they are wrong. Our biggest export is not Shallistones. It is gossip. Thank the stars the Magistrate of Battle decided to attend and brought reinforcements, or there is no way we would we have been able to secure this crowd."

Miranda finally found her voice. "Zalana, exactly what does this ceremony entail. I have no idea what I am supposed to do."

Zalana waved her hand, distracted by the gathering. "Nothing, Miranda. All you have to do is go to Zulien. He does everything else."

Miranda narrowed her eyes. "What 'else' does he do?"

"Professes his love and desire for you, promises to protect you and keep you near to him... it is a rather simple ceremony. Because you are his destined mate, there really is not any doubt that you will be together."

They had approached a four-foot wide aisle that the crowd had bordered. It led to the altar, and the flowers from the foyer carpeted the path. Miranda and Tempest began to get anxious when they saw their mates and Letang waiting for them. They had been separated for too long. "You better hold my hand, or I'm going to end up running up there," Tempest whispered.

"I know what you mean. I'm more nervous about being away from him than I am about the wedding."

The girls forced themselves to walk slowly. Murmurs of how beautiful they looked, comments about their 'ritual' flower crowns, an occasional Celestial Ancient remark, all went unheard as the young women passed by. Finally, they were at the altar, and Zulien held his hand out to Miranda. Taliquant held his out to Tempest, mirroring the ceremony.

Zulien turned Miranda so that she faced the crowd, and she continued to look up into his handsome, proud face. "I present to the people of Shallistone, the Celestial Ancient, Miranda. My mate."

Taliquant presented the Provider of Ritual Growing Things. The gathering was quiet, and Miranda found her gaze could not leave her warrior's eyes. Her mind drifted to their joining and she felt herself getting aroused. She did not realize she was in the ceremonial mating trance.

She never heard Zulien say, "I vow my love and desire for no other. I vow to protect and comfort you. No sound or request need be made. It is in my soul. Gaze once upon her beauty, and know that she is mine, mate of Zulien." With that, he removed the caftan with the bells and the entranced Miranda stood naked before the gathering.

Tempest was equally naked beside Taliquant, who was almost challenging anyone to find a single flaw on his beautiful wild mate. A minute passed unchallenged, and then the crowd erupted with applause.

The women came out of their trance. "Cripes..." Miranda snatched up the caftan from Letang's arms and pulled it over her head, sure she was redder than the darkest finisia flowers.

Tempest glared at Taliquant as she got dressed. "I do not know what the hell you did to me, but you are in deep shit, big guy."

The warriors were confused over their mates' obvious distress. "Tempest, why are you angry? There were no challenges. None," he said proudly. "You are mine."

"I am so talking to Zalana about this," Miranda said angrily.

"Why? My mother did not challenge." Zulien did not understand. The ceremony went perfectly.

"Strip," Tempest ordered, and Taliquant stared into her flashing eyes. "Now, big guy. No way am I going to stand in front of all your mother's friends and half the warriors in the galaxy butt naked and you do not."

"The witnesses do not challenge for us," Tali tried to explain.

Tempest reached for the top of his breeches. "Either you do it, or I will do it."

Zulien whispered quickly, "Miranda, stop her. If she does this, he can be challenged as not strong enough to protect her."

Miranda was pretty angry with him and did not understand what he meant, but she did understand the urgency in his voice. She had never heard him scared before. "Tempest, stop."

"What?"

"Stop. If you make him do this, he can't claim you any more. It makes you fair game for anyone out there."

Tempest's fingers were under the waistband of his breeches, and Tali was doing his best not to look panicked. Tempest slowly turned around and saw anticipation on one hundred warriors' faces. "Do not think you're off the hook," she hissed at him. She loudly exclaimed as she pulled on the waistband, stretching up for a kiss, "On my world, we end the ceremony with a kiss, my mate."

Disappointment shadowed the features of the onlookers as they realized the little mate could not kiss her warrior without pulling him down to her. Deliriously happy, Tali claimed her mouth, and stifled a yell when she bit his tongue.

They walked off the altar towards the feasting table. Miranda took her seat between Zule and his mother, and Miranda looked Zalana in the eye, "Absolutely no more ceremonies without complete descriptions first."

"Yes, daughter." Zalana had no idea why Miranda was upset.

The meal of unusual meats, fruits and vegetables was delicious. There was a table of pastries over to the side that people wandered by and chose from.

Tempest leaned behind Taliquant and Zulien, and tugged at Miranda's dress. "No wedding cake?"

"I guess they don't do that here."

"Look at the bottom of that pastry table. I think that will work." Tempest's eyes had a mischievous glint. "I owe the big guy one."

"Sounds good to me. How do we get them over there?"

"Everything you do is etched in stone around here. We are so going to give every mate who has ever had to stand butt-assed, a chance for payback."

Miranda giggled and she turned back to the table. A few minutes later, she announced, "Zulien, there is one part of the ceremonial feast from my world that I would like to share with you."

Zalana's eyes widened, and Terena was already memorizing. Miranda stood and led Zulien over to the table with different colored cakes, and Tempest pulled Taliquant to join them. Miranda cut four pieces off the large cake on the bottom.

The parents circled around them and friends looked on curiously. The two warriors stood proudly by their little mates. Miranda cleared her throat. "This signifies that you will always help provide for your mates."

She handed Zulien a piece of cake and Tempest handed one to Taliquant. The whole gathering that were within earshot, watched with anticipation. "You are to feed me the piece of cake," Miranda whispered.

Zulien and Taliquant carefully placed the small treats on their respective mates' tongues, and the gathering almost bowed their heads at the significance of the ritual. Miranda and Tempest turned back to the table and the two small pieces Miranda had cut off the large cake.

"Oh, I do not think so," Tempest said. She scooped up a huge piece and slammed it across Taliquant's face, and Miranda followed suit. The two warriors stood stunned, faces half covered in gooey blue frosting.

Tempest and Miranda looked at their shocked mates and the bewildered expressions on crowd and burst into laughter. Miranda pulled Zulien down and began licking the tasty cake off his face. Tempest decided that looked like fun. They licked and nibbled until their warriors' faces were clean and they were dripping with desire.

"Not exactly what I planned, but it works," Tempest murmured.

The warriors' shafts were practically exploding from their breeches. "This is a wise ritual, my mate," Zulien said in awe, and Miranda began laughing again and pulled him into a kiss.

The Magistrate of Battle had joined the cloistered group. Along with the others, he had watched the cake ritual and understood the significance of providing for your mate, and her answer of comfort and desire was not lost on him. "So many of the Old Religion's rituals have been forgotten," he said sadly. "Celestial, I am Vesario, the Magistrate of Battle. It is a great honor to meet you. I assure you that the Magistrates of Well Being and Divider of Realms are also pleased you are not decayed," he said reverently.

"Thank you, Magistrate. I am relieved not to be decayed, as well," she smiled. "Please, call me Miranda. This is Tempest."

"Yes, the Provider of Ritual Growing Things. We are most pleased you were procured as well." Vesario took Tempest's hand, and thought she looked too fragile to have been the Celestial's protector in the outer worlds.

"You're the dude that's giving us the planet, right?" Tempest grinned.

The statement had him flustered, and he decided that 'dude' must mean messenger. "I have been chosen to be that dude," he affirmed. "The other allies on Laquista are positioning themselves to protect the Celestial."

Vesario turned to Zulien. "The Magistrate of Well Being has stalled any edicts to demand the Celestial's presence before the hierarchy, for now. The Magistrate of the Divider of Realms agreed with my understanding of the Celestial's vision, and we have already arranged a temporary shelter on Vallastera large enough for your families and an initial pilgrimage."

"So far out?" Zalana whispered to Zibula.

"We suspected that planet to be part of the original Ancient's worlds. With Vesario controlling the battleships, it would be difficult for the enemies within the hierarchy to organize an attack," Zibula reasoned.

"As far as the other vision Zalana relayed to us, we are considering its meaning. It would have been helpful to have had the Magistrate of Old Ways to confer with, even if his ideas are diluted. Naturally, we are keeping the information only with those we know to be behind us."

Miranda spoke up. "Perhaps you should speak with Ballion. It sounds like his people may be a more reliable source for interpretation, and the Minocs are not interested in twisting what is remembered for personal gain."

Vesario's mouth dropped open. He glanced over to where Ballion stood by Ethram, antenna waving in the air and occasionally stroking his chin. "What would a Minoc know about these things?"

"It had not occurred to me either, Vesario. Apparently, after the Battles of Chaos, some of the lesser civilizations seemed to be supportive of the new hierarchy, when in fact they have been aggressively researching and protecting the Old Religion. These planets never posed a threat to the Magistrates, so they have been able to quietly conduct their studies unnoticed. Minocania has been researching Ancient civilizations, and Ballion was most helpful with his suggestions on the joinings. The wasted procurers on Garnella have located ruins and altars, and I would not be surprised if there are more supporters hidden among the lesser worlds," Zibula announced.

"The Quillant and Quistar will escort you to your new home after the ceremonies have concluded, and the Quibasta is already circling Vallastera. With one attempt already made on the Celestial, we feel it is imperative to get her moved to safety as quickly as possible," the Magistrate explained. "Zibula, I would like to discuss what you have learned about the lesser planets with Ballion and Ethram." The two warriors wandered off.

Zalana and Terena disappeared to make arrangements for the move. Zalana contacted the other visionaries, and they all expressed the desire to make the pilgrimage, excited that their ability might finally have meaning. As it looked as though the Quillant was to be a rather permanent fixture protecting Vallastera, the families of the warriors on board decided to make the move. The initial pilgrimage consisted of over seventy people from Shallistar.

Ethram offered to shuttle some of the travelers on the Isotant. After checking with the leaders on Garnella, they wanted him to remain close to the Ancient and relay information. Naturally, the Minocanians were beating their antennas with pride that Ballion should represent their interests.

The ceremony wound down, and the crowd slowly dispersed to their waiting shuttles. The newly joined mates and their parents, along with the warriors of the Quillant and their mates and the Magistrate of Battle, made their way back to the docking port for the Quillant.

Zulien and Taliquant flanked Vesario as he prepared to offer Letang his commission. Vasilla stood with their parents, pride shining in her chocolate eyes.

"The Quillant is being joined by three junior officers," Vesario began. "Lieutenants Bregan, Shiplant and Drapent have shown promise in their training, and are looking forward to joining your regiment."

Vesario noticed the confusion on the Quillant warriors' faces. They knew Berslan would need a replacement. Maybe it was decided to add to the regiment because of the importance of their new mission. The regiment and mates shook hands with the new additions with warm acceptance.

"Lieutenant Letang and Captain Seartock, please step forward for your commissioning," Vesario boomed.

Seartock looked questioningly at his friends. Everyone expected Letang to be promoted to Captain after all he had done for the mission, but Seartock had no idea why he was being included.

"All warriors on the Quillant are being commissioned up one grade."

The warriors and their mates beamed. They did not know what was going on, but the promotions were an unexpected boon. Sometimes they had to wait centuries for a battle that made them worthy.

"Commander Zulien and Major Taliquant are being promoted to on world Admirals for Vallastera, and it is with my utmost agreement with them that I announce this commissioning. Letang, you are now Commander of the Quillant. Seartock, you are now Major, and his second."

Just as Zulien had predicted, Vasilla fainted into the arms of her father, and Ebonisha burst into proud tears. The warriors erupted into congratulations. It was a very good day for the regiment.

Parents were brought on board the Quistar, while the other citizens making the pilgrimage shared procurement rooms on the Isotant. Arrangements were made to forward personal belongings, and businesses were transferred to family members and friends to watch over. The ships left the Shallistar atmosphere.

Zulien nervously led Miranda to his quarters. After centuries, it would be his last trip sleeping in them. He was certain when Letang moved into them, Vasilla would lighten his dungeon colors to the lavenders and light blues she liked to be surrounded in.

"Please understand, my mate, my apartments have been my own for many years. I did not have time to honor you with new furnishings, and my only explanation is the dark despair I was feeling over my long wait to find you." Zulien thought of the horrid place and the distaste he would see in Miranda's eyes.

"I am sure you have it set up like a bachelor's pad would be on my planet. Do not worry, Zulien. It is common for men to keep what makes them comfortable close on my planet, too."

He took a deep breath and opened the door, and he stared in amazement. Light green curtains and bedding now decorated his sleeping area. His desk had been organized and the maroon carpet had a golden rug covering most of the threadbare pacing paths. As Miranda entered the room, Zulien checked the plaque on the door to make sure he had the right room. Ebonisha and Vasilla stood at the end of the hall and smiled warmly, giving him a thumbs up and mouthing 'You're welcome'.

A bottle of wine sat on the nightstand with two glasses and a note. "Welcome, Miranda. If there is anything you need, please let us know." It was signed, "From your new family."

"Oh Zulien, this is wonderful. If this is what

your idea of a bachelor's hangout is, I am afraid you will not be impressed with my decorating ideas."

Zulien admitted that Vasilla and Ebonisha lightened the quarters, because mates kept no secrets from each other. They sipped wine, and Zulien promised to take her to the bridge later so she could look out the viewport to the stars he loved. They drank the rich, fruity beverage in silence while Zulien turned out all the lights except the glow from the shallistone on the desk.

They stripped off their clothes and lay back on the bed. Zulien's mouth found hers, and she felt sparks shoot through her while their tongues danced together. His big hand covered her breast and squeezed gently, pinching her nipples into hardened buds.

Miranda's hips began to squirm. She felt his erection pressing against the side of her thigh and she wrapped her fingers around as much of him as she could hold. Her fist lightly pumped, and she let her fingers stroke his length.

Zulien leaned over her and his hair brushed the pillow on either side of her pale cheeks. The liquid blue eyes shining up at him mirrored his desire for his beautiful mate. "I never hoped to be so lucky, Miranda."

Miranda searched his dark gaze. How could this incredible warrior be her husband? Although she had visions of him in the past, it still seemed surreal that such a magnificent man could exist... and for her. The desire reflected in his eyes reached into her soul, and her lips quivered with excitement. Her body ached to be filled by him.

Zulien's head traveled lower and his lips kissed sparks down her flesh. Her hands rested on his shoulders, squeezing while he suckled at her breast and his finger burrowed between her legs. "I need you, Zulien. I need you to fill me," she moaned.

His head dipped lower, scenting her arousal, and passion flared deep within him. His hands trembled as he pinned her hips, and his tongue swept over her. Miranda reached for him and fisted his hair, trying to pull him back up to her so he would enter her and calm the fire inside her. Zulien took her wrists and held them to her sides while he continued his oral ministrations.

Miranda was panting, trying to squeeze her thighs together while lightly bucking her hips towards his tongue, and when he began to suck at her, she gasped. "No, please, Zulien, I need you in me," she begged.

Zulien continued his teasing onslaught until he felt the shuddering spasm of her climax and he saw the distant gaze in her eyes as the vision filled her mind.

She stood before the glass pyramid, the light beam from her hand still aimed towards the blackness of space. The star that had gathered at the end of the beam flared brightly, and a million colored shards burst from its center.

CHAPTER X

Even with the added information, Miranda did not understand the vision. She lay curled up on her warriors' chest while her breathing returned to normal and she reclaimed her senses.

When all seemed in order, she rolled over and straddled his waist with her thighs. "You're going to have to stop doing that. I really feel like I'm going to shatter." Miranda scooted her bare bottom down until she felt the bulbous end of his shaft centered. She sunk down in a single plunge and groaned in pleasurable fulfillment.

Her hips rolled as she ground him deep inside her, and she rubbed seductively on his pubic bone as she felt her need tighten on him. Zulien was growling with the erotic sensation as slender fingers reached around and stroked Miranda. She was so lost in passion that the brushing on her sex took a moment to register. Miranda looked down to where their bodies were joined, and screamed.

Zulien's eyes flew open, and their bodies separated with a moist sucking sound as he rolled her protectively behind him.

"Commander, I sense your passion and need. My tongue salivates to stoke along your lusty length. My nipples harden to..."

"Voice off, dammit."

"Zulien, who is she?" Miranda whispered. She studied the slender woman. Her skin was dark red, and she had white hair... at least, on her head. The rest of her appeared to be completely denuded, and everything sexual about her seemed exaggerated. When the five-inch split tongue sensually ran over her lips, Miranda shivered. "What is she?" Miranda thought she must be another kind of alien.

The Parina's arms reached out to stroke Zulien's chest. "Stop," he ordered. Zulien pulled Miranda back to his side. "It is the ship Parina. I guess in all the confusion she has not been programmed to the new junior officers." Zulien saw the question in his mate's eyes. "She is an android. The unmated warriors share her to alleviate tension."

Miranda was beginning to understand. "I see, and this would be your night with her?"

The Parina's eyes flashed as she rapidly organized data and purred, "You are the Celestial. You are the Commander's mate. Thought of you fills the warriors with desire, and their sacks to fill with..."

"I said voice off. Go to the bridge for instructions."

The Parina rose and shrugged into her robe before she left the room.

"Yes," Zulien admitted. "I hate the thing. She does serve her purpose, though."

"You will not be needing her any more?" Miranda wanted confirmation that the sexual toy was not to be part of their relationship.

"Oh, I do not think so, my little Ancient," he chuckled. Zulien threw her onto her back and Miranda squealed in delight. He positioned himself and entered in a single thrust, resuming their sexual tryst. Miranda felt an uncontrollable claiming desire rise, and her nails scored down his chest in mindless passion.

More colorful shards exploded from the star as Zulien roared his seeds' eruption, and Miranda disappeared in climatic vision.

The next afternoon, they finally exited his quarters. Both wore the quietly smiling expressions of thoroughly satisfied mates as

Zulien took her hand and led her to the bridge.

Miranda walked into the crescent shaped room. Letang sat behind the navigation screen, and Seartock hovered over star charts relaying coordinates. Vallastera was a planet in the Shatung Quadrant. Most of the worlds on the northern edge of the inner worlds were uninhabited, and so far out in the hierarchy that they were rarely visited.

Miranda paid the men no attention as her eyes fixed on the viewport that made up the entire outside wall of the room. She was hardly aware of her feet moving her forward until she stepped up on the low, carpeted platform and rested her fingers against the translucent wall. Seartock and Letang watched her glide across the room with wide eyes and an expression of overwhelming rapture.

"I wonder if that was the look on my face the first time I entered space?" Letang mused.

Zulien was delighted at her enthrallment, and he walked up behind her as the officers returned to their tasks. "Zulien, it's beautiful." Miranda leaned back against her warrior's chest.

"Even after centuries, I am still awed by its magnificence," he agreed. "How long before we are on planet?" he called back to Letang.

"We are picking up staticky transmissions from the Quibasta. We have been able to make out the surface preparations are ready, but they are still too distant for us to lock onto their course. I am guessing we will get a better fix by this evening, and I anticipate docking sometime tomorrow morning."

Seartock added, "It is pretty far out there, Commander. I have only been to the Shatung Quadrant one time, so we are still working out the exact coordinates. Celestial, turn a little to the left. See the hazy pink disk with the blue center?"

Miranda nodded.

"That is where your new home will be," Seartock informed her.

"It looks like the eye of the goddess." Miranda traced the curved galaxy on the pane and smiled.

Zulien led her to the lounge. By the time they arrived there, Tempest was sitting in Taliquant's lap, holding court. She was answering questions about what life was like on her primitive planet, and the mates were laughing at her descriptions.

Tali was holding a breast in each of his big palms. Apparently, it was a compromise, because Tempest only moved his fingers when they began stroking her nipples. Miranda heard her say, "Easy boy, I may never get to cruise in a spaceship again, and I am not spending the entire time locked away in your quarters."

Tali smiled and gave her a squeeze as his hands retreated to cupping her mounds. The look of adoration on his face for her wild friend made Miranda happy. The warrior was clearly in love with her.

She thanked the mates for their welcoming note, and Zulien thanked Ebonisha and Vasilla for making his quarters more presentable. They assured him it was no problem and that they were pleased to do something for the Ancient.

Two of the junior officers entered the lounge with the Parina following behind them. The men walked over to a couch and the Parina approached Miranda. "You are the Celestial. You are the Commander's mate. Thought of you fills the warriors with desire and their sacks fill with need," she said, in a throaty, seductive purr. Her eyes blinked rapidly as her data banks processed information.

"Zulien, can you get her away from me? She makes me nervous," Miranda admitted.

"Who the hell is that?" Tempest asked.

"That is your mate's former girlfriend," Miranda told her.

"Tali?"

"I no longer require the Parina's services, my wild mate." Taliquant briefly filled Tempest in on the android's function.

"She's a robot?"

The Parina never approached the women, and Zulien was mystified as to the android's apparent interest in Miranda. "Why do you speak to my mate?"

The Parina focused her eyes on him. "While Major Berslan thrust his manly cock into my tight channel and his heavy sack pounded against my crevice in sexual heat, he was inflamed in passion with thoughts of finding the Celestial. While the Commander grips my..."

"Voice off, dammit," Zulien squirmed.

"More info than we needed, red woman," Tempest squirmed.

"She cannot help it. Her programming is such that everything she says or does has to have sexual overtones," Taliquant explained.

"That still does not tell me why you are approaching my mate," Zulien responded. "Speak."

"After Major Berslan's magnificent, engorged staff exploded its warm fluid deep within my quivering channel, he asked me to scan the ship for the Celestial. I told him her life gave no signal. He rose from the bed, and I watched as his sinewy muscles flexed when he communicated to the Makers that she was decayed." The Parina looked at Miranda. "You can decay and rebuild?"

"Leave us," Zulien ordered. When the Parina walked over to the men on the sofa, Zulien turned to Taliquant. "Have you ever known a Parina to ask questions like that?"

"No, but I guess if she was processing the cause for Berslan's passion she may have wanted to know if it was something she could use to seduce him again," Tali suggested.

"It never occurred to me he would use her to find Miranda. She must have reported to him that our rumor of her decay was true. Now she thinks that, like her, Miranda can be rebuilt. I hope she does not use my mate in sexual responses to arouse the men."

The Parina's hands were rubbing the swollen bulges in the junior officers' breeches. Tali chuckled. "It takes a while for them to adjust to having her always ready and willing."

The group went back to their discussion with Tempest about her primitive beginnings and what they thought Vallastera would be like. They had done some research and knew what the planet's basic physical attributes were. It had been uninhabited since the Battles of Chaos because it was so far out and had nothing of unique interest to the hierarchy.

In the evening, the Quibasta's communications were clearer, and the three ships journeying to Vallastera were able to align their navigation systems to track to the planet. The Quibasta confirmed that the planet's surface had been prepared with supplies and shelter for the travelers' arrival.

They rendezvoused with the battleship late the next morning. Zulien and Taliquant met the crew of the Quillant on the bridge. They wished the men luck, and even though the ship would maintain orbit within the planet's quadrant, it was an emotional goodbye.

"Commander Letang, I turn over the helm to you, sir." Zulien's voice cracked a little towards the end, as he glanced around the bridge that had been his world for so many years.

Letang shook his hand. "Thank you, Admiral. I can only hope to do as good a job as you did."

The mates decided to shuttle to the surface with the Celestial's group, and rejoin their families while they settled in. They knew the warriors would be distracted for a few days while they decided the strategy for best protecting the isolated world.

The shuttles began delivering the pilgrims to the surface. Miranda was delighted with the golden grass and unique, flowering trees. The temporary housing that had been constructed was comfortable and arranged around natural rocky outcrops.

Taliquant's father had the Isotant tow a barge of colorful shallistones that were brought to the surface to be distributed to the new citizens of Vallastera. The next few weeks were busy as they settled in.

Zulien and Taliquant discussed the courses for the three battleships with their commanders, and had a comfortable, protective arrangement shielding the planet. The Isotant traveled back to Garnella and Minocania to bring back excited researchers who wanted to join the citizenry of Vallastera.

The tall Garnellians would pace around the settlement, usually in heavy discussion with a Minoc whose antenna would be stroking its chin in concentration as they compared information. There were still frustratingly empty pockets of knowledge that were lost, but many threads of research were connected when the secretive learnings could finally be joined.

Ballion puffed with pride when he introduced his friends to Miranda, and she never failed to compliment him on his sensitivity and help with her procurement. Secretly, she loved to watch his antenna beat uncontrollably with emotion at her obvious affection, and she had made a game of it.

It seemed new people arrived daily, shuttling shelters to the surface and joining in the discussions of the true Old Religion. There was a palpable excitement throughout the citizenry.

Tempest was engrossed with the plant life, and with Terena's help she learned the names of various vegetation and herbs. She slowly began to figure out plants that were comparable to those she had used on her old planet. A collection of herbs was growing in colorful pots, and Miranda was relieved that Tempest had found a herb that seemed to be a cross between valerian root and chamomile, with the same calming affects when brewed. Now, it was a ritual for all the women to be sipping the tea in the evening, and it reminded Miranda how closely her actions were observed and duplicated.

The Garnellans were thrilled when Miranda asked if they would help build an altar. With Tempest's guidance, the stones were being placed. The Minocs questioned everything, and it seemed for every large, brooding procurer, a little lizard man was by his side. They made odd pairs, and their friendships caused Miranda to smile.

In the evening, Zulien would stand with her and gaze into space. "You must miss it terribly."

Miranda squeezed her warrior's hand. "I thought I would, but for some reason I am comfortable here. I know most of it is because of you, but it just feels right for me to be here."

Miranda was watching the moons, and remembered her vision. They were both crescents tonight, one filling as the other declined. She realized one would darken as the other grew, and knew that when the full moon was joined by the crescent, something was going to happen. Something big.

"Vesario is enroute. He should be here tomorrow," Zulien informed her.

"I wonder what's going on back there. It must be frustrating for him to work around the politicians."

"I think this is something he has been wanting for a long time. He was probably afraid it would not happen before his decay."

"I'm sure glad he is on our side," Miranda said as Zulien pulled her inside their apartment. She gazed up into his dark eyes and rested her fingers on his broad chest. "I feel such a sense of peace, Zulien."

"I know. I can feel it too." He leaned down and met her lips, ending their reflective musings.

Miranda felt her passion stirring. The strong feelings still amazed her whenever her mate touched her, and she wondered how her heart did not burst with love.

Zulien lowered her caftan to the floor, and she lay on the bed as he undressed. She studied the strength of his muscles as he approached, and the spasm of welcome from her scented the pallet. Zulien was already swollen with arousal, and the light from the shallistone by their bed glistened off the end of his shaft.

Miranda groaned and began trembling with anticipation of his touch. He lay down beside her, and her hands moved to his sex. One hand encircled him while with the other she gently ran her fingers over, under and around.

Zulien's mouth found her distended nipple and he sucked greedily. She shuddered as his teeth scraped across her sensitive nerves.

He rose over her and she spread her thighs willingly, needing him to fill her. As he plunged into her, she wrapped her legs around his hips and they began a slow, undulating grind into each other. His tempo increased, and Miranda's grip tightened on his shoulders, slipping occasionally on the sweat of his exertions.

She squeezed against his movements until they erupted, and her vision was of complete darkness followed by a blinding light. It held no meaning other than to make her anxious and fearful. Whatever it was, it was going to be bad.

The Magistrate of Battle arrived, and the admirals, their parents and the mates met him in Zulien's quarters.

"The Magistrate of Old Ways has dropped in commissioning. People have stopped going to his temples and are calling him a heretic. They are ignoring his threats of decay over abandoning his preachings. I did not realize how thin an influence he had. It is no wonder he sided with the Magistrate of Commerce to get to the Celestial."

"How are things sitting within the hierarchy?" Zibula asked.

"The Magistrates of Commerce, Building, Law and of course, Old Ways are demanding the Celestial be returned to Laquista, presumably to discredit her. All of them realize their precarious position. If Miranda returns the Old Religion, the Magistrates of Law and Building will be dismissed. She will bring back the true laws instead of his self-motivated decrees, and with her rebuilding the temples the Magistrate of Building will not be able to construct his monstrosities. Who knows what the people will do about the temples he has destroyed, and everything is tied into the Magistrate of Commerce's taxation and financial support. I think he is afraid he will be assassinated."

"What are their plans to convince the hierarchy to order her return?" Zulien was nervous about that much strength determined to obtain his mate.

"Those are the four Magistrates who have the most to lose. As allies, I have the Magistrate of Well Being, the Divider of Realms, Star Charts and Drafting, and thanks to Tempest, the Magistrate of Growing Things. He raised two levels in commissioning with Tempest's connection to the Ancient."

"Cool, I can't wait to meet him." Tempest was pleased to finally contribute something of her own, and Tali hugged her as she sat in his lap. The thoughts of tractors and shovels were replaced by beautiful robes and walks with the unknown Magistrate through gardens of flowers she would grow.

Zulien was pleased. "Our allies are strong, but what about the other three?"

"They are staying out of it. Whatever their beliefs, they just want to make sure they keep their commissions when the dust settles," Vesario explained. "The Magistrate of Well Being has drafted an edict that the citizens would be too upset if the Ancient was forcibly brought to Laquista. It is keeping things at a halt, until the Magistrates of the Divider of Realms and Star Charts and Drafting can declare the north inner worlds as its own hierarchy, with Vallastera the capitol."

"By the stars! They are trying to split the monarchy?" Zibula was stunned.

Vaserio nodded. "I think they might succeed, because a lot of the citizenry is behind them. They are tired of the taxation, and the data banks are flooded with requests about the Shatung Quadrant. People are already preparing to move to the northern planets as soon as the decision is made."

"What about our allies? They could lose their importance if the people leave their hierarchy," Zulien stated.

"They are not worried about it. Ultimately, they hope to see everything brought back to a single government with the Old Religion's teachings guiding everyone, and if they have to split it up until the other four Magistrates are discredited, they are willing to go that route." Vesario was pleased. He knew his allies would be protected by the Celestial because of their backing.

Miranda had begun fidgeting in Zulien's lap. Her teeth nibbled her lip, and he could tell she was upset. "Miranda, what is wrong, my mate?"

"If I am following what you're saying, you're trying to make me some kind of ruler of the Shatung Quadrant." Now, she was almost trembling.

"That is exactly what we are suggesting," Vesario smiled in triumph. "They will not be able to order you to do anything in your own worlds."

"If that's what happens, can I appoint our allies as part of my hierarchy? I don't want the responsibility of trying to re-build this civilization you're organizing. With your guidance, I would like to appoint a governing body that does not require me to be much more than a figurehead."

Vesario beamed. "Miranda, that is precisely

what I wanted to hear. I promised the allies I would allow you to suggest it, so they would know you were not manipulated into seeking their support. I cannot wait to see the expressions on the faces of the Magistrate enemies when they find they are left out. The raising of commissioning for our allies when they rule both governments will probably sway the three that are undecided. With their commissions lowered and their importance diminished, it will just be a matter of time before the other four are dissolved."

While the men discussed even more stringent protection for the Celestial, Miranda and Tempest wandered outside. Tempest began calling Miranda, 'your highness', and it was driving her crazy. "Please stop that. Cripes, I am nervous enough about all this. As soon as all this political junk is settled, I am going to figure out a way to get myself out of this mess."

"But, you're going to be like a queen for a bunch of planets. How cool is that?" Tempest danced around one of the altar stones.

"It's not so cool, Tempest. All of these people are going to be depending on my decisions. It's bad enough having everything I do turned into a ritual." Miranda was exasperated, and briefly flashed with fondness about her boring life in the cabin. She waved in recognition at a couple of women who had raised their teacups, showing her they were following the new ritual protocol. "Cripes," Miranda muttered.

The warriors stayed busy organizing the paths for the two additional protective battleships that were being left behind. If the hierarchy split was passed, and now it looked like more of a question of when, Miranda would have to be assassinated for the four excluded Magistrates to save anything of their power.

Miranda decided to sit by the altar while Tempest joined Terena in the garden they were planting. She saw the women discussing different plants, and she left the stone structure and wandered aimlessly towards the edge of the settlement, deep in thought.

"It is pretty here, Celestial."

Miranda turned to see a warrior leaning against the back of one of the buildings. "It is beautiful," she agreed. She studied the man's uniform. "Are you from the Quillant?" She did not remember seeing him before, and she was sure he was not one of the new officers.

"I used to be third officer," the friendly warrior informed her as he walked forward with his hand extended. Miranda was confused, and she tried to remember the warriors she had met.

"I feel your arousal and passion, Major Berslan. Allow me to fulfill your desires." Miranda gaped as the Pirana came into view. Berslan grabbed Miranda's arm and shoved a rag of strong smelling liquid over her face, and she faded into darkness.

"Shall I take care of your need?" the Parina purred.

"Stay, you stupid 'droid'."

Berslan had snuck onto the Quillant when it docked with the Quibista, and when he discovered the Celestial had already been shuttled on planet he made his way to a battle cruiser. In all the confusion of the shuttles and surfacing, no one noticed him leave. Unfortunately, he had not noticed the Parina on board waiting for a tryst with one of the junior officers.

She had been very helpful in locating the Celestial. Apparently, they had met, and her lifeforce was scanned into her data banks. He did not have the time or patience to deal with her seductions now. He needed to get the Celestial back to the hierarchy before she was discovered missing. He carried the small woman back to the cruiser, leaving the Parina disoriented with no one to guide her.

The Parina walked to the other side of the structure and located the wild haired woman she had seen with the Celestial. Maybe she could instruct her on how to get to Major Berslan and ease his arousal. Her data banks were almost smoking as they tried to assimilate the reason the Celestial caused such passion.

Tempest looked up as a hand brushed her shoulder. "What the hell are you doing here? You're not after my mate, are you?"

The Parina's eyes flashed, as she rationalized the question. "No, Admiral Taliquant is mated now and no longer requires my services to suck his mighty cock. Major Berslan's sack is heavy with arousal. His cock is in need of my wet sheath, and his passion fills with quivering lust from obtaining the Celestial. It bursts within him."

"What the hell? Did you say Major Berslan has Miranda?"

"Major Berslan is filled with heated need over obtaining the Celestial," the Parina confirmed.

Terena's face turned white and she screamed. "Zule, Tali! Hurry!"

The Parina repeated her seductive rantings, and Zulien yelled for his mate. His hand stroked absently over his heart. He knew she was gone.

The other warriors had joined the admirals, and Vesario said, "Where did he take her?"

"His swollen cock is readying to leave this planet without satisfying its passion." The Parina pointed to where Berslan had hidden the cruiser.

The warriors ran in the direction she pointed, and when they rounded the barge of shallistones they saw him loading the unconscious woman onto the cruiser.

Berslan had taken his time, not realizing the Parina would relay his actions. He had been thinking about the honor the pompous Magistrate would bestow on him for bringing the Ancient back to Laquista. As he leaned to place her on the floor of the shuttle, massive hands ripped him from the doorway.

Zulien punched him so hard that his nose crunched and tilted to the side. He hurried to his unconscious mate while Taliquant kept up the assault until Vesario and Zibula pulled him off the beaten man.

Zulien ran with Miranda in his arms and placed her on the sleeping pallet, while Terena, Zilana and Tempest tried to figure out how to help her. "Zulien, I smell dillint on her. We need a healer immediately," Zilana said. She had recognized the residual odor on Miranda's face. The powerful drug could kill the fragile woman if it was not neutralized.

Two guards held Berslan outside while Vesario and the other warriors entered the room. "Are you sure it is dillint, Zalana?"

"Yes, Vesario." Zalana's face had the unhealthy yellow cast of fear.

Vesario lifted his communicator. "How far off is the Quanza?"

"They are due to be in orbit in an hour, sir," was the distant reply.

"Tell them to speed up," he ordered. "I need the Magistrate of Well Being. The Celestial has been injured."

There was silence as the information was

absorbed, and then, "Yes, Magistrate. At top speed they can be here in fifteen minutes. I will tell them to prepare the Magistrate of Well Being's shuttle."

The group waited in agonizing silence as Miranda's breathing became shallow. Zulien was alternating between holding her hand and pacing angrily, wanting to kill Berslan.

"Zulien, you need to hold your mate. If she feels you close, it will help her until the healer arrives." Zalana guided him back over to Miranda.

The Magistrate of Well Being burst into the room. "What has happened?"

"It is dillint. Berslan was trying to kidnap her and bring her back to Laquista," Vesario informed him.

"As what? A decayed corpse?" The Magistrate threw his staff into the corner as he approached the pallet. "By the stars, she is so small. She would not have made it out of the quadrant." The big man knelt by Miranda's head. He laid his hand on her forehead and blew across her face.

He reached into his cloak and pulled out a vial, and then measured the blue liquid into a dropper. He looked at Miranda again, and put two drops back. "She is so small," he repeated in a whisper. He placed the drops in her mouth and, keeping one hand on her forehead, he placed the other on her stomach and closed his eyes. He envisioned the poison leaving her, and after a few seconds a green fog rose out of her body, dissipating quickly.

The Magistrate fell back. "Her will is strong. I have never felt such power." He looked up at the worried faces, and then at Zulien. "She will sleep for a while and be fine. The baby lives as well." He noted Zulien's shocked expression. "You did not know? Your mate is with child."

The Magistrate walked over to Tempest, who was shaking with relief in Tali's arms. "Your babies will be born close to the same time."

Tempest looked up in shock. "Are you telling me I'm knocked up?"

Her reply confused him. "I do not sense an injury. Were you hurt as well?"

"What? Oh no, I'm all right. Did you say I was pregnant?"

The Magistrate shook his head, bewildered. "Perhaps it is because you are a primitive that you were unaware of your condition."

Tempest rolled her eyes. "I wish people would stop calling me that." She smiled as she put her hand over Tali's where it rested on her stomach. "Cripes!"

Miranda slept safe in Zulien's arms until morning. He felt her stiffen as she awoke, and she sat bolt upright. "Zule!" she exclaimed.

"I am here. I have got you, Miranda. You are all right, my little Ancient."

Miranda settled back onto his chest. "That man..."

"We caught him, and Vesario is taking him back to Laquista. He is using his confession to discredit the Magistrate of Commerce. With the Magistrate of Well Being's signed statement that the drug he used would have killed you, they plan to bring them all up on assassination attempt charges. The Magistrate's daughter is still promised to Berslan, so he would not be able to separate himself from the treachery."

"I was so scared. As soon as I saw the Parina, I realized I had walked into a trap."

"Actually, the android saved you. Berslan left

her when he headed to the cruiser with you, and being on planet she had no warriors to serve. She was disoriented. The only man she could sense in need was Berslan, and he was with you. She found Tempest and asked her what she should do."

"I bet that was an interesting discussion," Miranda smiled.

Zulien chuckled. "It does take some patience to work through the innuendo to obtain the facts."

"I guess I should thank her." Miranda's brow furrowed.

"She is back on ship, happily servicing her three officers. To her, being of service is her reward," Zulien explained. "Did you know you are with child?"

Miranda looked up at him. "How did you find out?"

"When the Magistrate of Well Being healed you, he told us the baby was all right. Why did you not tell me?"

"Because I was afraid you would not let me out of your sight so you could do your job," she admitted.

"You are right. I intend to keep you beside me. If you had been with me, Berslan could not have made his attempt on you."

"Or he would have killed you, knowing it would be the only way to get to me," she rationalized.

There was a knock on the door, and Tempest called, "Is she awake yet?"

"Come on in, Tempest. I'm fine," Miranda answered.

Tempest walked in with Tali on her heels, bursting with pride. "My mate is with child." He had been announcing it to everyone.

Tempest rolled her eyes. "It's official. Everyone on this planet and on all three battleships knows now." She smiled at Miranda. "You too, huh?"

Miranda nodded. "That was some joining."

Zibula appeared at the open door and came in. "Vesario is already entering Laquista air space. They must have been on full throttle the whole way back."

Another large man came in, and Miranda recognized the cloak and staff of a Magistrate. "How are you feeling, Miranda? You gave us quite a scare."

"I feel fine. Are you the one who healed me?"

"Yes, I am Feriston, the Magistrate of Well Being. It is so good to finally meet you. You continue to cause excitement, for one so fragile," he chuckled.

"Well, I hope the excitement stops soon. I am reeling with all the changes."

"It will. The Magistrate of The Unexplained joined our alliance when he heard of the assassination attempt. We are expecting the other two will announce their intentions as soon as the formal charges are drafted. The indecisive idiots are still waiting to see how many people are supporting us." The Magistrate shrugged.

"What happens then?" Miranda asked.

"Our allies will insist on space decay for the parties involved. The Magistrate of Law is in charge of the proceedings and will argue against it. I do not see how he can get around it, though. He is the one that drafted the law. When he did it, he was afraid of an attempt on his own life, and he figured the strong penalty would make whoever was after him second-guess his decision. Now, he is stuck with using it on his ally." The

Magistrate smiled. "Hopefully, they will tie his insipid daughter into the plan because she was Berslan's promised mate."

Tempest spoke up. "What, exactly, is space decay?"

Tali kissed her forehead. "You are with child and should not concern yourself with such things."

"Do not patronize me, big guy. What the heck is it?"

Zulien sighed. He held Miranda tighter, instinctively knowing the explanation would unsettle her. "If they are convicted, they are taken to the border of the outer worlds and released in shariver suits. It is left to the gods whether or not they make it to a habitable planet before their air supply and fuel are exhausted."

"That's horrible," Miranda gasped. "Zulien, I can't let that happen. Please, stop it. These people are only trying to protect their way of life."

"Miranda, I have no control over what the audition decides."

Miranda thought for a minute. "Have they split the hierarchies yet?"

"No, it takes time to draft the borders and get them agreed upon."

Miranda struggled out of Zulien's arms. She stood in front of the Magistrate of Well Being and looked up at him. "Magistrate, I refuse to press charges. I will not be a part of this. You say that everyone is pleased I've been found so peace can once again rule, and yet the first audition concerning me will result in three deaths."

"Miranda, it is the way this is done. The laws will slowly change as the support shifts," the Magistrate explained.

"If this sentence is carried out, I will not

perform any rituals or relay any visions. It would be hypocrisy to say I am to return the Old Religion on the backs of three murders."

Zulien whispered, "Miranda, the hierarchy..."

"No, Zule. You may as well return me to the outer worlds. I promise I will be useless to you." Miranda's lip quivered with her statement.

Zulien was stunned into silence, and the rest of the people in the room were just as shocked. "We have waited centuries for an Ancient." Zalana's eyes were filling.

"You've created a civilization that thrives on clawing up the backs of others, and with all your advancements you are no more civilized than the primitive outer world you procured me from." There was true sadness in Miranda's voice. "If these people die because of me, there will be no cleansing ritual that could ever bring me balance. Whether or not I wanted to continue to help you re-build, the power would be lost to me." She sat on the sleeping pallet and stared at the floor.

Zibula quickly communicated to Vesario to stay in orbit and not transport Berslan on planet. He told him what the Celestial said. "Vesario wants to know what you want us to do, Miranda."

She was quiet for a minute, and then looked up at her father-in-law. "Ask the Magistrate to bring Berslan back here. Even without an audition, he would be assassinated on Laquista to protect the people who ordered him to do this."

"Miranda, he has tried to kill you twice. You cannot bring him back to Vallastera," Zibula declared.

"It's the only way I know that I can ensure he will not be murdered because of me," she explained.

"The only reason I did not murder him was because I knew they would order it on Laquista, and perhaps round up his conspirators as well." Zulien was clearly agitated at the thought of his mate's attempted assassin returning.

"Do any of you really think he meant to kill me?" Miranda asked.

"But, the dillint..." Zalana began.

"Berslan is no herbalist, Zalana. He is a warrior. If he meant to kill me, he could have strangled me or used a knife. I believe he meant to bring me to Laquista, based on whatever lies and promises they made him. Whoever gave him the drug to use on me and told him it was harmless is the one responsible," Miranda reasoned.

"All of you have been so surprised at his actions, because he was an honorable warrior alongside of you for centuries. I, for one, do not believe he is beyond redemption. Instead of thinking the worst of the man, suppose he was told I would be honored and celebrated on Laquista, and that is what he thought he was returning me to. They may have made it sound a heck of a lot better for me than being evicted to some uninhabited world on the edge of the hierarchy with a handful of warriors and family to protect me."

Miranda continued, "Do not misunderstand me. I love being with you here. I am just saying, that if this is what they led Berslan to believe, his actions were not totally without merit. Zulien, you backed him into a corner, forcing him to trust them when you stripped away his commission. It was the only honorable thing he had to hold onto."

Zulien was frustrated and angry. "Why do you support this theory that he acted with honor instead of self-righteous gain?"

Miranda smiled. "Because of the Parina. She

is an android and cannot devise political motivations."

"The Parina? What does she have to do with it?" Feriston asked.

The Magistrate remained silent, digesting all the Celestial had been saying.

"The Parina said that every thought Berslan had concerning the Celestial brought him passion and desire. Berslan likes me. He has been the unwitting agent of these people. If you interview him yourself and tell him what the drug he had used could have done, I think you would be very surprised at his reaction. No one from either side has included him in any conversations of what the hierarchy really wants me for, and now he's only getting the information they want him to hear."

Zulien silently dropped into a chair. What Miranda said was true. They had carefully hidden their suspicions from Berslan because they thought he had been working with the Magistrate of Commerce with full knowledge of their enemies' plans. Perhaps, he did not know. The only thing of which he would be guilty was trying to take the Celestial to a place they told him was safer and where she could receive the tribute she deserved. Obviously, he would benefit from her acquisition, but not from her death.

Miranda knelt down by her mate. "Do you see why I can not abide by his murder, Zule? Bring him back here. Help your friend regain his pride. I think you will discover he is not nearly as committed to the people who have been advising him once he learns they were using him to kill me."

The Magistrate of Well Being was already communicating with Vesario. "Miranda, they are returning Berslan to Vallastera. We would like to place one condition."

"What is it?"

"We want you to ask him where he got the drug. It is the only way we can prove our enemies meant to have you killed, and we need to get the hierarchy straightened out," he explained.

"I have a condition of my own. If I obtain the names of the people involved, instead of space decay I want them sent to an uninhabited planet with enough supplies to survive, but where they can no longer be a threat."

"I can suggest to the Magistrate of Law that he give them the choice of their fates. Of course, that is depending on whether or not he gets implicated in this mess too. Enough of our allies will understand your request to push it through," Feriston replied. "You look tired, Celestial. The ship will not get back until tomorrow. Rest with your mate. You carry an Ancient gene, and we do not need additional risks to your pregnancy."

Everyone left the room, leaving Zulien alone with Miranda. "I do not understand your compassion for a man who almost killed you. Even if it was unintentional, do you not feel any anger towards him?"

"I am angry with the people that made him their puppet. From what I can tell, they have taken an honorable man and disgraced him," she replied. "Zule, when he gets back here, please give him a chance to explain his motives. Remember your history with him."

Zulien hugged her. "For you, Miranda, I will try." He led her to their sleeping pallet, and they lay together his hand on her stomach as he rubbed across it gently. "By the stars, Miranda, I am to be a father."

His light touch inflamed her, and she ran her fingers across his golden chest. Her nipples peaked and she leaned into him as his lips met hers, and her hands wound in his long hair as she held him close to her. She was already pulsing with need for her warrior.

Zulien pulled up and knelt between her thighs. He tried to enter her slowly, still awed by the thought of their child within her. Miranda wrapped her legs around him and pulled him deeper, forcing the motion she craved. The warrior lost himself in passion and plunged them to their climax.

Miranda smiled in the wonder of her vision. In the morning, it was Tempest she relayed it to, and she told her friend to keep it to herself, not wanting her to be a target for the hierarchy as well.

CHAPTER XI

Berslan was flanked by two warriors and by the Magistrate of Battle when they shuttled to the planet, and he was held in Taliquant's quarters until he was called for.

Miranda had asked the Quillant to send the Parina to the surface. They thought it a most unusual request. She assured them the android would be returned quickly.

The Parina was led into Zulien's quarters, where the Admirals Vesario, Zibula and Feriston waited with the Celestial. As soon as the Parina entered the room, she approached Miranda. "You are the Celestial. You are the Commander's mate. Thought of you fills the warriors with desire, and their sacks fill with need," she purred.

"Why is that important to you?" Miranda asked.

The Parina's eyes flashed as the data was confirmed and the proper answer to the request deciphered. "My purpose is to serve the manly cocks of the warriors, and I am to encourage the filling of their sack with desire. My processors relayed two of the warriors' passion to be driven with thoughts of the Celestial, and I am unsure how to integrate this desire into my programming," the Parina responded.

"You're trying to figure out how to duplicate the warriors' response to me?" Miranda asked.

The Parina's data flashed for over a minute. "I have been designed to incorporate any seduction that brings the warrior pleasure. There is no data on why thoughts of the Celestial brings the warriors to lusty need, and I have scanned their aroused response and can decipher no physical contact with the Celestial to drive this passion and encourage their cocks to swell."

Zulien replied nervously, "When Berslan thinks of the Celestial, his feelings of passion are like mine?" The thought of Berslan using a vision of his mate to become aroused was unsettling. "What would he say?"

"Major Berslan's mighty cock fills with great need when he envisions the Celestial, and he has said the Celestial would save them all. I could not decipher what danger the Major was in that he should need to be saved. I sensed no fear in his life force. He was filled with overwhelming joy, and spilled mightily when I stroked gently on his bloated sack. I seek knowledge of the Celestial so I can bring this desire to all I serve," the Parina finished.

"See? Berslan thought of me as someone to help. He did not want to see me harmed," Miranda concluded.

The Parina began speaking again. "You are the Celestial. What is it you do to cause the Commander's mighty cock to fairly burst with..."

"Voice off, dammit," Zulien muttered.

"Tali, is there a recorder or transmitter in your quarters?" Miranda asked.

"No, but we have a portable viewer," he answered.

"Can you get it?" Miranda walked over to Zulien. "I want to meet with Berslan alone, Zule."

He began to interrupt, terrified of the potential danger.

"Zulien, he is not going to hurt me, and I will let him know you are all watching. I think, after fear of you, humiliation for his actions stands a close second. He is never going to speak with warriors in the room. Please, I know I am right about him."

"I do not like this, Miranda. He could snap your neck in an instant."

"To what gain? He's had the opportunity to do that and has chosen not to. Besides," she grinned, "he knows you would kill him. If he hurts me, the hierarchy will not claim him, so what is the possible benefit to him?" Miranda asked.

They all had to reluctantly admit she was right. Tali retrieved the communicator and handed it to Zulien, and they walked to Taliquant's quarters. The warriors guarding the door stood at alert as Zulien and the Celestial entered the room. Zule placed the recorder, glared at Berslan, and left.

Miranda looked at the shadow of the man sitting at the table. The big warrior folded in on himself, with his head on the table and his hands clasped behind it.

"Berslan?" Miranda said softly.

The man looked up with his bruised and broken nose and blackened eyes. The warriors had beaten him severely when he had abducted her. "Oh, goddess," she exclaimed. She hurried to the side cart and brought him some juice.

He tried to smile, and lifted the glass in his shaking hands. "Thank you, Celestial," he rasped. His eyes filled, "I am so sorry."

"What are you sorry for, Berslan?"

"I am sorry for trying to take you from your mate. They told me he would join you as soon as suitable quarters were arranged," he replied miserably.

"The Magistrates told you my mate would be joining me on Laquista?"

"Of course. Mates are not separated. Your procurement was a surprise. The Magistrate was truly speechless when I told him, and then, when they learned three Debayluth crafts had already made an attempt on you, they knew a single battleship could not protect you. The Magistrates met, and concluded the Commander was thinking only of claiming his mate and his thoughts were irrationally compromised by your procurement. I was so upset when I heard you had decayed, and when I reported to my betrothed that you were being transferred to Shallistar for mourning, she convinced me to put off our own ceremony so you could be mourned publicly within the hierarchy.

"When the Commander decommissioned me, my heart ached for his loss. He asked why I aided the hierarchy in transporting you to Laquista, and I could not let his judgment be in question over his mourning over you. I told him it was because he chose Taliquant for second. Tali was offered his own ship more than a century ago, and I know I am no candidate for commander, Celestial. I was a good warrior, but my strength is in support and defense. It is why my failure in acquiring you, to defend you while the Commander was disoriented about your procurement, is such a disaster."

"Berslan, obviously I am not decayed. Why did you try to take me from Vallastera?" Miranda asked.

"Celestial, you have the ability to bring back our Old Religion. To sequester you on an outer planet under the guise of keeping you safe, is ridiculous. You are open to attack from anyone out here... and too far for the hierarchy to get defense to you. The Magistrates realize Commander Zulien is now working without benefit of my defense guidance, and I have heard talk that he does not wish you to share your knowledge. He has, perhaps, become a possessive mate who desires to keep you to himself. The Magistrates know you are unfamiliar with our ways, and the mating gene may keep you from seeing Zulien's misjudgment. Once they had you safely on Laquista in apartments suitable for your station, they were going to convince Zulien of their wisdom and have him join you."

"So you kidnapped me?"

"I certainly misjudged the Commander's desire to keep you to himself." Berslan managed a grin, as he rubbed his chin. "He is obviously still in joining passion."

"Berslan, what did you drug me with?" Miranda put her hand on his.

Berslan shrugged. "Something Sharpina gave me. She said she uses a small amount for aching head, and that if I coated the rag you would sleep peacefully and wake refreshed when we reached Laquista."

Miranda decided to drop the bombshell, and see his reaction. "It was dillint."

The battered man looked confused. "What?"

"You drugged me with dillint, and I almost died before a healer arrived," Miranda continued to watch him.

He shook his head and looked at her with confusion clearly showing in his eyes. "No. Celestial, it was Sharpina's medicine." Berslan saw the truth in her sad expression, and he paled as his eyes began to fill. "Please, Celestial, it was Sharpina's medicine. She gave it to me herself. Who told you this?"

"I am sorry, Berslan, it was dillint. The Magistrate of Well Being was transported here to save me, and he said I would have been dead before we made it out of the quadrant."

Berslan's tears were flowing, and he whispered, "They think I was trying to kill you, and that is why they have been so cruel."

"Berslan, was Sharpina speaking with her father when she gave you the medicine?" Miranda pressed.

"Yes, he went back to her compartments with the Magistrate of Law to retrieve it. The Magistrate of Building and Magistrate of Old Ways were telling me how you were to be honored on Laquista, and how important it was to all citizens to bring you back quickly. They arranged for my transport aboard the Magistrate of Battle's ship. I was only working in the loading dock, but still I was on a war ship."

"The Magistrate of Battle was unaware you were on board," Miranda informed him.

"Oh no, Celestial, the Magistrate of Law said he was handling the paperwork personally. He said he knew I would be uncomfortable with my recent decommissioning and did not want me to be embarrassed, so he had them position me in the hold."

Miranda could see the anxiety in Berslan's eyes as he began to understand he had been used. "It was dillint," he whispered, and he covered his face. "I almost killed you." It took him a moment to compose himself, and then he raised his head and mustered as much pride as he could manage. "Celestial, I swear to you, I did not know that was the drug I was given to use. Nevertheless, I accept responsibility for my actions and await your decision. I am grateful my despicable act did not succeed."

Miranda turned to the portable communicator. "Zulien, why don't you and the Magistrates join us?"

Berslan steadied his jaw in resignation. Zulien would certainly want to tear him apart again, knowing his mate almost died, and the

Magistrates would transport him back to Laquista in disgrace for attempting to assassinate the Celestial Ancient. There, undoubtedly, they would sentence him to space decay. He certainly did not expect the reception he received.

The Magistrate of Well Being walked up and held his jaw as he pulled a vial from his cloak. "Open." Berslan was slightly nervous that they intended to circumvent his return to Laquista for audition and were going to poison him there and then. He rationalized it would probably be quicker than space decay, and opened his mouth. The medicine was dispensed, and the Magistrate put his hands on either side of the tilted nose and snapped it back. Miranda watched in amazement as cuts and bruises healed within minutes.

Zulien stood against the wall with his arms folded across his chest while the Magistrate worked, and then he spoke up. "Berslan, who are the Magistrates that convinced you my mate needed to be returned to Laquista?"

"Commander, I am so sorry. I never sensed the treachery."

"Who were they?"

"The Magistrates of Commerce, Law, Building and Old Ways. They told me they wanted to keep her safe and honor her," he replied miserably. He squinted his eyes in concentration. "Commander, I have copies of my transmissions with them."

"What?"

"My communications on the Quillant, I automatically record them all. I began doing it after the battle in Starquist Two. Remember? We were audited for being out of position. I knew we were not, but I could not prove our orders, so after that I have had my communications automatically recorded."

Zulien ordered the transcripts downloaded to

the portable communicator from the Quillant, and the Magistrates listened as Berslan was coerced into believing he was acting in the Celestial's best interest for the hierarchy. Berslan began shaking his head sadly, as he now understood how they had used him.

"Commander, there is no punishment harsh enough for how badly I have discredited myself, abused my position, and most of all, dishonored you and your mate. Magistrates, I will not argue the audition on Laquista. I am ready to face charges."

The Magistrate of Battle rubbed his chin in contemplation. "Berslan, from what I gather, everything you did was under orders of the hierarchy. You made no decisions to engage in this duplicity on your own. Zulien?"

"Naturally, I am upset about the treatment of my mate and that you would question my rationality, even in mating procurement. I have to agree, Vaserio, Berslan meant no threat."

"We can use these tapes, and we finally have direct implication concerning the Debayluth attacks."

"How?" Zulien asked.

"Because they ordered her retrieval before the attacks were reported, and Berslan did not even mention them until after the Magistrate did. The Quistar had not logged in for the boon, so the only way the Magistrates could have told Berslan to collect her to protect her from future attacks was because they had ordered the attacks," Vesario concluded.

Berslan's eyes widened. "By the stars, they have meant for the Ancient to be destroyed from the beginning?" It was obvious he had absolutely no knowledge of the hierarchy's true designs for Miranda.

"Don't expect me to apologize for knocking you out for what you did to my mate, Berslan." Zulien's eyes pierced him, and then he smiled. "I am relieved to know you are still a loyal warrior."

Berslan looked at him in disbelief as Zulien continued, "Vesario, I would like Berslan re-commissioned. I think his defense strategy will complete the protection on planet we need for the Celestial, and he will, of course, be made available for any auditions."

Two strange transmissions were received in the afternoon while Berslan was shown the on planet operations station and given quarters. He was resting when his communication band buzzed, and he looked at the incoming transmission. "By the stars," he whispered, and went in search of Zulien.

"Admiral, they do not know," he blurted.

"What are you talking about?" Zulien was in the station, studying the star charts with Vesario.

"The Magistrates, they do not know what has happened. I just received an incoming message from Sharpina, and she wants to know when I am arriving with the Celestial. Her father wants to know if Miranda is well," Berslan informed them.

Feriston walked in on the discussion. "I think we can use this, Vesario."

The men sat down, and Berslan helped them organize their plan. "I know this will work. I wonder why the Magistrate of the Unexplained did not tell them I had failed?"

Feriston walked outside and lifted his communication band. He returned a few minutes later, smiling. "Ah, the intrigue. It seems our formerly uncommitted Magistrates have been organizing their own tryst to help, and they have been supporting us all along. They decided not to announce their allegiance so they could keep an undetected eye on our enemies while we have been busy planning," he chuckled.

"They did not know about Berslan's actions until we told them, and they decided they needed someone closer to our enemies to keep us informed. The Magistrate of Acquisitions is pretending to grumble to them about not being included in the habitation of the north planets, and he is making it seem he is being swayed to their side. He intends to become involved with them and warn us if there is going to be another attempt on the Celestial."

"I've confirmed this with the Magistrate of the Divider of Realms. He says all three have signed the edict to separate the hierarchy, but made him promise to keep the knowledge secret. I would not believe the Magistrate of Knowledge could be so devious. We had drinks two nights ago, and he let me go on for hours trying to convince him to join us." Feriston shook his head, smiling at the duplicity.

An incoming transmission from the main communication terminal caught their attention. A nasal whine was heard. "I would like to speak with Commander Zulien."

"By the stars, how did the Debayluths get our bandwidth?" Zulien stalked over to the terminal. "Who is this?" he demanded.

"This is Commander Geershane. I wish to speak with Commander Zulien," came the nasal reply.

"This is Admiral Zulien." He grinned back at the men at the table. "What do you want?"

There was a pause. "Congratulations on your promotion, Admiral. I ask your indulgence for a moment."

"I owe you nothing, Commander. Three of your ships tried to destroy my ship and murder my mate," Zulien replied angrily.

"I work with a greedy lot, Admiral. The three ships did not communicate their intentions when the hierarchy contacted them. I believe their hope was to complete their mission and raise their standing," the Debayluth replied.

"You admit the hierarchy ordered the attack?" Zulien looked at his friends, confused by the confession.

"Admiral, I can send you the communication. It was transmitted as a general request to all our ships in the quadrant at the time. Luckily, the other four ships that received it thought it might be a trap and contacted our leader before they agreed."

Zulien paled. If the other four ships had joined in the battle, it could have been a disaster. "Vesario, why do you think he ordered the other four ships not to proceed?"

Berslan interrupted, "I do not think they want the Ancient destroyed. Zulien, I think you should hear him out. If he is really willing to send the communication from the hierarchy, the way they duped me is almost minor."

Zulien turned back to transmit. "Why did you not order the other four ships to engage?"

"We have no allegiance to the hierarchy. We are the last to hold out against them since the Battles of Chaos." The Debayluth paused. "Admiral, is it true? Has an Ancient finally come back to us? Please, Admiral, we have struggled for centuries and been labeled the lowest vermin in the inner worlds because we refuse to submit to the new ways. You owe us nothing, we are aware of that, but it would be an act of compassion to let us know our commitment has not been in vain."

All the warriors in the room were stunned

into silence.

"Admiral, please, let us know if the Old Religion is to come back to us." The Commander was almost begging for the news.

Vesario nodded and whispered, "Zulien, if he is willing to give us those tapes, and truly stopped four ships from engaging... we never have understood why the Debayluths chose to become marauders. If they considered themselves the last to remain faithful to the Old Religion, they are perhaps more honorable than the rest of us have been."

Zulien cleared his throat. "Commander, my mate is an Atlantian Priestess."

Before he could continue, the warriors could hear loud cheers erupting through the speakers. The Debayluths were clearly overjoyed with the news, and it was several minutes before they quieted enough for their Commander to continue. "Admiral, we would like to meet with an allied Magistrate. Those of us who have committed crimes will stand audition, but we would like our citizens who have been in hiding for so long to be able to integrate back into the worlds and practice our beliefs in the open once again."

"Zulien, we have seven battleships in the area. Perhaps we should have the Commander shuttle to Vallaserio, if he allows his ship to be surrounded and boarded before they are in orbit," Vesario suggested. "If he is willing to take that kind of chance, I would like to hear him out."

Zulien suggested Vesario's idea, and they were surprised at how quickly the Debayluth Commander agreed. "Admiral, may I bring my mate to the surface? She will have me space decayed if I deny her a chance to see the Ancient."

Zulien chuckled. "Yes, Commander, no harm

will come to her."

While they waited for news from the Quillant that the Debayluth vessel had arrived and was secured, the warriors discussed the unexpected turn of events. "How come we did not know that was what all their bickering had been about?" Zulien asked.

"It is strange. They cannot wait to divulge battle strategy, yet manage to keep their true designs hidden for centuries. I guess over the years we were responsible for turning them into pirates."

Berslan's band buzzed again. "Admiral, I am going to have to transmit something to her. Perhaps I should tell her the Celestial is declining, and I will have to communicate later? She will probably welcome the news."

It was agreed, and the warriors remained silent as Sharpina cooed, "Oh Berslan, I hope she will be all right. You know father expects you to return her to Laquista safely."

Berslan rolled his eyes at her mock concern. "Yes, my betrothed. It will be nice to have this business concluded so we can finally be joined."

There was a long pause before Sharpina's voice was heard. "Of course, we will have to wait until all the ceremonies honoring the ancient have concluded." She quickly signed off.

"You know, I do not think my betrothed is as dedicated to our joining as I thought she was," Berslan frowned, and the warriors laughed.

Miranda walked into the room with Ethram. He had been discussing his ability to cloak. The warriors informed them of what was happening. "Those poor people. Centuries of letting themselves be considered the worst of civilizations just so they could protect their beliefs," Miranda commiserated.

"It still does not lessen the fact that three of their ships tried to destroy you," Ethram reminded them.

"Have they sent the hierarchy plea?" Vesario asked.

Berslan checked their data. "Yes, sir. Would you like me to play it?"

Vesario rubbed his hands together and nodded.

The tape began, "This is a Magistrate of the hierarchy. I have a commission for the Debayluth warriors."

"It sounds like he has dealt with them before. How else would he know their communication channel?" Berslan queried.

Next came the whiney reply of a Debayluth. "Magistrate, this is Commander Helixer on the battleship Dishton. Go ahead."

"Commander, this is the Magistrate of Commerce. It has come to our attention that the battleship Quillant is due to rendezvous and procure an Ancient who holds the gene for those responsible for the destruction of the Old Religion."

"Has this been verified?"

"Yes, Commander, we have the communication from the Procurement Ship Isotant. They managed to locate her in the outer worlds. No wonder these enemies have remained unnoticed. The hierarchy has learned the Garnellan's have been secretly searching for them during procurements."

"The cloakers! You have told us for years they were not to be trusted."

Ethram was red with anger. "Those despicable dremonts. This explains why the Debayluths have singled out our procurement vessels."

The Debayluth continued, "I have two other ships that will engage to destroy the threat, and one is already within tracking distance of the Quillant. You will of course offer boon?"

"The Magistrate of Law has agreed to look the other way as to the destruction of the Quillant, and the Magistrates of Building and Old Ways have agreed to the boon. This threat to our worlds must be stopped."

"Why do you not engage your own ships?" the whiney voice questioned.

"The Magistrate of Battle holds a lesser commissioned position, as you know, and we are not entirely sure he can be trusted. It is one of his Commanders the ancient enemy is to mate with. It is possible that whole commissioning is corrupt."

Now Vesario exploded. "How dare he question my loyalties!"

The rest of the communication outlined the plan and the payment arrangements. After the Debayluth failure, two more communications were posted from the Magistrate to the pirates that went unanswered.

"I apologize, Admiral Zulien," Ethram said. "The hierarchy must have heard our original hailing to you on the open line."

"There is no way you could have known this would be their reaction, Ethram," Zulien replied. "Vesario, by the Debayluths' own transmission, they thought the Celestial was an enemy Ancient. The Magistrates are responsible for the destruction of the three ships under a misinformed allegiance."

"And the Magistrate of Commerce directly implicated the other three Magistrates," Vesario noted.

"If they have caught any of our recent transmissions, they are liable to try to run to where they think their riches have been stashed," Zulien suggested.

Vesario swept his arm around the room. "Where do you think the financing for all this has been coming from? Our enemies were also kind enough to pay those large procurement boons for Miranda and Tempest."

Everyone laughed over the thought that their enemies' 'secured' wealth had supported the entire move, and Miranda shook her head in amazement. "No wonder the hierarchy is so messed up."

Word was sent that the Debayluth shuttle was on its way to the surface. Zulien had to get Letang to repeat it twice because of all the noise. "Where in Dremonia are you, Letang?"

"I transported with the warriors to secure the Debayluth battleship. Admiral, you have never seen such a celebration. They had all their sidearms locked in the hold before we had docked. Even for Debayluths they are going nuts up here, and they are pestering us for information about the Celestial. Are we allowed to talk about her?"

"It sounds like you had better say something, or you will all be going back to the Quillant with aching heads," Zulien laughed.

The shuttle arrived and everyone walked out to greet them. Zulien suggested Miranda remain hidden until they were positive it was not an elaborate trap.

"Don't be ridiculous, Zulien. You said yourself they are not any good at subterfuge. If these poor people have been hiding for centuries, I am not going to put them through that." She whisked by him to greet the Commander.

When Miranda thought of warriors, she always thought of the big men like the Shallistarians. What exited the ship was a little man who only came up to her waist. His skin was light pink; he had golden eyes surrounded by light blue hair, and his mate was an even smaller version of him. "They are quite colorful," Miranda noted. To think, these tiny people had been waging war for centuries against the hierarchy.

The Commander expected to be shackled by Zulien as soon as he left the shuttle. Instead, he faced two warriors and two Magistrates who stood back as a golden vision moved towards him with her hand extended. "Commander, I am Miranda. It is so very nice to meet you."

His hand slowly raised to take hers, and his eyes never left her face. He was speechless, and Miranda turned to his mate. The woman, equally stunned into silence, had trails of tears wetting her pink cheeks, and Miranda knelt down and hugged her. "I can not imagine the sacrifice you have had to endure."

There was absolutely no question as to the Debayluths' dedication. The warriors and Commander retired to the operations station for long discussions, and Miranda showed Letana the settlement. They spent a long time sitting by the altar drinking tea.

Tempest was fascinated by the small woman and led her through the gardens. They invited her to the cleansing ritual in two days, and Letana was ecstatic and asked if her best friend could watch.

"I think the more people who see the rituals, the quicker they can be remembered and spread. It's a real kick, and I think you're going to enjoy it."

A plan was in place to collect the wayward

Magistrates, and Berslan called Sharpina. "The celestial continues to decline, so I am surfacing on Rentang."

"What the dremont for? Bring her back here," Sharpina ordered, irritation clearly edging her shrewish voice.

The Magistrate of Commerce came on line. "Berslan, Rentang is uninhabited and there is no way to help her there. Bring her to Laquista so we can have the Magistrate of Well Being tend to her. He has already been advised of her condition."

Feriston raised his eyebrow and muttered, "Dremont."

"I am sorry, Magistrate, but I cannot concentrate on operating the ship with the Celestial in such a state. I am already shuttling to surface. Perhaps you can meet me here? Oh, I do not know what to do," Berslan replied in a bemoaning tone.

"Bring her to Laquista," the Magistrate thundered.

"Oh, I think her breathing is even shallower. I will see you here." Berslan signed off. There was immediate buzzing of his communicator, which they ignored.

Zulien looked at the Debayluth Commander. "Everything is set?"

"Yes, Admiral. I really am surprised you never suspected us on Rentang. It is so close to Laquista, and has been our major planet for centuries," he smiled. "We have coordinated Major Berslan's communication wave to the Commander on the surface, so we will not even have to look for them when they land. They will come to us. We are in agreement that some of the royal guard may be sacrificed?"

"Yes, Commander, it cannot be helped. Just

make sure your warriors do not injure the Magistrates before they are shuttled to Vallastera," Zulien reminded him.

The group had a leisurely dinner, and several shuttles traveled back and forth to the Debayluth battleship so that more of their citizens could meet Miranda. She was exhausted, and finally had to excuse herself to lie down.

Zulien joined her in their quarters and he held her in his arms as she quickly fell asleep. "My poor little Ancient. I hope things settle down for us soon. This business has been tiring for both of us," he whispered.

Miranda woke in the morning extremely nervous about finally seeing the people who wanted her dead. "Remember, Zulien, you promised me they would not be killed."

Letana walked over and took her hand. "They will live in exile on Rentang. We have given our word they will not be harmed. Their lives of ill-gained luxury will end, however. They will live out their days in the primitive life we have endured. For us, it is quite comfortable, but after golden domed buildings and matching trappings, they might not see the beauty and enjoy our caves on the dark side of the planet."

The shuttle landed, and to everyone's surprise all the Magistrates exited with their mates and a shrieking Sharpina in tow. She pulled herself from the grasp of the warrior holding her and stormed up to Berslan. "How dare you allow your betrothed to be handled this way!"

Berslan looked down, shuffled his feet for a moment, and then he looked at the shrew. "Sharpina, about the joining. I do not think it is going to work out. I am afraid I am going to have to release you from our commitment."

Her mouth fell open, and her head slowly swiveled as she finally began to observe her surroundings. Only three Magistrates and their mates stood with her father. The rest were smiling and shaking hands with a golden haired woman. Sharpina narrowed her eyes, realizing this was the Celestial who had caused so much trouble. She also realized her precarious position if she did not change alliances pretty quick.

"Berslan, surely you do not mean that," she purred, and she waltzed over to Miranda. "I am Sharpina. It is so good to finally meet you. I was so upset to hear the problems my father has caused you. It truly aches my head. Thank goodness you are well."

Miranda smiled. "Thank you, Sharpina, and as for your aching head, you're in luck. Berslan was kind enough to hand me your medicine, so now you can relieve that ache." Miranda held up the vial containing the remaining dillint. "Here you are, dear. Drink up, and I am sure you will feel better in no time."

Sharpina backed away in horror. "Do not come near me with that," she cried.

"Why, one would think you knew what was in this little bottle. I must agree with the Major. The two of you are completely unsuited for each other. Perhaps you will find a mate on Rentang?"

"Rentang? My apartments are on Laquista," Sharpina huffed.

"No, dear. I have been kind enough to suggest you be moved to Rentang... in lieu of space decay," she added.

Sharpina stumbled back to her father screeching, "What have you done to me?"

He was not listening. All the Magistrates heard Miranda's decree, and when Terena read the charges and evidence stacked against them, verbatim from testimony and tapes, they knew they either had to accept her compassionate sentence of exile or face their own penalty of space decay.

The alliance spent the afternoon in heavy discussion about the new hierarchy. Miranda sat through endless hours of arguments, as everyone agreed they had to abide by the Ancient's decision. She wearily stood up. "I've heard enough. I will return with my pronouncement in an hour." Tempest found her sitting in the altar clearing.

"How is the new altar going?" Miranda asked.

"It will be ready for tomorrow night. Cripes, I can't believe I thought it would be cool for you to be a ruler. With everybody trying to promote their agenda, how are you going to decide?" Tempest hugged her friend.

"I already know what I am going to do. I just figured it might make it easier for them to accept if they think I really deliberated over it," Miranda sighed.

"What? Will it get you out of this mess?"

"It will take care of most of it. Come on, let's get back to them before they tear each other apart." Miranda rose.

When they walked back into the room, everyone sat down and looked at the Celestial in expectation. They all felt they presented a good case towards their support of her, and they had no idea what ranking she would give them in the new commissioning.

Miranda sat next to Zulien and studied the faces quietly before she began. "All allied Magistrates will be keeping their titles, and to replace the Magistrates that have been decommissioned, I have decided on the following: "Ethram's father, Jefrot, is the new Magistrate of

Building, and with the help of the other Garnellans we should be able to rebuild the temples and altars."

Ethram shook his father's hand, pleased that the wasted procurers would all play an important role in the new hierarchy.

"Tempest, you are the new Magistrate of Commerce. You always charged a fair price, hate taxes and handled our finances back home."

"Cripes Miranda, no wonder you wouldn't tell me your decision," Tempest complained.

"The Magistrate of the Old Ways commission is to be replaced with Terena, the Magistrate of Scribes of Truth. With the shared knowledge that has been pouring in, she has got the only mind I know that can possibly remember it all."

Terena beamed and hugged Tempest.

"The Magistrate of Law commission is to be replaced by Zalana. Mother, you have the most important task. You are my new Magistrate of Mercy and Redemption. I could see you understood my feelings about space decay, and understood my choice of exile for our enemies. Space decay is abolished, as of right now."

Zalana nodded in agreement.

"I am adding one more Magistrate. Letana, you are the Magistrate of Patience and Virtue. Your centuries of devotion and sacrifice can stand as a role model for us all. I am also charging you to have the Debayluths find other civilizations that may be in hiding after the Battles of Chaos. You will know how to help them integrate into the hierarchy."

The Debayluth Commander straightened with pride at his mate's commissioning within the new hierarchy.

"The commissions must be of equal importance for the hierarchy to flourish, and I will not have them tiered so that anyone's contribution is considered less than another's. With thirteen Magistrates, all auditions will result in a majority vote, and my input should not be necessary. I have chosen Magistrates I feel represent my ideals, so I will abide by your decisions.

"My primary focus needs to be on re-building the Old Religion. This is what all this deception has been about, and I will not let myself get distracted by things that can be resolved by a commissioned hierarchy that now has the same goal."

The evening was spent with the Magistrates, comparing ideas and agreeing that Miranda had made a wise decision. Zalana questioned whether women could even hold Magistrate positions because it had never been done before. Miranda shrugged her shoulders. "It's my hierarchy, so I guess I can appoint whoever I want for now."

The Magistrates decided on a schedule that would allow them to hold auditions twice a month on Laquista. Everyone else could reside on the planet of their choosing, with an agreement that a conference communication to keep everyone attuned to what was happening would be mandatory three times a week.

CHAPTER XII

Miranda left the Magistrates busily making plans, and sat by the gardens with some tea. She had an uneasy feeling she was being watched, but did not see anyone in the moonlight. "Is someone there?"

"You are the Celestial. You are the Commander's mate. Thoughts of you fill the warriors with desire and their sacks to fill with need," a voice softly purred.

"Parina? What are you doing here?" Miranda looked around for the trap as the red woman approached, and she noticed that the Parina looked sad.

"Thoughts of you fill the warrior, Major Berslan, with desire, and his sack to fill with need. I have not been able to retrieve and decipher data on this passion." The Parina's eyes blinked rapidly.

Miranda studied the android. "You like him? Are you able to do that?" If she had been talking to a human, she would have thought the Parina was slightly jealous, but mostly she seemed sad she could not provide Major Berslan with the arousal she thought he deserved.

"The warrior's sack withered in sorrow over his decayed mate. I tried to swell his cock and could not until he heard of your discovery. I have learned much about desire as he spoke to me while I licked and sucked him in pleasure. He has great need of me," she said softly.

Miranda remembered Zulien telling her the Parina's greatest reward was to service the warriors in need. Apparently, her sensors detected Major Berslan was the warrior who needed her most. "Parina, why is Major Berslan so sure his mate is decayed?"

The Parina rubbed a slender hand over her heart. "There was great sorrow over the discovery, and his cock could no longer swell. Commander Ethram's sorrow was just as great, but I sense his pain and need have lessened."

"Commander Ethram? His mate is decayed?"

"When Major Berslan brought me on planet for his meeting with Commander Ethram, there was such sadness in the quarters where the sisters lay decayed. My sensors determined no seduction would swell their cocks." The Parina said this as if she had failed.

Miranda figured out what had happened, of course. Ethram and Berslan's mates were sisters, and they were discovered too late. The Parina's interest in the Major's suffering was interesting. It seemed as though it would be a high honor for her to serve the desires of the warrior who needed her most: Major Berslan.

Miranda still felt she owed the Parina for saving her life. Berslan was destined to remain on planet with no hope for a mate... and no Parina. "Come with me, Parina."

"You are filling with passion, Celestial. Is this what arouses Major Berslan?"

"Come." She took the Parina's warm red hand while they walked to Berslan's quarters, and she knocked. She kept the Parina against the wall, out of sight.

"Celestial? Is something wrong?" Berslan looked over her shoulder for any trouble.

"Zulien told me you thought your mate was decayed. You lied, Berslan. You knew she was."

Berslan's eyes began to tear. "Ethram told you?"

"No, someone who cares a great deal about

your needs and happiness informed me." She pulled the Parina into view.

Berslan looked confused. "Parina, why are you not on the Quillant?"

"I watched your muscles flex with proud strength while you brought the shuttle to surface. I stored the maneuvers I observed," she replied seductively.

"You stole a shuttle?" Miranda was astounded.

"The shuttle is not stolen. It is where Major Berslan kept it when his cock filled with seeing you," she replied.

"Why? Why did you take it?" Berslan asked.

"Though I can not decipher how the Celestial brings you passion, you are still in need of me and your need is far greater than the warriors on the Quillant."

"Berslan, if I thought it was possible, I would say the Parina is in love with you. Throughout all of this, you're the one she refers to, and if she asks me one more time what it is that I do to arouse you, I am going to throttle her," Miranda laughed. "It is the closest thing to jealousy I could imagine."

He looked at the android that had held him in her arms for so many years after he discovered his decayed mate. Eventually she stopped trying to arouse him, and sensed he wanted to be held and ramble on about his sadness over his lost mate. She sensed exactly when he needed a soft kiss or a brushing stroke. In the darkness, she had been his lover, and now he realized he had never been sure if he could follow through on his commitment with Sharpina. "Miranda, she is issued to the Quillant."

"I will order them a new one. I owe the Parina as much as I owe you. Please, Berslan, you need each other."

Berslan looked at the ground. "People will laugh that I am with an android."

"No they won't. I think you will find they are much happier to see you with her instead of that horrid Magistrate's daughter," Miranda smiled.

The Parina purred, "Your sack fills with need." Her eyes flashed while she sorted the data, and she almost looked confused when she glanced at Miranda and then back at Berslan. "Your cock swells for me. I am here, Major, and I will fulfill your desires." She pushed him through the door and shut it behind her.

Miranda saw Ethram talking to his father when she headed back towards her quarters, and she pulled him aside. "You never told Zulien your mate's sister belonged to Berslan?"

"He asked me not to, because he was afraid Taliquant and Zulien would give up hope. I am so happy he told you. I felt miserable with all the suspicion on him."

"He didn't tell me. The Parina did."

"When?"

"A little while ago. Apparently, she is quite attached to the Major, and she stole a shuttle from the Quillant to get back to him." Miranda had not realized that Zulien had walked up behind her.

"The Parina did what?"

Miranda wished Ethram and his father goodnight, and filled Zulien in on what had happened.

"You are right," Zulien said. "I would rather see him with the android. Did he seem okay with it?"

"In the Parina's words, he swelled for her," Miranda laughed.

"I will have another one issued to the Quillant. I hope he is not uncomfortable with the knowledge his companion has been with half the men on the battleship," Zulien chuckled.

"I'm sure she will share her experiences with him." They headed towards their quarters. "Let's share our own experiences," she smiled as they entered their rooms, and she let her caftan drift to the floor.

Zulien lay beside her, running his hand gently from her throat to the curls of her mound and back again. Miranda felt the liquid heat of her desire slowly spread through her, and involuntary little shudders electrified her nerves. She reached over and wrapped her hand around him, feeling him already swelling with desire.

Zulien's lips found hers already parted, and she met his tongue in a warm dance of passion that her fist kept rhythm to. He groaned into her mouth and his fingers stalled in her soft curls, stroking her gently.

The unbearable heat of her arousal forced a spasmed quiver of her muscles, and when his finger brushed over her, it delivered a quickened flick over the sensitive bundle of nerves. She gasped.

"I need you, Zule. Please, I need you now."

Zulien rolled onto his back and pulled her on top of him. She spread her legs wide so that she kneeled over his hips, and her hair brushed along his thighs like heated sparks of molten wax. Miranda centered herself above him, and she felt him enter her as his big hands rested on her hips, pulling her down.

When he was fully imbedded within her, she ground against him for a moment before she began lifting and controlling the plunging movements.

Zulien's breath became ragged with his need for release, and he guided her moves into a quicker pace. Miranda felt the eruption building within her as their climax culminated in convulsive, gripping shudders.

The vision she had at the height of her orgasm completed the questioning scenes that had previously flashed in her mind. She knew what she was to do, and finally she was certain that she really was the Celestial Ancient these people had been waiting for.

The next day, it seemed everyone just wanted to relax. Finishing touches were added to the large altar on the hill, and Ballion had several of his friends stock the fire pit with the white logs of the yassah trees that shaded the settlement. He carefully explained to the other Minocs to take only wood that was already on the ground and to thank the tree for its gift as the Celestial had instructed.

Berslan brought the Parina to the operations station and asked the Makers if there was any way to tone down her seductive speech patterns. He lifted the nail on her little finger and pushed the catch that disengaged the tip. The Parina inserted the raw wires into the socket, and Berslan waited ten long minutes for the upload to complete.

When they left the building, the android was suitable for the company of royals, and Miranda smiled as she watched them wander through the settlement. Berslan anxiously waited for people to make fun of him but it never happened. The closest to an insult he received was one of the women suggesting he change her name, and Berslan was considering it. As the day wore on, he began to relax and his Parina continued to fawn over him.

Miranda and Tempest climbed the hill to make sure everything was prepared for the evening's ritual. They turned and looked back over the surface of Vallastero. "We need to remember this, Tempest. It will never look this way again after tonight." They held hands and smiled.

As the afternoon wore on, the women became excited as they looked forward to nightfall when the first on planet ritual was to be held at the new altar built on a hill overlooking the settlement. Zulien wrapped his arms around Miranda and ran his hand over her sapphire caftan where it swelled with their baby.

"The mates from the Quillant are going to join the ceremony tonight. I am so excited, Zulien. Everything has been so crazy since we arrived here, and it is good to have things finally adjusting to more of a routine. Letana was thrilled when I told her all the mates from their ship were invited as well." Miranda smiled. "They're so cute... and they come in so many colors," she laughed softly. All the Debayluths were pastel in color, in just about any combination, but the mates always matched, she noticed.

Zalana knocked on the door. "Miranda, it is almost time. I will walk up the hill with you."

As darkness fell, Zulien climbed with them and set the fire. He stood outside the stones while the women made a circle around his mate, with Tempest by her side.

"They are so beautiful, Zule." Taliquant was watching Tempest and Miranda lit by the glow of the moons.

"Never in the centuries could I imagine this outcome to our journey, Tali," Zulien agreed as he gazed at his mate.

Miranda stood on the hill, surrounded by the altar and her friends. She raised one hand to the moon and began her blessings. Slowly, the light from the crescent and full moons converged and wavered just beyond her reach.

"Zulien, I think you need to join me this time," Miranda called.

Zulien walked up beside her. "I do not know what to do."

"Put your hand in mine," she whispered.

The light flowed through their joined hands, and Zulien became aware of her vision. Tempest felt the warmth of the energy enter through the hand clasped in Miranda's, and for the first time, she felt an unexpected trance-like feeling.

The Celestial continued to absorb the light, and an Ancient knowledge filled her mind. Miranda was completely aware of her shared vision, and she released Tempest's hand and pointed out towards the blackness of space.

Tempest immediately lost the trance until she put her hand on Miranda's shoulder, and then it reentered her mind. "Oh goddess, Miranda, it's beautiful." Tears flowed from her emerald eyes, as she saw what her friend was to do.

Zulien was speechless at the sight, and in the background he thought he heard muffled gasps and cries from the women who made up the circle as they all shared the vision through their connected hands.

The light filling Miranda traveled through her, causing both her and Tempest to glow. Tempest released Zalana's hand, and each of the women freed one hand and placed the other on the shoulder of the woman standing beside her. Instinct told them to point their free hand at the surface of Vallastera, and the beam left Miranda in a 'V', entering from one hand and exiting into the darkness of space.

A small light blinked into view in the vast emptiness, and it grew steadily in size until it became a large star. Miranda experienced a clearing in her soul far greater than any cleansing ritual she had ever performed. Without warning, the light at the end of the beam exploded into rays of colorful starbursts. It reminded Tempest of fireworks.

As the new star exploded, the colorful shards assaulted Miranda's hand and traveled through the women. They slowly waved their arms as the shards exited her fingers, leaving the crystal pyramids, altars and Temples of Atlantia in their wake. For long moments, the colorful fragments traveled from Miranda through Tempest who was the catalyst of the extraordinary event, and then on to the visionaries where they were waved across the surface.

When the beams finally finished disbursing the translucent colors, the settlement had been transformed into a breathtaking sight, reflecting off the moons and back into the darkness like a beacon for all the worlds. The great pyramid of the Temple of Knowledge glowed, and the light from the altars was almost blinding in its brilliance.

The visionaries standing around them began silently weeping in joy as the planet's surface was rebuilt with the glass shrines that were thought to have been destroyed so long ago. "We should have known," Zalana whispered. "We should have known they would have found a way to protect them."

Miranda lowered her hands and collapsed into Zulien's arms. The women's mates ran up to them, holding them until they were able to compose themselves.

"By the stars, Miranda, look what you have done." Zulien held his tired mate and stroked her golden hair while he looked at the ancient civilization's renewal.

Miranda and Tempest were finally able to stand again, and they walked towards the beautiful city. The Celestial stood at the edge of the hill and began speaking. "I do not know why I know these things, but I do. The Atlantian visionaries knew they could not hope to win the war because too many had turned their back on the Old Religion for the promise of wealth. They knew it would take many centuries for the people to realize they had been misled by greed, and in the end they used their remaining strength to save the knowledge until it could safely renew. Six were sent out from the Temple to leave a messenger to guide the people when they were ready."

Miranda smiled and pointed to a lavender crystal structure with carved pillars and sweeping curved roof. "That is the palace. It will be home to the priests and priestesses." She continued to instruct. "The three buildings on either side are filled with rooms and apartments for those that wish to visit the Temple. The blue crystal pyramid across from the palace is the Temple of Knowledge."

Miranda smiled at Terena. "The scrolls are safely ensconced in glass cases, so I am afraid you are going to be very busy."

Terena was slowly composing herself, as she gazed with wonder at the great pyramid. "I am sure I will have help from the Minocanians. They have spent so many centuries trying to remember the lost knowledge, and with the Debayluths' help it will be a wonderful quest."

Miranda looked at Jefrot, her Magistrate of Building. "The Garnellans will want to study the altars and temples. They should be built throughout the worlds where all who desire to visit can be near one. The visionary priestesses will help the people re-learn the rituals," Miranda said.

"Priestesses?" Zalana whispered.

"Yes, Zalana, that is the power I have felt within the visionaries. I don't know why I know this, but I am sure it is true. It is you and your friends who have struggled to understand the Old Religion who will bring the rituals back to the worlds. There will be a peace throughout the inner worlds that will stretch for eternity." Miranda took Zulien's hand and they walked down the hill. Slowly, the people followed, still gazing in awe.

Epilogue

Miranda brought back the wheel of the year, with an extra sabbat due to Vallasteria's rotation around its suns. The esbat rituals were being learned throughout the inner worlds, and the wasted Garnellans were accompanied by their Minocanian friends as they built the temples and altars.

The hierarchy stabilized to such a degree that auditions were held only once a month, usually over minor issues. The Magistrates seemed to find agreement on almost every issue, determined not to burden the Celestial with politics.

With the prediction of a long-term peace, Berslan set the strategy for protection, and then he joined Ethram on the Isotant with his companion, Parina. He could not bring himself to change her name. Ballion decided to stay on planet as an honored Minoc, finally admitting his emotions made him unsuitable for a procurement vessel. Ethram and Berslan were noted for their unfailing commitment and sensitivity procuring their precious cargo.

The exiled Magistrates made a short quest for freedom, and were quickly captured and moved further back into the dark caves of Renteng. The Debayluths said they preferred to be left alone, and the only time they heard from them was Sharpina's shriek at her father when they collected their supplies.

Tempest's son was born with emerald eyes and golden skin. Tali liked to pull his dark curls into spiky clumps, and defied anyone to say he was not the most handsome warrior in the inner worlds.

Three days later, Miranda gave birth to a

daughter. She had pale, luminescent skin with a soft golden glow, and Miranda's liquid blue eyes. Her smile radiated peace to everyone who watched her rock in the cradle Zulien carved with stars and moons and suns. Miranda had a vision the day before her birth, and inexplicably named her Mahana.

The End

ABOUT THE AUTHOR

Candace raises miniature horses on a small Florida ranch. She enjoys kayaking on the river, and has been an avid pool player for years.

Her writing includes fantasy erotica and erotic romances.

www.ingramcontent.com/pod-product-compliance
Lightning Source LLC
Chambersburg PA
CBHW050016180626
46810CB00002B/441